All In

Center Point
Large Print

Also by Shelley Shepard Gray and available from
Center Point Large Print:

The Bridgeport Social Club Series
Take a Chance

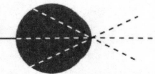

**This Large Print Book carries the
Seal of Approval of N.A.V.H.**

All In

The Bridgeport Social Club Series

SHELLEY SHEPARD GRAY

CENTER POINT LARGE PRINT
THORNDIKE, MAINE

To Annette Friesner,
Pilates Instructor Extraordinaire,
thanks for everything.

. . . .

This Center Point Large Print edition
is published in the year 2020 by arrangement with
Blackstone Publishing.

The text of this Large Print edition is unabridged.
In other aspects, this book may vary
from the original edition.
Printed in the United States of America
on permanent paper.
Set in 16-point Times New Roman type.

ISBN: 978-1-64358-688-5

The Library of Congress has cataloged this record
under Library of Congress Control Number: 2020942067

Letter to Readers

The realization caught me by surprise. About two years ago, I was having lunch with an editor and searching for things to talk about besides work. That's when it occurred to me that I didn't actually do a whole lot besides write books and walk my dogs. Oh, my husband and I travel quite a bit, and I have a great group of friends. But somehow, around the time I became an empty nester and my husband's travel schedule picked up, I began to fill all my extra time with work. And while I love to write, I realized in the middle of that lunch that my life had gotten pretty unbalanced. I didn't actually need to work fifty to sixty hours a week.

Something had to change.

When I got back home, I thought more about my schedule and did a little bit of praying, too.

And that's when I decided to take a Pilates class.

I'd been thinking about starting some kind of exercise routine for a while. However, I also had lots of excuses about why that couldn't happen! I was busy. I had deadlines. I was out of town a lot. Then, one evening, I admitted to myself the real reason I had been holding back—I was afraid to fail. I knew I was out of shape, not very strong, and not all that young anymore. I wasn't especially eager to have sore muscles, embarrass myself in front of other women, or admit to my husband that I had both started and quit yet another exercise routine.

But then I reminded myself how scared I used to be when I first started writing. I figured if I could get used to showing things I made up to complete strangers, I could commit to Pilates.

Years ago, I read something about how it takes forty times of anything to make a routine. That always made sense to me, so I decided to commit to forty private sessions. I was going to go to my Pilates class once a week—no matter what. I wasn't going to schedule appointments or give myself excuses why I "couldn't go." I was just going to do it.

In other words, I decided to go all in.

I'm not going to lie. It wasn't easy for me. It still isn't! But I have gotten stronger, I've met some great people, and it's been a wonderful stress reliever. And yes, it's even given me something else to talk about besides writing.

This idea of committing to something whole-heartedly was my inspiration behind *All In*. I wanted to write a novel about a group of people who were starting over—and who ultimately realized that achieving their dreams was only going to happen by committing 100 percent. Maybe you, too, have done this very same thing a time or two?

I hope you enjoy getting to know Ace and Meredith and returning to the fictional town of Bridgeport, Ohio. Look for *Hold on Tight*, the third book in the Bridgeport Social Club series, in June.

With my thanks and blessings,
Shelley Shepard Gray

1

From Les Larke's
Terms for Poker Success:

All In: When a player bets everything he's got. Be advised that this can be a risky undertaking. If you lose, there's nothing left.

SATURDAY

The shove came out of nowhere, hitting Meredith Hunt hard on her shoulder and knocking her down onto the paved walking path. Feeling both shocked and confused, she threw out her hands in a weak attempt to break her fall. But instead of helping the situation, a sharp, fierce pain reverberated along her right hand. Pebbles tore into her other palm, her knees, and parts of her thighs. She felt dizzy. Stunned. Half in shock.

What the heck had just happened?

Panic overtook her as she realized that whoever had just rammed her to the ground had taken off with her backpack—the backpack that would have been secure on her back with its chest clip had she not been retrieving her water bottle at that exact moment.

Just like that, a dozen images of what was stashed in there flitted through her head. Her wallet. Her phone. Her keys . . . Her *address*. The idea of any of that coming into a stranger's hands was enough to make her jump to her feet.

Well, she would've jumped up—or even simply sat up—if she hadn't been feeling so dizzy.

"Hey. Hey, are you all right?"

Opening one eye, she realized a man was kneeling next to her. He had short black hair, dark eyes, scruff on his cheeks, and a very concerned expression. He was what her best friend in high school would have called "dreamy."

"I think so," she muttered, horrified to realize that she sounded gritty and hoarse. Like she was barely hanging on. Which, unfortunately, pretty much summed up exactly how she felt.

The guy's expression grew more concerned. "I saw some punk push you down. Looks like you hit the ground hard."

Hating that she was still sprawled out in front of him, she stretched a leg experimentally. "I need to get up."

"Hold on. What hurts, darlin'?" he drawled. Though she knew better than to be taken in by a drawl and a cast-off endearment, she relaxed a little. This man was a stranger but he didn't seem dangerous. Just as her conscience started to remind her that good looks and charm really didn't mean anything at all, he reached out to slip a hand under her head. "Is your neck okay?" he asked quietly. "Can you move?"

Thinking that was a good idea, she moved her head, realizing as she did that it was being supported by a very big hand. "I'm all right. I hit my head, but I think my hand got the worst of it."

He shifted and took a knee, which was covered in faded denim. "Just your hand?"

She knew what he was getting at. She was acting a little peaked for someone who had just a cut palm. Thinking of all her students who powered through her classes even when they were struggling or in pain, Meredith tried to get a grip on herself. "Maybe . . . I guess I hit the ground kind of hard. I'm a little stunned." Maybe a lot stunned, since she'd just mentally compared the color of his eyes to her favorite dark Ghirardelli chocolate bar.

After studying her a moment longer, he slid his hand out from under her head to her arm. "Ma'am, I'm going to take your elbow, okay? We need to get you sitting up."

Ma'am? She swallowed. Did she really look that old?

"Dad, what are you doing?" a voice called out. "Oh my gosh. Miss Hunt?"

Surprised, Meredith focused on the person just beyond her rescuer. Finn. He was a sophomore at Bridgeport High—one of the kids she helped out when she volunteered in a friend's class once a week. Finn was fifteen, muscular, almost six foot, and a little on the chunky side. He was built like the football player she'd recently learned he was.

However, in spite of all that brawn, there was still a sweetness to him. His face still had a touch of peach fuzz that most underclassmen boys at the school had. He also had dark-brown eyes and dark hair. Pretty much the spitting image of the man who was still kneeling by her side.

"Hey Finn. Fancy seeing you here." Inwardly she winced. Had she really just said that?

Finn blinked, then grinned, like she'd really amused him. The man by her side, the one whose hand was still curved protectively around her elbow, looked confused.

No doubt that was not only because his kid knew her, but also because she'd spouted such an idiotic phrase while lying on the ground. When she noticed that his free hand was hovering in her general direction, that he didn't want to manhandle her without her permission, she tentatively smiled at him.

That was all he needed to wrap that hovering hand around her side. A little above her waist. A little below her breast. Not that she should be noticing anything like that. After all, she was a Pilates instructor. She knew that positioning other people didn't mean anything personal. Usually, it really was just an offer of assistance.

But still, she was aware of his touch as she moved to a sitting position. She breathed deep, hoping to get her bearings. But all she got was a good whiff of him. He smelled like soap and tobacco and peppermint. It shouldn't have been a good combination. Neither should have been his underlying scent—the one that signaled he was all man.

She really needed to get her bearings. Like, immediately.

"You all right?" he murmured.

"Um-hum," she whispered back, though why she was whispering, she didn't really know.

Finn stepped closer and looked down at her. "Miss Hunt?"

She summoned what she hoped was a sunny smile. "I'm going to be just fine."

The man looked from her to the boy in confusion. "I'm guessing y'all know each other."

"I help out in one of his classes," she replied. "Finn, well, he's currently my favorite sophomore."

Blushing, Finley ducked his head as he dropped to one knee next to his dad. "You tell everyone that."

"Maybe. But right now it's true." Looking at his dad, she attempted to act like the situation was normal, even though she was lying on the

13

ground in the middle of the bike trail. "Hi. I'm Meredith Hunt."

"You work at the high school?"

"Work? No, not really. I'm just a volunteer."

"She helps out in Miss Springer's classroom, Dad," Finley explained before turning back to her. "Miss Hunt, are you really gonna be all right? That guy who shoved you was really big."

Still feeling out of sorts, she tried to nod, but was immediately hit with a monster headache. "He grabbed my backpack."

Finn frowned. "I thought that was what he did. Sorry we weren't close enough to grab him."

Even imagining Finn getting tangled up with the man who'd shoved her made her tense up. "I'm glad you weren't any closer! He was kind of big. You could have been hurt. No backpack is worth that."

While Finn looked like he was about to start laughing, his dad looked affronted. "That kid wouldn't have hurt us. But to be honest, I wasn't thinking about your pack."

He'd been thinking about her.

"I wish I'd been more aware of what was going on. My life is in that backpack."

"Like you just said, it's just a backpack," Finn's dad said softly, a thick drawl accentuating every word. "We've also got more important things to worry about."

"Oh?"

He smiled sympathetically. "In case you didn't realize it, you're bleeding."

She looked down at her bare legs. In spite of it being January, she'd decided to wear shorts to run. The sun and fifty-degree temperature were too welcome to ignore. But now, seeing the scrapes, she was coming to regret that decision. They did look kind of bad, but there wasn't that much blood. "My knees will be fine."

"I was talking about your hand, Meredith."

To her surprise, he pulled out a worn, soft bandanna from a pocket and pressed it over a cut on her hand. Right then, a slicing sharp pain entered her wound. She sucked in a sharp breath.

Finn's dad curved a palm around her shoulder. "Easy, now. It's deep. You need stitches." Still looking at her hand, he frowned. "It's swelling, too. You might need an X-ray."

Finn pointed to her head. "I think you're gonna have a big bruise on your head, too. You might have a concussion."

Shifting, Meredith looked at her hand in confusion. Blood oozed from her palm. "Gosh. You're right. I guess I better go . . . " Her memory returned—as well as the knowledge that everything she'd been carrying had been stolen. "I don't know what I'm going to do. I don't have my license or keys." Or her insurance card. Or any money. Or her phone.

Crap!

Panicked, she struggled to her feet. "I need to—"

Resting both hands on her arms, Finley's dad held her steady. "Hold on, now," he drawled. "You're gonna hurt yourself."

"You don't understand. My phone was in there with my wallet." Which, for once, was full. And her credit cards.

Crap again!

Oblivious to the minor meltdown she was having in front of them, Finn said, "Dad's right, Miss Hunt. You need to be careful. Sorry, but you look pretty bad."

She felt pretty bad, too. Though she was feeling fuzzy, she had recovered enough to start making sense of the situation. "Do you think that guy might have only taken cash then dropped my bag or something?"

"It's worth a try. Finn, go look up ahead. Maybe go a couple hundred yards or so. What color is the pack, Meredith?"

"Teal blue."

"I'm on it." Finn got to his feet but his attention was still on her. "You gonna be okay?"

Everything inside of her turned to mush. Just mush. In the three weeks since he'd arrived in Bridgeport, Finn Vance had been kind of hard to read.

At first, she'd thought it was simply because he was the new kid. That would be hard for anyone.

But then she heard from one of the coaches she worked with that Finn was destined to be a starter on the varsity team in the fall. She'd also heard from her friend Emily that he seemed to be struggling in her class.

She'd also noticed that he never looked all that happy in class, either. Always serious.

That serious attitude, combined with his fake diamond earrings, faded jeans, and collection of black concert T-shirts made him definitely stand out in the school.

But though he also seemed tough, he behaved well and always watched her like he was trying to figure her out. Just last week, when her arms were full of notebooks, and she was having trouble managing them all, he'd helped her carry them to her car.

She'd suspected then what he was proving now. Underneath all those muscles, T-shirts, and attitude was a kid who'd been raised to be something of a gentleman. "Finn, I wish every kid in Bridgeport was like you. Thanks."

The blush that reached the roots of his hair made her smile. When he trotted off, she turned to his father. "I think I can stand up now."

He nodded, but looked at her steadily. And, if she wasn't mistaken, in a completely new way. "Careful, now."

Feeling awkward, she stood up, accepting his hands on her elbow and waist again. Once they were both on their feet, she blinked as she lifted her head another couple of inches to meet his gaze. "Thank you again. And, um, I guess we should probably introduce ourselves a little better. As I said, I'm Meredith Hunt."

"And I'm Ace Vance, Finn's dad."

His voice was serious, gravelly. Meredith thought that it went well with his eyes, which looked like they had seen too much and were ready to take on anyone's burdens. "Thank you for coming to my rescue. I don't know what I would have done if you and Finley hadn't arrived."

His dark eyes turned stormy. "Don't thank me. I haven't done anything yet." Before she could refute that, he visibly scanned her from top to bottom. "We need to get that hand taken care of."

Looking at the bandanna that was slowly getting soaked, she resigned herself that he was right. "I guess I better call the police. Maybe they can help me?" Of course, that was going to be kind of hard to do, since she no longer had a phone. Thinking of all she'd lost, panic set in. "Could I borrow your phone for a minute? Would you mind?"

"If you need the cops, I'll call. But give Finn a sec, okay? I think there's a good chance he might find it nearby. Most muggers are only after cash, not backpacks and keys."

Imagining the worst, she said, "I hope that mugger isn't nearby. I'd hate for Finn to get hurt."

"Finn already weighs one eighty. He's played football since he was six. No backpack-stealing punk is going to get the best of him."

Releasing a ragged sigh, she knew he was right. One step at a time. Seeking to take her mind off her misery, she said, "Um, your son is really great."

"Thanks."

"No, I'm not just saying that. He helped me carry some equipment to my car the other day. Half the kids I work with wouldn't do something like that. That's how we met."

His eyebrows lowered. "They should be helping you."

"What I'm trying to say is that he's really composed and mature for his age. You should be proud of him, Mr. Vance."

A reluctant smile appeared on his lips. "Thanks. Finn's not much of a student, but he's a good person. At least, I've always thought that. You know, when he's not being a teenager with a chip on his shoulder."

She laughed. "I'd guess half the kids at Bridgeport High have chips on their shoulders, Mr. Vance. My friend Emily says it comes with the territory."

A reluctant smile crossed his features. "Why don't you call me Ace, Meredith? I've never been the type of guy to be called 'mister' anything."

"That's reserved for your father?" she teased.

"Nah, he ain't that kind of man either." Looking bemused, he said, "Now that I think about it, I can't think of a single person to ever call my dad anything but Hank."

Hank. Ace. Finn. Interesting names. Country names. "All right." She smiled slightly, thinking how odd it was that she felt so at ease with a man who looked so different than the majority of the men she knew. He had to be at least ten years older than she was, seemed to favor black as much as his kid, and had earrings in his ears as well. Two tiny silver hoops. One of his arms had a bunch of tattoos, all inked in black.

Startled by the direction of her own thoughts— of the way she wondered when he'd gotten his ears pierced, what he did for a living, and why he was in Bridgeport, she held up her bleeding hand and pretended to be completely fascinated about the way blood was oozing out of her palm.

"It'll be okay," he said in a soothing tone. "I bet you won't even have much of a scar."

She was an adult. She'd taken CPR. She'd had extensive training when she became a certified Pilates trainer. She dealt with clients recovering from injuries on a daily basis. She definitely did not need some unfamiliar man coddling her and murmuring sweet things in her ear.

So why did she kind of feel giddy around him? Why did she feel like he might even be making her feel better?

She turned to stare at the path behind her. Maybe if she stared down the empty path long enough she could suddenly conjure this whole thing to be over.

And then she saw her savior. Again.

"Here comes Finley!" she called out like he was returning from battle. "And he's holding my pack." Relief flooded through her.

Ace looked in that direction as well. When Finn got within speaking distance, Ace grinned. "Good job, kid."

Finn smiled broadly. "It weren't nothing. It was laying on the ground just around the bend. I didn't see the guy who took it, though."

"S'okay. You got her bag," his dad said quietly, in that same soothing tone that sounded so mesmerizing. "That's most important."

Finley nodded before turning to her, then he said, "It was already opened, Miss Hunt. I didn't open it."

"Of course you didn't." Impulsively, she squeezed his hand with her good one. Before she thought the better of it, she waved her fingers toward the zipper. "Well, go ahead and check it out. What's inside?"

He opened it. "Keys," he said, pulling out her heavy Minnie Mouse key ring. "And your phone."

"That's a relief. Do you see my wallet?"

Ace frowned. "Nope. Sorry."

She was sorry, too, especially since her wallet had all of her vital information in it. Determined to not show the extent of her dismay in front of the teenager, she reached for the pack with her good hand. "Thanks, Finn. That's too bad about my wallet, but at least I can get home now." Already making plans, she said, "I'll cancel my credit cards when I get home. And if I get pulled over for driving without a license, I'll just have to explain to the policeman what happened. He should understand, right?"

Finn was staring at her like she'd grown another head but nodded. "Yeah, maybe."

But Ace frowned. "You need to get to the doctor first before you do anything. And you shouldn't be driving. Not until you get checked out."

"That's sweet advice, but I don't really have a choice." She wasn't going to burden a girlfriend, and her mom lived in Tampa.

Ace sighed. "Why don't you let us take you to urgent care? There's one of those doc-in-the-box places in the center of town. After we get you seen to, I'll drive you back to your car."

"I couldn't let you do that."

Studying her hand, he nodded. "Would you rather go to the hospital? We could do that . . . "

Ace Vance was really too kind. Cutting him off, she said, "I hate to point out the obvious, but I don't have any money on me. I can't pay right now."

He shrugged. "If they charge you something up front, I'll pay it."

"I could never ask you to do something like that."

He raised an eyebrow while his son remained silent. "You didn't ask. I offered. There's a difference. Right?"

He did have a point. But how could she take advantage of him like that? It wasn't even like she knew Finn all that well.

Then there was the little matter that they had also just spent time and energy getting her on her feet and retrieving her backpack. That was more than enough good works for two strangers. "I'm sure you've got other things to do. This isn't your problem."

Finn lifted his chin. "We don't have anything else to do, do we, Dad?"

"Nothing as important as making sure you are okay." Settling his eyes on her, Ace said, "You don't want to drive if you're woozy. Trust me on that one."

"I hate to impose. I mean, you've rescued me, found my backpack, and gave me your bandanna to ruin."

"My dad doesn't take no for an answer real well." Looking like he was fighting back a grin, Finn continued, "You might as well give in now."

Glancing at his father, she saw a new light shine in his eyes. He was pleased about his son.

Pleased about how Finn was reaching out to her and joking around a little bit.

That, in the end, was what did it. Sure, she was still a little shaky on her feet. She also needed help paying for the clinic visit. But what mattered most to her was that it seemed like Finn needed to help her as much as she needed his help. She could ignore a lot of things, but she could never ignore that.

"In that case, thank you," she said finally. "I really do appreciate your help."

2

From Les Larke's
Terms for Poker Success:

Forced Bet: A bet that starts the action during the first round of a poker hand. This first move can set the tone for the whole game. Place your first bet with care.

They'd only been sitting in the waiting room of the walk-in clinic for ten minutes when a nurse appeared at the doorway.

"Miss Hunt, you can come on back now." Looking at the blood-soaked bandanna on Meredith's hand, and maybe the way she was still looking peaked as well, the older nurse glanced at Finn and Ace. "You can come on back, too. We might need your help."

Though Finn jumped to his feet, Ace didn't feel as certain that that was the right decision. Most people didn't like to get poked and prodded in front of strangers. And Meredith? Well, she seemed more reserved than most other women he knew, which meant she really wasn't going to want them watching her get checked out. Those examining rooms were real small.

But when he saw her looking his way and how stiffly she was holding herself, Ace realized that she was either more scared or in more pain than she'd been letting on.

He got to his feet and followed the other three through the door and into one of the examining rooms.

It had been a while since he'd been in one of these things. He didn't get sick often and Finn? Well, Finn was blessed to be healthy for the most part, too.

As he breathed deep, wincing as he inhaled the pungent odor of antiseptic, he was reminded of the time Liz had called him in a panic because Finn had fallen off the monkey bars and had broken two fingers and his nose. Liz had been freaked out and worried about taking time off work. And because she hadn't been the type of person to keep a job even in the best of circumstances, he'd dropped everything to take their boy to the doctor.

He'd sat with their seven-year-old, held Finn's hand while he'd gotten his scrapes cleaned up and his fingers bandaged, and then taken him home for grilled cheese sandwiches and a vanilla shake. Finn had fallen asleep on the couch next to their old Labrador, Lucy, while Ace had looked on, wondering if Liz was ever going to put their kid's needs first.

He should have guessed then that she never would. If he'd done that, it would have saved him a heap of trouble and aggravation in the long run.

"Dad," Finn hissed. "Sit down."

That was enough to pull him out of the past. "Sorry. My mind drifted off." He gave his attention back to Meredith and to Finn. Meredith sat on one of those paper-covered tables and Ace stood against the wall.

Taking the lone chair in the room felt rude, though he couldn't really say why.

After taking Meredith's vitals, the nurse put on gloves and reached for Meredith's cut hand. "What happened?" she asked in a chipper voice.

"I fell on the bike trail."

"Someone mugged her," Finn corrected. "He pushed her down and she cut her hand."

"My word!" the nurse said. "That had to have been scary."

"It happened so quick, I didn't even realize what had happened at first."

Still poking around Meredith's palm, the nurse said, "It must have been quite a fall."

"There was some glass," Meredith added around a quick intake of breath as the nurse started peeling off Ace's bandanna from her skin. She gripped the side of the table hard, showing—to Ace, at least—that she wasn't nearly as tough as she was pretending to be.

Before he realized he was doing it, Ace was at

27

her side. He wasn't really a nurturer, but something in her blue eyes called to him.

"You okay?" he said quietly.

Meredith nodded. "It just stings."

The nurse looked sympathetic. "I'm sure it does," she murmured as she continued to unwrap the cloth and gently pry away the fabric that stuck to the wound. Once it was free, she tossed the cloth on the tray then carefully moved Meredith's hand one way and then the other. "You've got a couple of glass shards stuck in there real good."

"I kind of figured that."

"I'm going to get some tweezers and clean this up. It's going to hurt like the dickens." Setting Meredith's hand back down, she said, "The doctor will be in soon."

"Doctor? Is that really necessary?"

"Yep. He likes to look at everything first. He'll give you some shots before I clean it."

"I'm going to need a shot?"

"More than one, dear. But don't fret. I promise, you're going to want them." She winked. "Good thing you've got your men here to hold your other hand and fuss over you," she said as she closed the door behind her.

When they were alone, Ace noticed her shudder. Unable to stop himself, he rubbed her back. "I know this sucks but it'll be over soon."

She released a ragged sigh. Tried to smile. "You're right. This is no big deal."

He was pretty sure she was lying through her teeth. "Hey, it's real good you came in. Pulling out stuck glass is never easy. Sometimes it just settles in no matter how hard you poke and pull."

Finn groaned. "Dad."

"What?"

"You can tell she's scared," he said under his breath. "You can't talk to her like that."

Taken aback, Ace swallowed. "I'm sorry. Sometimes my mouth gets the best of me. It's . . . well, it's been a while since I've tried to offer reassurance at the doctor's."

"Don't worry about it."

"I think you're doing real good, Miss Hunt," Finn said. "I stepped on a big chunk of glass once and cut the pad of my foot real deep. I had to have two shots in it before they could stitch me. Remember that, Dad?"

"I remember. You were all of ten. Made a real mess of my favorite shirt, too."

Finn laughed. "I was bleeding like a stuck pig. Worse than when I broke my nose."

"Could we stop talking about blood, please?" Meredith asked.

Ace grinned sheepishly. "It seems Finn inherited my poor manners after all. I guess you can tell that neither of us is used to taking care of women. Delicate sensibilities are beyond us."

Her smile broadened. "I'm hardly delicate. And I'm sure you take good care of your mom, Finn."

When Finn's relaxed manner stiffened, Ace silently cursed. If there was one way to ensure that Finn's good mood disintegrated, it was to bring up his mom. "His mom isn't around," he blurted, maybe more harshly than was necessary.

Immediately, Meredith looked contrite. "I'm sorry, Finn. Did you lose her a long time ago?"

"Nah," Finn said, his whole body tight. "My mom's not dead, she's just not around."

Meredith glanced his way. Confusion and hurt and maybe disappointment filled her gaze. Ace realized she thought he was married. "Finn's mom is out of the picture. She's back in West Virginia."

Finn, who was obviously trying to act as if he wasn't embarrassed as all get out, stared straight ahead.

Meredith's cheeks and neck turned pink. "Well, now I'm really embarrassed. Sorry, I shouldn't have said anything. Your personal life isn't any of my business."

Before Ace could say something, Finn spoke. "It's okay. You didn't know."

Darting a glance toward him, Meredith shot Ace another apologetic look.

"No need to worry. Finn and I are doing just fine on our own." Ace knew he probably should have given her more information, but he didn't know how to do that. He sure wasn't going to say anything more about Liz with his boy standing in the room.

But there was no mistaking that the warm current that had been running between them had stalled out.

Before he could figure out how to set things right, the door opened. A doctor who looked to be about the age of his father came in, followed by their nurse in her green scrubs.

"I'm Dr. Owens," he said.

"Meredith Hunt. This is Ace and Finn."

After smiling at Ace and his son absently, the doctor picked up Meredith's hand and manipulated her wrist and fingers. Then, after he poked a little and she winced, he turned to the nurse. "Let's numb the area and clean it well."

When the nurse picked up a needle, Meredith looked at Ace again. This time, however, her look was so pleading, Ace didn't hesitate.

He reached for her good hand. "You gonna be okay?" he whispered.

"Yeah. I just hate needles." She rolled her eyes. "And yes, I realize that I'm a little old to be carrying on like this."

Seeing the hypodermic that the nurse was holding, he leaned closer, practically pressing his lips to her ear. "Close your eyes and squeeze my hand, 'kay?"

To his amazement, she did just that. When she squeaked as she was pricked the second time, Ace wrapped an arm around her shoulders. "Breathe deep, honey. It's almost over."

Again, she did exactly as he suggested, making him feel like he was something special. He sensed Finley was staring at him in astonishment. Ace wasn't surprised about that. He hadn't coddled his boy much, not since he was a little guy and his mother had let him down.

It had been a hell of a long time since he'd tried to comfort a woman when she was hurting. He'd sure never done that with Liz.

He'd taken care not to bring any women he'd been dating around the boy as well. But now that they were living together permanently, he supposed that would probably change, too.

"All done," the nurse said brightly. After tossing the needles into a red container, she walked to the door. "I've got to get something to irrigate that wound. I'll be right back."

The moment they were alone again, Meredith released his hand with a shaky breath. "Thank you. I'm so sorry. I bet you both think I'm the biggest baby."

"Nah. I think getting a shot in the hand hurts."

She turned slightly to look at Finn. "What do you think? Is my reputation of being a tough-as-nails volunteer in jeopardy now that you've seen me fall on the ground and get all squeamish when I get a shot?"

He grinned. "Yep, though you should probably know that everyone already thinks you're a pushover."

Ace reckoned that wasn't the way to put her at ease. "Hey, now."

Meredith just laughed. "I'm not offended. Finn's exactly right." But then her bright smile faded as the nurse bustled back into the room. "Oh, boy."

After setting down a metal tray that was loosely covered with a paper towel, the nurse put back on gloves and picked up a syringe filled with some kind of liquid. "You might want to keep looking away, hon. I'm going to have to irrigate the wound. I'm getting the idea this isn't going to be your favorite thing to see."

She swallowed hard. "You guessed right." Meredith didn't need to be told twice. Looking up at him, she held out her hand. "Would you mind?"

He shook his head. "Not at all." Clasping her hand in his again, he whispered to her to keep breathing.

Then he tried really hard not to notice how soft and slim her hand was. Or how many shades of red were in her long auburn hair.

Or how nice it was to be needed by someone who wasn't looking to take advantage of him.

Thirty minutes later, the doctor peered into her eyes. "Your pupils are still a little dilated. You need to take it easy for a couple of days. Can you do that?"

"I own and run my own business. I need to

work. How long do you think I'll be out of commission?"

"At least forty-eight hours. What do you do?"

"I'm a Pilates instructor. I mean, I have my own studio."

"I don't know a lot about Pilates, but I'm thinking you aren't going to be much good if you're sitting in the corner of the room. Am I right?"

"Yes."

"Then you need to let your clients know that you're taking a few days off."

Ace could practically see Meredith mentally calculate the money she was going to be losing right in front of his eyes. Though he knew how she was feeling—it wasn't like anyone was standing around, giving him sick days either—but he agreed with the doctor.

At last, she pulled her shoulders back and smiled again. "I understand. Thank you for patching me up."

"It's my job." After smiling at her again, he tapped the screen he was holding in his hands. "I'll send a nurse in to give you the paperwork and the prescriptions."

"Thank you, Doctor."

Looking like his mind was already on his next patient, he smiled before walking out.

When the three of them were alone again, Meredith turned to Ace and Finn. "Hopefully this won't take too much longer."

"Don't worry about it."

"This has already taken up a lot of your time. Too much. Um, I'm happy to take an Uber or something home so you guys can get on your way."

Ace shook his head. "One more time, that's not how I do things. There's not a single thing more important than making sure you get home safe with everything you need."

Doubt, together with pure gratitude, shone in her face. "I don't know how I can repay the two of you."

"Maybe we don't need to be repaid," he said lightly. "Maybe we just want to help you out today."

She looked doubtful but kept her silence.

Only later did Ace realize that Finn had been keeping his silence, too.

3

From Les Larke's
Terms for Poker Success:

Live One: A player who isn't very knowledgeable. He usually plays too long and makes simple mistakes. Obviously, this is who you don't want to be!

As the minutes stretched like hours, Meredith realized she hadn't let herself feel so vulnerable in years. She liked being in control of herself and of the situation. It was why she had her own business and lived by herself.

And, a small voice interjected, why she had never been able to commit to a meaningful relationship before. She had too many insecurities about herself to let her guard down. Most men got tired of having to jump the emotional fences she'd erected—and she didn't blame them. She'd kept them so high, the men would have to be emotional warriors to scale them.

Why did time seem to go so slowly now that the whole experience was almost over? Meredith had run out of things to say, especially since her attempts to apologize, pay Ace back, or even get him to leave had fallen on stubborn ears.

Now the three of them were sitting in awkward silence in the small examining room. Someone had decided to paint it bright blue and add fluffy clouds and rainbows on one wall. The vibrant colors made the space seem claustrophobic instead of happy. Finn had pulled out his phone and was thumbing at his screen like it was the most interesting thing in the world.

And Ace? Well, his expression was carefully masked. She was getting the feeling it was like that a lot.

Finally, he coughed and held out his phone. "You know what? I didn't even ask if you had anyone you wanted to call. Your boyfriend, maybe?"

"Oh. I don't have a boyfriend."

Finn, looking more uncomfortable by the minute, groaned.

Ace's brows lowered. "I see."

Her personal relationships weren't any of his business. She didn't owe him any explanations. But instead of letting her statement hang there between them, she started talking. "I used to have a boyfriend." Well, she and Scott had dated. "But we broke up." After she'd realized he didn't believe in commitments, and he'd realized she had a tough time trusting people.

That had been over a year ago.

The nurse appeared at the doorway. "Miss

37

Hunt? Here's your prescriptions and paperwork."

Breathing a sigh of relief, Meredith hopped off the table. As the nurse read through the forms, she made Meredith initial each page. Finally, she was asked to sign the last page.

"Okay, you're free to go. You can settle your bill on your way out."

"Thank you."

Ace edged to the door. "I'll take care of things while you get yourself together."

Seconds later, he was heading out of the examining room, Finn on his heels.

The nurse chuckled. "All men are like that. They hate sitting around and waiting."

Meredith kind of thought women were like that, too, but she kept that to herself. "I think they wanted to give me some privacy. We don't know each other real well."

"Ah, a new relationship. I love those."

"You do?"

"Oh, sure. Everything is bright and exciting and the men try so hard and are so gentlemanly." She frowned. "After a while? Well, you're lucky if you can get them to pick their boxers up off the floor in the bathroom."

Meredith glanced at the nurse's simple bridal set on her left finger. "Sounds like you have some experience with that?"

"Boy, do I. Six years of marriage and three kids later? Honey, the honeymoon is over."

"It sounds kind of nice to me."

"Oh, it is. I wouldn't change a thing. Don't worry, hon. He looks like a keeper to me. Before you know it, you and him will be back here holding a sick kid with strep throat."

Before Meredith could say that motherhood wasn't likely in the cards anytime soon, the nurse looked at her watch. "Oops. I've got to get on my way. Don't forget to take it easy now."

"Thanks. I won't."

She took a moment and washed her unbandaged hand as best she could, smoothed out her ponytail in the mirror above the sink, then grabbed her backpack and headed down the hall to meet the guys.

Now all she had to do was hang in there until Ace and Finn dropped her off at her car. Then she could try to figure out how to get ahold of all of her clients and tell them that she was going to need to cancel their classes for a couple of days.

Ace and Finn were standing by the door. To her surprise, the waiting room had filled up. Half the people seemed to be holding boxes of tissue or coughing uncontrollably.

"Are we all set?" she asked.

"Yep." After holding the door for her, the three of them walked outside. Handing her a folded sheet of paper, Ace said, "I've got some good news for you."

"What is that?"

"I told the receptionist about what happened to you, and she only charged you the minimum for right now."

"Really?"

"They only made Dad pay twenty-five bucks," Finn said as they got back into Ace's truck.

Meredith felt like cheering. She was so glad that Ace hadn't had to pay a hundred dollars, money he might not have, just to get her hand stitched up. "Wow, that was really nice of them. I'm kind of surprised, too. I didn't think anything ever got between a doctor's visit and their payment."

"I was surprised, too, but glad. I'm thinking that the receptionist felt sorry for you," Ace said. "Nobody wants to hear about a woman getting mugged on the bike trail."

"I guess not."

"The receptionist was also flirting with you, Dad," Finn said, amusement thick in his voice. "I think she was hoping you'd ask for her number or something."

Ace stiffened. "We don't need to be talking about that."

She wasn't positive, but she thought Ace was blushing. That amused her. He was so tough looking, she wouldn't have thought anything could embarrass him. It seemed she was wrong. "Is the office going to send me a bill later?"

"Yeah. She said she had everything she needed on that sheet you filled out when you arrived,"

Ace said as he pulled out of the parking spot. "Where to?"

"I need to get my car, so if you could drop me off at the bike trail, that would be great."

Ace pulled over to the side and stopped. "Meredith, I don't think you should be driving right now."

"I don't have a choice. I mean, I need to get my car."

"I can get a buddy to help me pick it up for you later this afternoon."

She shook her head. "I can't ask you to do one more thing for me."

"That's why I didn't ask."

"Ace—"

"Honey, where's your house?" he drawled.

After glancing at Finn, who was giving her a look that said his father wasn't going to budge, she decided to give in. "I don't live too far away. Just take a right out of here and another right at the light."

"Gotcha." Ace turned as she directed, one hand resting lazily on the steering wheel.

Now that she had stopped bleeding and she was all stitched up, the inside of his truck felt even smaller. Maybe it was also because she was noticing more things about Ace. Like that he wore his ball cap low over his forehead, as if he was trying to block out the sun without putting on sunglasses. Or the fact that he had a pack of

Marlboro Reds in the opening at the bottom of his dash. She'd never dated a man who smoked before. Had never wanted to have much to do with anyone who smoked.

But with Ace? Well, not that she was dating him or anything, but she secretly thought it added to his attractiveness. He was a poster boy for men she never would have thought she'd want to date. He called women by endearments, he drove a gas-guzzling vehicle, he had tattoos and earrings, and he was built like a football player. He was completely rough around the edges.

And now she was sure that he smoked, too.

He was everything Scott hadn't been. Everything the opposite of the type of men she'd ever dated. So why couldn't she seem to stop herself from looking at him?

As if he knew she was staring, he cleared his throat. "You okay over there?"

"Oh, yes. I was just watching the road."

"So . . . keep going straight?"

"Yes. Then turn left on West Avenue."

Ace smiled as he maneuvered his truck through the light traffic. Sandwiched between them, Finn stayed quiet.

When they got to her neighborhood, she continued to give Ace directions to get to her house, which was in an older section of Bridgeport.

She was proud that she owned her own house. She'd put down the money for it three years before, when she realized that renting wasn't helping her finances at all. It was in the middle of a line of houses originally constructed in the fifties. It was in need of new paint and could use a handyman to fix one of her front lights and maybe even replace some rotten wood around her back door. But she kept it as neat and clean as she could.

When they pulled onto her street, Finn spoke at last. "You live two streets over from us, Miss Hunt."

She turned around to stare at Finn. "Really?" Bridgeport wasn't that big, but realizing he was living so close to her made her feel like their town might be a whole lot smaller than she'd imagined.

"Yeah. We live over on Maple."

"Small world, hmm?"

Ace glanced at her. "So did we do good? Is this a nice neighborhood?"

It felt like a trick question even though it wasn't. "I think so. It's, well, it's not in the really fancier sections of Bridgeport, but all my neighbors are friendly. Most everyone works hard and keeps up with their yards." Looking at her hedges, she made a mental note to hire someone to plant some new bushes and shrubs in the spring.

"I got the same sense about it," Ace said. "We looked at some of the newest subdivisions, but the houses were too big. Finn and I don't need that much."

"Yeah, my grandpa Hank always says you can only stand in one room at a time," Finn said.

She'd never heard that saying before, but she liked it. "He's absolutely right."

"I'm just glad I didn't have to buy too much furniture for the place."

Meredith blinked and looked at him more closely. If he looked at bigger houses and was talking about buying rooms of furniture, maybe he had a whole lot more money than she'd imagined. And . . . there was yet another difference between them. She was living on a tighter than tight budget.

"Well, I guess I better get out of your hair. Thank you both so much. I don't know what I would have done if you hadn't come along."

"I'm just glad we were there." Ace leaned over the seat. "I'm going to walk Meredith into her house and make sure she's settled and get her car keys. You good, Finn, or do you want to come along?"

"I'm good." He turned to her. "See you, Miss Hunt."

She opened her door. "Yes, see you soon. I hope you have a better rest of your Saturday."

Finn shrugged like it didn't matter.

She wondered about that as she slipped off her seat—only to realize Ace was standing right next to her. Before she knew what he was about, he'd rested his hands on one of her arms and her waist and helped her down. Then he snatched up that backpack and carried it to the front door.

"I can carry it myself, you know."

"I figured you could."

"But . . . "

"But, it was my mother's way to teach her sons to look out for women." When she stood at her front door, debating whether to inform him that most women liked to do things on their own, he lifted up the backpack. "Keys?"

It was on the tip of her tongue to mention how bossy he was, but since she needed them anyway, she unzipped the front pocket. "Thank goodness these weren't stolen."

"That is a blessing."

A blessing. What forty-year-old man said things like that?

Before she knew what he was about, he was inserting her key in the slot and turning the handle. "You got an alarm, sweetheart?"

"No."

He looked around, frowning slightly. "It looks a little dark in here. Want me to turn on some lights for you?"

Warmth threaded through her. This was the first time she'd had a man enter her house and try to help her get settled before taking off. Until that minute, she hadn't even realized that walking into an empty house had ever been a cause for concern.

Afraid she might even start liking that attention, she shook her head. "I'm drawing the line at you turning on my table lamps. I've got it."

"Okay, then. Hand me your car keys and tell me what you drive and where you parked."

"Are you sure about this?"

He didn't answer. Just kept his hand out.

"Fine. Here you go," she said as she tossed the key fob in his hand. "I parked in the same lot you and Finn did. In a space a couple of rows down. It's a red Honda Accord." She bit her lip. "I don't remember the license plate number, but—"

"I can find a red Honda Accord. I'll bring it by in a couple of hours."

"All right. Thank you."

"Let me give you my phone number."

She was about to refuse, then realized she was definitely going to want to text him later to say thanks again. She walked into the kitchen, turned on the cheery overhead lamp, which was Tiffany-style stained glass, and pulled out a scrap sheet of paper and pencil from her junk drawer.

After taking a look around, he scribbled his name, address, and phone number on the piece of paper. Then tore off the bottom of it and wrote down her name. "Give me your phone number."

She gave it to him before she thought the better of it. When he folded it and slipped it in his wallet, she smiled at him. "Did your mother also teach you to be bossy?"

He grinned. "Nope. I figured that out all by myself." Reaching out, he took her injured hand and kind of cradled it in between his own. "You take care and get some rest, Meredith Hunt."

"I will."

"Good." After treating her to another half smile, he turned and walked back to her front door. "Lock up."

"I will. And thanks again."

Just as he was about to turn away, he stopped and stared down at her. "Don't thank me, honey. I'm glad I was there."

Then, while she was just about to tell him not to call her honey, he was walking back out to his truck. She stood in the doorway as he sat down and buckled up. Then lit a cigarette. It perched between his lips as he pulled out, his window now partly rolled down.

Finn waved just as they drove out of sight.

In spite of her relief of being home at last, she couldn't help but feel a little at loose ends as she closed the door and locked both the locks.

For the first time in ages, being alone in her house had lost some of its appeal.

Or maybe she'd finally realized that it never had been all that good—she'd just been trying not to notice.

4

From Meredith Hunt's
Guidebook to SHINE Pilates:

Tip #7: Be Forgiving! Part of Pilates is learning about self-forgiveness and acceptance. You are not going to grasp everything the first time. That's okay! Just take a deep breath and try it again.

SATURDAY

After Meredith waved off Ace and Finn, she placed Ace's number on the kitchen counter with a sigh. She thought about sitting down and inspecting her backpack more thoroughly, just in case something else was missing that she hadn't realized.

She also considered getting right on the phone and calling those credit card companies. Perhaps even make a late lunch and starting a to-do list.

Instead of all that, she decided to take a bath. She felt grubby after her run, her fall on the trail, and sitting in the clinic. Her whole body was feeling sore, too. She might have only cut her hand, but her muscles were acting like she'd just gone two rounds in a boxing ring.

Then, there was her mental state. She was thirty-one years old, had dealt with a lot of things in her life, but had never felt so unsafe or off-kilter.

She'd always regarded Bridgeport as about the safest place in America. No longer, though. She realized she might even start being afraid to go running by herself on the bike trail. Every bit of her felt vulnerable, too.

Then there was Ace and Finn. For some unknown reason, she'd felt comfortable by Ace's side. She'd trusted him enough to get into his truck and let him take her to the hospital. She'd certainly never thought she'd trust another person so easily ever again.

After fumbling around with her clothes, doing her best to get out of them without hurting her bandaged palm in the process, she gingerly stepped into the hot bathwater.

Immediately, her muscles contracted, then slowly relaxed. Bringing with the action an immediate sense of relief. She poured in some lavender bath salts and let the scent soothe her.

Closing her eyes, she sank down farther. But while the water soothed her body, it was becoming apparent that her mind wasn't going to be quieted as easily.

She couldn't believe the way that Ace had

volunteered to give up several hours of his Saturday to help her. How he was still going to help by retrieving her car.

Then there was Finn. She was no expert on teenage boys, but she knew enough to realize that there weren't many who would go along to the urgent care clinic without complaining or trying to get out of it.

"No, what has you spun up isn't Finn's actions, or even Ace volunteering to pick up your car. It was what Ace said," she murmured to the empty room, her voice echoing and bouncing against the walls of the bathroom. "When he said that he wasn't that kind of man to leave a person in need, it struck a chord with you."

Maybe it was hearing the words aloud, but Meredith couldn't deny that she'd noticed how different her situation was from Ace's. She was an only child of a father who'd taken off when she was five and a mother who hadn't been shy about how much she'd resented her very existence.

Meredith didn't have to search far to locate the feelings of abandonment that she'd carried with her like a too-heavy coat in the middle of January. It felt cumbersome, but the fear of being caught without a way to keep herself warm weighed on her mind, so she kept wearing it.

Growing up, she'd tried so hard to become worthy in her mother's eyes. Her mother had worked in a bank and prized education, so Meredith had made sure she made straight As.

Mom had valued money and appearances, so Meredith had started working after school as soon as the closest fast-food restaurant would hire her.

Then, when her mother had fallen in love with Ken Marko—who she'd met at the bank and who was older and had money—Meredith had tried to act like she didn't mind moving to a new school or living in a new house.

She actually hadn't minded Ken. He'd been nice enough to her. However, it had always been pretty obvious that he would have rather had her mother all to himself.

Meredith had graduated at the top of her class and gotten a scholarship to Miami University. She'd lived in the dorms, worked various jobs on campus, and had majored in accounting. When she'd graduated, she'd gotten several offers from well-known financial institutions.

Feeling like her mother was finally proud of her, Meredith picked the best-paying job, bought herself a couple of conservative navy suits, and started working fifty hours a week.

She'd hated every minute of it.

She found the pressure stressful, the offices confining, and she was constantly afraid that she would inadvertently make a mistake and ruin someone's life.

Just when she'd begun to realize that she wasn't ever going to be happy working in finance—and that she was never going to have the relationship with her mother that she'd always yearned for—she got in serious car accident. A distracted driver hit her car on the highway.

Meredith had broken an arm, sustained a variety of cuts on her arms and face, and had been badly bruised. She'd also strained her neck and back.

Her recovery had been slow. So slow that she'd realized that she needed to take care of herself better—all of herself, not just where she'd been injured.

She'd started Pilates on her doctor's advice and had continued her training when she realized that it had made her feel centered and calm for the first time in forever.

She began to make plans. She scaled back her hours at the office and used the extra time to become a certified Pilates instructor. She got out of her fancy townhouse and bought a small house in Bridgeport, much to her mother's dismay.

Then, a year after her accident, she quit her job and opened her own Pilates studio. It was one of the best moments of her life.

It was also the day that her mother had said that she couldn't be more disappointed in her.

And *that,* she figured, was her life in a nutshell. One step backward, lots of ragged, painful steps forward, an attempt to hang on by her fingertips . . . just to realize that she still had a lot to learn in the relationship department.

Her experience with Scott had been the worst. She'd met him online, and had stumbled forward in their relationship in small, hesitant steps. She'd communicated with him for several weeks before agreeing to give him her phone number. Another month passed before she had consented to meet him in person.

That first meeting had changed everything. He'd seemed perfect—everything she'd dreamed he would be when she'd been sitting at her computer at home. Handsome and fit, charming and classy-looking. He'd gone to Ohio State, had a Land Rover, and had given her looks of appreciation that she couldn't ignore.

In short, he was everything her mother would have approved of. Everything she had on her list of attributes for a "perfect man." They'd dated, then gone exclusive, then become intimate. She had been so sure he'd been biding his time, waiting to propose marriage. In the middle of all that, she'd even introduced him to her mother and stepfather when they'd come up from Tampa to visit.

Her mother had looked at her like she'd done something good. Finally. Meredith had even begun to believe that her life was about to be charmed.

Then one of her clients stayed after class one

day and haltingly told Meredith that she'd seen Scott with another woman downtown.

The water in her bath rocked as she shifted. Splashed against the side as she recalled how irritated she'd been, hating that the woman had felt the need to ruin her happiness.

But it turned out that she'd been fooling herself. Scott actually had been lying to her. For months.

And when she confronted him?

Well, the things he'd said still hurt too much to remember word for word.

Since then, she'd kept to herself and focused on work and her house and volunteering. Things that mattered, made her feel good about herself, but didn't touch her heart. Until she met Ace, she'd been pretty proud of herself for keeping her life so steady. Actually, she'd almost convinced herself that she didn't need a serious relationship anymore. She was better off alone and keeping control.

Now, though, it felt kind of empty.

Afraid to dwell too much more on her past, she got out of the tub, threw on a pair of old leggings and a Miami sweatshirt, and then went to her computer and started calling her credit card and insurance companies. She needed to get her life back in order as soon as possible.

And hour later, Ace knocked on her door.

"Your car is in the drive," he said as he smiled at her. "You look like you feel better."

Feeling self-conscious in her old clothes and bare feet, she laughed. "I do feel better."

"I'm glad." He gazed at her again, then held up a hand. "Here are your keys."

She clutched them in her good hand. "Thank you. I can't thank you enough."

"You already have." He smiled again. "I'm going to take off. My buddy Kurt's outside waiting for me."

"Oh! Of course."

"Take it easy, okay? And put on some socks, darlin'. It's January."

"Anyone ever told you that you're pretty bossy?"

"Just about everyone I ever met." He winked. "I'll call you. Bye, now," he said as he strode back down her walkway and got in the passenger side of a big black truck.

Watching him drive off with his friend, Meredith couldn't help wondering if he really was one of those people who did what they said.

Who was as good as he seemed.

Who really would call her.

If he was? Well, she'd take that call and be friendly. Not expect anything more than a simple phone call.

And if he didn't?

She could handle that, too.

As she closed the door and wandered into her bedroom to put on a pair of socks, Meredith firmly reminded herself that it might be for the best if she put Ace and his tats and drawl and biceps out of her mind. She had a lot of other things going on in her life. Positive things. Good things. Like all her clients. And the great reviews her business was getting online.

And the money she was slowly making.

It was just too bad that none of those things kept her warm at night or made her feel all that loved.

5

From Les Larke's
Terms for Poker Success:

*Floorman: An employee of the cardroom who
makes the decisions. His or her opinion is
not always appreciated. The floorman is like
taking your dad on a date. His opinion is
useful but not always wanted.*

Later that afternoon, after Kurt had dropped him
off at his house, Ace ran Finn to the sporting-
goods store to pick up a new pair of running
shoes. The kid needed those shoes for Monday's
practice, and Ace had promised they'd get them
that afternoon.

Finn had acted pleased Ace hadn't forgotten
about the errand. But beyond the necessities,
neither of them had much to say to each other
during the short outing.

Ace was grateful for the quiet. He needed a
couple of minutes to think about his reaction to
Meredith. She'd summoned up a whole host of
emotions and tender feelings he'd assumed he'd
forgotten.

Now he realized that patience and compassion,

protectiveness, and old-school Southern manners were all things his mother had attempted to drill into his thick skull at a young age—and he'd ignored.

During the last two hours, he'd been everything he hadn't known he could be, at least not any-more.

No wonder Finn had kept looking so uncom-fortable! The kid probably hadn't been aware that his father could act so sweet.

It wasn't like he'd been all alone since Liz. He'd dated. Through the years, he'd even had a couple of casual relationships. But he hadn't been ready for anything more than that. He had Finn, and he had been determined to give the kid whatever attention he could whenever they had time together.

Then there had been his scars from Liz. She'd burned him good, constantly changing things between them, playing games with visitations. Lying to him about her social life.

Eventually, his parents had encouraged him to get lawyers involved. His lawyer, a sharp fifty-year-old woman named Marcie, had proven to be invaluable. It was because of her that he'd been able to form a real relationship with his son. But Marcie's services hadn't come cheap. After refusing to let his parents help with her fees, he'd begun working more overtime to pay the bills.

All that meant he was used to keeping a careful

distance from women, especially women who he found attractive.

So it was really ironic, like *really* ironic that he'd moved to Bridgeport to be all about Finn all the time—and what had he done? Found himself doing more for one red-headed Pilates teacher in need of a hand than he'd done for any woman in over a decade.

It just didn't make sense. He figured that he needed to get his head wrapped around that—and soon, too. Meredith Hunt was a nice lady, and she already had a connection with Finn. He was going to need to get his feelings figured out.

Why had he not only helped her, but refused every offer she'd made to let him leave? Why had he given her his cell phone number in case she needed something? Why had he walked her inside her house, just to make sure she was okay and safe? Why had he insisted on retrieving her car for her, even though it had taken another hour out of his day?

Though those actions had been nice, he couldn't ever remember being that nice.

So had he done all that because she'd been hurt, because she had been obviously kind to his kid . . . or because he found her really attractive?

"Hey, Dad?"

Realizing that he was going to have to dissect things later, Ace tried to clear his head. "Yeah?"

"What do you think of Miss Hunt?"

Guess he wasn't the only one with Meredith on his mind. "She seems sweet." No, she was a sweetheart, that's what she was.

Finn shifted in his seat. "I think she's pretty. I mean, she is for an older woman and all."

"She ain't that old. I bet she's ten years younger than me."

"You know what I mean."

"I know. And you're right. She is pretty." No, make that gorgeous. He'd never been a huge fan of redheads, but Meredith's looks had gotten him to thinking that he'd been wrong about that. "Does she act like that at school?"

"Like what?" Finn asked.

"That sweet?" That naive? That tender, like she needed someone to run interference in between her and the world? The question was out before he could take it back.

"Pretty much." His lips curved. "Everyone knows she's kind of a marshmallow. I heard that she sometimes even volunteers to help with some of the student athletes, like in their training or when they get hurt."

"Huh. I guess that makes sense. I don't know much about Pilates, but she must know a lot about bones and muscles."

"I don't know. Maybe."

He tried to imagine her on some football field and couldn't. "The kids don't take advantage of her?"

"I don't know for sure, but a couple of the people in Miss Springer's class told me that everyone's pretty cool around her." He shifted in his seat, stretching one of his legs out. "It's probably because the coaches act like they'd freak out on anyone who didn't speak to her real respectfully. Plus, everyone knows she's volunteering."

"What do you mean?"

"You know, she's not just at school for the money. Even kids appreciate that."

"Ah."

Finn glanced at him. "Now that I saw her house, that's kind of surprising, huh? I mean, it's not that fancy or anything."

"Money isn't everything."

Finn snorted. "Grandpa says that, too."

"A lot of people do."

Finn laughed, showing him that he wasn't buying Ace's excuse for a minute. "Grandpa ain't gonna believe that we've both been quoting him today."

"Don't you go telling him. If you do, he's never going to give us a moment's peace."

"You mean give *you* a moment's peace. Grandpa will just say that he's glad I haven't forgotten him."

The words stung a bit. It was true, Ace missed his family. He'd thought getting Finn away from his mother had been the right thing to do, that it trumped the loss he'd feel from losing his grandparents and aunts and uncles, but maybe he'd been wrong. "Grandpa knows you haven't forgotten him."

Finn shrugged. "I'll call him soon."

"Good idea." He parked the truck in the driveway and got out.

Finn pushed the garage door button and they walked inside. There were still some boxes from the move that Ace hadn't sorted through yet. When they walked into their house, Finn glanced at all the white walls. "Was her house pretty inside?" he asked, letting Ace know that Meredith was still on his mind.

"I didn't see much. I only stood in the doorway."

"But . . ."

"But, yeah, it was. Kind of girlie."

"Dad, did finding out she lives near us seem weird?"

"Why do you ask that?"

"I don't know." He shrugged. "I guess I thought she was fancier."

"We don't know much about her, Finn."

"Yeah. You're right."

Finn sounded embarrassed. Ace thought about giving him a break and telling him that he'd thought she was richer, too. His first impression of her had been that she was high-class. Everything he'd noticed about her had practically screamed that. Her neat nails—unpolished but neatly filed and cared for. The diamond solitaire earrings in her ears. The designer logo backpack that had gotten yanked. And maybe even the way she acted about all of it. Almost like those things weren't all that important to her.

Maybe they weren't.

Things weren't all that important to him either, but for a different reason. He'd never had a lot. Well, not until his mechanic job started taking off. He'd been making a boatload of money for some of the classic cars he'd been working on. He'd socked most of it in the bank, which had enabled him to pay for over half the house they were in, and to be able to be picky when he chose the new shop he worked for.

"Hey, we did a good thing today. If we hadn't been jogging on the trail, she could've really been in trouble."

"I thought about that, too." He was grateful that he and his boy had been nearby and Meredith hadn't been forced to deal with everything all by herself.

After tossing his keys and his wallet on the counter, he said, "I don't know about you, but I'm starved. What do you think about ordering a pizza? I'll even let you choose the place."

"Hey, Dad?"

"Yeah?"

"Do you think you'll see Miss Hunt again?"

"I don't know." Though everything inside of him wanted to blow off his kid's question, Ace didn't. "You mean like ask her out?"

Finn nodded.

"I'm not sure. I mean, I didn't come to Bridge-port to date."

After taking off his new shoes and putting them carefully on the bench by the back door, Finn looked at him sideways again. "If you don't want to date her, why did you hold her hand and stuff?"

So, that's where they were going. Feeling like this conversation meant something pretty important to his son, Ace thought about his actions and wished he had a concrete answer.

But all he could do was tell Finn the truth. "I don't know."

"Dad."

When had Finn perfected the art of making one word sound like an entire novel? Hating that he felt as awkward as he did, Ace rolled his shoulders. "Really, it's the truth. At first, it just seemed like I should. Then she asked me to." To cover up how affected he'd been by the small act, he attempted to lighten the mood. "Some girls get scared of needles and blood, you know."

"She was freaked out," Finn said with a smile.

"Holding her hand was just the right thing to do. The kind thing. Something your grandpa would have done. She was scared and I happened to be there."

Looking reflective, Finley nodded.

Ace felt like he'd just passed a test. "Let's order that pizza."

"Did you ever act that way with my mom?"

"With Liz?" He tried to act like he was trying to remember, but there wasn't anything to remember that had been so sweet. Taking care to not make her sound like a complete bitch, he murmured, "Nah. She wasn't that kind of girl."

"Oh."

Still facing each other in the middle of the kitchen, Ace said quietly, "We both know how your mother is, Finn. As hard as it is for me to tell you this, I can't think of a time when your mother was soft, shy, or needy." There was no reason to start reinventing the past. Liz was a lot of things, but no one could ever accuse her of ever acting vulnerable.

"I know." Frowning, he turned away. "I'll find that number. I think it's in the junk drawer." Watching Finn sort through a bunch of coupons and flyers, Ace walked to his side. "You mad at me? I promise, I wasn't making the moves on Meredith."

He shook his head. "I'm not mad. I just never saw you act like that before. You were real patient with her." Finn glanced back at him. He looked like he was about to say something more, but stopped himself.

Ace figured a better parent would have something good and meaningful to say, but he couldn't think of anything worthwhile.

So he just shrugged. "Like I said, some women just need their hands held from time to time. One of these days, you're going to be discovering that for yourself."

"I hope not. I've got a lot other things to worry about besides a needy girlfriend."

"I hear you," he said, smiling. "But listen, sooner or later a girl like that might come your way."

"I hope it's later."

"Still, when it does, I'd advise you to hold that hand. It's the right thing to do."

"If I do start holding some girl's hand, it's going to be because I feel sorry for her, not because I'm sweet on her or anything."

"Understood." Ace grinned, thinking that Finn's decision to not give any girls a second look was a relief. The boy had school and football to concentrate on—and a mother's cold shoulder to get over. The last thing he needed was a relationship.

Pulling out a blue flyer from one of the drawers, Finn said, "I'm gonna order pizza from Blue Ribbon, okay?"

"Blue Ribbon sounds good. Don't forget to

order bread sticks and ask for jalapeños on half of the pie."

"I'm on it."

After tossing a couple of bills on the counter, Ace walked to his bedroom. He realized that this was the first afternoon he'd felt that he had his boy back since the move.

Here, he'd taken him out on the bike trail in a half-baked attempt to get Finn to talk to him about how he was doing. But what had done the trick was a petite redhead in need of a helping hand.

No, it had been Meredith's sweet personality and gentle manner that had reached deep into both of them and brought out qualities that had long been buried.

He never was the type of man to give thanks for anything that had happened to him. But at that moment—even though he knew he shouldn't feel right about it—he was real pleased that pretty Meredith Hunt had gotten robbed right in front of them.

He'd been glad to help her . . . and he was starting to get the feeling she had helped them both even more than that.

6

From Les Larke's
Terms for Poker Success:

Gut Shot: To hit an inside straight. If you get this, consider yourself lucky, you had the right cards at the right time. Wouldn't it be great if this happened more often in life?

"Hey, Ace, you got a minute?" Cliff Malone called out from the front office.

"Yeah." After double-checking the bolt he'd just tightened one last time, Ace edged out from under the hood of the '68 Camaro RS he'd been working on for the last week. He'd practically salivated when the owner had brought it in, complaining of some suspicious knocks and pings whenever he took the vehicle above fifty miles an hour. Working on classic cars was what Ace excelled at.

Even better had been that the man had brought the car to Bridgeport Automotive specifically for Ace. Turned out his buddy owned the vintage E-type Jaguar that Ace had synchronized the carburetor to three weeks earlier.

After wiping his hands on one of the many white rags he kept on hand, Ace walked to the office door. "What's up?"

But instead of giving him an order like he usually did, Cliff rested an elbow on his old scarred desk. "Close the door, would you? It's cold as hell out there."

It was cold. After the unexpectedly spring-like weekend, typical January had returned with a vengeance. The daytime temperatures were supposed to hover around freezing the rest of the week. However, the heater was on in the office, and Cliff was wearing a couple of layers. Compared to the garage, the office felt like Florida.

Concerned, he closed the door and looked at his boss a little more carefully. "You all right, boss?"

As he'd hoped, Cliff's expression folded into amusement. "I've been running this shop for twenty-five years, and you're the only kid who continually calls me boss."

Ace sat down. "I'm hardly a kid. And it ain't my fault you're hiring workers who don't pay you no respect," he added lightly. That wasn't true. The other five mechanics in the shop were top-notch guys.

"Point taken. You should remember that next time we need to hire on again."

"Me?"

"Yeah. That's what I'm trying to say. I got my

results back from my last physical and the news wasn't good. I've got a blockage in one of my arteries. The doc thinks I'm going to need to get Roto-Rootered out."

"Damn. I'm sorry."

"Me, too." Looking grim, he said, "Wendy took it even worse than I did. She said she's not ready to be a widow."

Ace inhaled sharply. "It's as bad as that?"

"Nah," Cliff said quickly before taking a gulp of air. "I mean, I don't think so. But it isn't good. The doctor said I finally have to change some things, and he's right. I need to eat better and move more." His gaze flickered back to Ace. "And work less. Wendy and me talked, and we agreed that after I get better, we need to take some time and do things together. Travel, maybe."

Ace nodded. "She's right."

"That means I need a manager. And that means I need you."

"But I just started here."

Gray eyes fastened on him and held tight. "You told me when I hired you on that your long-term goal was to run your own shop. I'm asking you to start thinking about doing it sooner than later."

"But the other guys—aren't they going to be upset?"

He shrugged. "Maybe. A lot of them are real good mechanics, even though none of them are as good as you." Resting his elbows on the desk, he continued. "Emerson and the guys also know a lot about working in a garage, I wouldn't trust them with the shop's bank account or taking over the reins. I worked too hard for one of them to accidentally blow it up. However, I do trust you." Still eyeing him steadily, Cliff said, "I'm talking putting you on salary. It would give you a real nice raise. Full benefits for you and your kid, too."

Ace would have taken on the responsibility simply to help Cliff out. Getting a full package, too? He would never pass that up. "When would you want me to start?"

"Next week or so," Cliff replied, looking pleased. "The doc wants me to get fixed up soon."

Ace knew Cliff hadn't made the offer lightly. He didn't take it for granted either. But he also knew if he took it, his long-range plans would have to change. He'd been hoping to work for Cliff for a year or so before leaving to open his own shop. If he took Cliff up on his offer, he would need to honor the commitment and stay at Cliff's shop as long as he was needed.

Of course, the upside was that he wouldn't have to use all his savings. He could have that set aside in case Finn didn't get the scholarships his coaches seemed sure he was going to receive.

"Cliff, thank you. I'll be glad to accept."

"Ha. I thought you were going to make me wait a day or two."

Ace shook his head. "Nah, I don't work that way. I need a good job, and you're offering me one that's better than I expected. I appreciate your faith in me."

"You just gave me one less thing to worry about and made Wendy real happy." Cliff stood up and held out his hand. "Let's shake on it then."

Standing up as well, Ace shook the older man's hand, thinking that Cliff's hand probably felt a lot like his own. Rough and scarred from years of hard work. Firm, like he knew his mind and stood behind it. Ace hoped he'd do him proud. "Thanks again, boss. Now, do you need anything else?"

"Yeah, after you help me get the shop cleaned up, get on out of here. It's heading toward four o'clock. You were already here at seven, when I got here."

Ace grinned. "Will do."

He was pleased that Emerson and JD had already cleaned up the worst of the mess when he got into the garage. All he had to do was put away a couple of the tools and write down some notes about some of the problems he'd discovered with the Camaro he'd been working on.

After closing and locking the garage doors, JD looked his way. "Everything okay?"

"Yeah."

"Good. I'm out of here, then."

"I'll be right behind y'all."

Twenty minutes later, he was getting into his own Chevy Silverado 1500 and blasting the heat. While the engine warmed up, he checked his phone. Seeing that Finn was already home and doing homework, Ace texted Kurt to see if he was around. His buddy's reply was immediate and succinct.

I'm bored as sin. Come on over.

Grinning at the words, Ace knew Kurt had intentionally quoted Ace's father. Hank Vance lived for spouting clichéd sayings. It bugged the heck out of him when he'd been a kid. But now? Hearing one of his dad's sayings made him homesick.

As he drove over to Kurt's house, he made a mental note to call his parents later on and tell his father about Cliff's offer. Since moving to Bridgeport, he'd come to realize just how much he'd taken his parents and brother and sister for granted. He hadn't seen them every week back in Spartan, but it was a rare occurrence when he didn't cross paths with one of his family members within a two-week period. He realized now that if *he* was missing them, Finn was no doubt feeling their loss even more.

As he drove down the windy streets of

Bridgeport, looking at the bare branches and wondering what spring would look like, he also thought about Meredith, and wondered how she was faring. Though he told her he'd call, he was starting to have second thoughts about it. He knew there was something about her that he liked, and a phone call wasn't going to change that.

If he wasn't careful, he'd be trying to see her, then who knows what would happen after that.

He found Kurt in his garage, sipping a beer and looking at a calendar.

"Hey. What's going on?"

"I was just trying to figure out when I can go on another college visit with Sam."

Kurt had left Spartan for his little brother, who was their parents' " oops baby" and the smartest kid to come out of their town—at least by anybody's recollection. Kurt had moved him to Bridgeport so he could take college prep classes and get noticed by some Ivy League colleges. Then, Kurt had fallen in love with Emily, Sam had gotten himself a steady girl—and had also started talking about how he didn't want to move so far away.

Kurt often had confided to Ace that it all had been a good lesson on never thinking anything was a done deal.

"Where are y'all headed this time?"

"University of Dayton."

Ace froze in midnod. "Wait, Dayton, Ohio?"

Kurt grinned. "Emily swears it's terrific, but I had the same reaction. The kid got a letter from Vanderbilt two days ago. *Vanderbilt*, Ace. They offered a full ride, too. Emily thinks Stanford might even step up to the plate, too. But instead of getting excited about all that, he's been carrying around the packet from Dayton and says he thinks we need to go take a second look."

Ace grabbed a beer and sat down across from the guy he used to sit next to in kindergarten. "Is it all about the girl?" Sam had fallen for a pretty cheerleader named Kayla soon after he started the school year. Now they were practically inseparable.

"Maybe."

"What are you going to do about that?"

"Me? Nothing." He took another sip of his beer. Then he pushed the calendar away. "The truth is, I've learned that Sam's got a mind of his own. And there's no way I'm going to say boo about Kayla." His voice softened. "There's a part of me that hopes that the two of them do stay together. She's a sweet thing, and they've been through a lot."

Ace couldn't believe Kurt was okay with Sam being so serious about some girl. But maybe it was more of a case of him not being able to think of any teenaged girl without thinking about eighteen-year-old Liz. He'd hooked up with her and gotten her pregnant with Finn. And though he would never regret Finn—hell, that boy was the best thing in his life—he wouldn't encourage any eighteen-year-old to rush into a relationship.

Kurt leaned back. "I'm guessing you don't agree."

"Like you said, it's not my choice to make. Besides, I've got some news I need you to help me think on."

"Oh, yeah?" Kurt opened a pack of cards and started dealing gin. "What's going on?"

"My new boss Cliff is going to have to have some surgery and wants to step back. He asked me to be the new manager."

"Really? But you just got here."

"I know. It's too sudden. But he said a lot of complimentary things. And I am older than two of the other guys."

"What did you say?"

"I told him yes. He offered me a raise and benefits. Plus, the guy needs help."

"If you already said yes, what are you worried about?"

As they played a round of gin, Ace relayed his pros and cons. Kurt discarded, picked up cards, and listened a lot. Then, just as they heard two car doors slam in the driveway, he said, "I think you should relax. You did the right thing."

Ace nodded. "Me, too," he said slowly. "Hearing me talk to you about the options makes everything seem a lot more real. Thanks."

"Glad you came by," he said, just as both Sam and Kurt's girlfriend, Emily, stepped inside.

"Hey, Ace!" Sam said.

Ace got to his feet. "Hey, buddy. Congrats on all the college offers."

Sam frowned. "Did Kurt start talking to you about Dayton?"

"A little bit. He really just told me how proud he was of you."

Sam chuckled. "Yeah, right." Turning to Kurt, who had just given Emily a heck of a kiss, he said, "Did you go to the store?"

"Yep. I bought three frozen pizzas and a ton of lunch meat. Go eat."

"Awesome. See ya, Ace."

"See ya." After Sam disappeared into the house, Ace smiled at Emily. "Good to see you, Em. I'll get on my way now."

"One sec," Kurt said, a new sparkle in his eye. "Emily was just telling me that she got a call from someone you know at school today."

"Who is that?"

"Meredith Hunt."

"Meredith?" He tried to play it cool. "Oh. Yeah. Finn and I met her over the weekend."

"According to her, you did more than that. You helped her out of a tight spot and took her to urgent care. What happened?"

Feeling self-conscious, he said, "Finn and I saw some kid steal her backpack and knock her down.

Finn found the backpack but her wallet was gone. Since she needed stitches, we took her there."

"That was decent of you."

"You would have done it. Anyone would have."

"She was sure grateful," Emily said as a slow smile lit her face. "And, when she realized that I knew you, she asked all kinds of questions."

"She did? Huh."

"Um-hum. I think she thought you were cute."

"Pretty old to be considered cute, Emily."

She grinned. "She actually said some other things, but I think I'll keep those to myself."

Kurt raised his eyebrows. "What's she like? Single?"

"She's single, redheaded, and gorgeous," Emily answered before he could.

"Is that right?" Kurt's eyes lit up. "You ought to give Ace her phone number, Em."

"I already have it." Damn. He probably didn't need to admit that.

Kurt's grin widened. "So you've called her?"

"He hasn't," Emily supplied before Ace could answer.

"Why the hell not?" Kurt asked.

Feeling like he was on a crazy roller coaster at Kings Island, Ace tried to sidestep and shut the conversation down. "Because I'm not really in the market for a woman."

Emily wrinkled her nose. "Why not? Meredith is really nice."

"It's nothing against Meredith." *Like, not at all.* "It's just that I've got other things to focus on right now. I moved here for Finn, you know."

"I get it," Kurt said. "I mean, I moved here for Sam, but I still fell in love."

Ace shook his head. "No offense, but your situation was different."

"Because?"

"Sam is your little brother. Finn's my son. There's different expectations, especially given that his mother is, um . . ." What could he say that Emily wouldn't find offensive?

"A slut?" Kurt asked, one eyebrow raised.

Ace swallowed, then went with it. After all, a spade was a spade. "Yeah. Because Liz is . . . what she is. Finn already had to deal with a lot, and I don't plan to . . ." He trailed off when he saw the expression on Kurt's face.

Looking like he had all the answers in the world, Kurt leaned back in his chair and crossed his boot-covered feet. "Sometimes it doesn't matter what you've got planned," he drawled. "Take it from me—life has a way of doing its own thing, whether you're in or not."

If Emily hadn't been sitting there with them, Ace would have commented on his buddy's smug demeanor. Maybe teased him a bit about being whipped.

But she was, and so he didn't.

Then, too, was the nagging feeling that

79

Kurt's statement had a lot of truth to it. A lot of important things in his life had happened in spite of himself—Finn, Liz's shenanigans, and football. Now Cliff was offering him a great job managing a great garage—a garage where, a couple of years ago, he wouldn't even have dreamed of working.

And then there was Meredith.

He'd never been an especially religious guy, but it certainly seemed like God was arranging things to His own liking. Maybe he should pay attention to that.

He decided to give Meredith a call soon.

7

From Meredith Hunt's
Guidebook to SHINE Pilates:

*"You will feel better in ten sessions, look
better in twenty sessions, and have a
completely new body in thirty sessions."*
—JOSEPH PILATES

THURSDAY

About two years ago, when Meredith hit twenty-
nine and was starting to wonder if marriage and
motherhood was ever going to happen, she had
started volunteering at the high school once a
week.

She wasn't exactly sure why she'd decided that
devoting three hours of every Thursday afternoon
to teenagers was going to fill the gap created by her
lack of a love life, but she'd gone and done it. She'd
called up her friend Emily and asked if there was
anything she could do to help her out at school.

Emily hadn't even given her an hour to wait.
She'd told her to come into her classroom that
very afternoon.

So she had. Feeling nervous and strangely unqualified to help Emily's freshman honors class, Meredith had hesitantly stood at the door of the classroom, staring at the assortment of twenty-five teenagers—each of them looked both more savvy and smarter than she felt.

Just as she started trying to think of a way to back out of the idea, Emily'd spied her standing there. Hardly waiting a second, she greeted Meredith like a returning soldier and introduced her to the kids as one of her best friends. Then, instead of putting Meredith in the back of the room grading papers, Emily had given her a group of four students, and told them to start reading *A Tale of Two Cities* together.

Meredith had done her best but hadn't found the first two chapters any more appealing than she had the first time she'd read it. When her small group had looked just as unimpressed by the Dickens masterpiece, they'd bonded.

She'd found something with those freshmen that she hadn't even known she'd been looking for. Yes, it was acceptance, but it was more than that. It was humor and sarcasm, and maybe even a little bit the chance to revisit high school again—but this time feeling more confident and self-assured.

She'd never looked back.

Now, even though she owned her own company and often worked far more than just forty hours a week, she continued to volunteer. Being around the kids rejuvenated her. She liked being around the teens. Liked their humor, liked their excitement about things. Simply liked feeling like she was helping them, even if it was just giving them another adult to connect with.

All that was why she'd come back into Emily Springer's classroom on Thursday, not quite a week after her fall, even though her hand was still bandaged up and the bruise on her face had turned to a blob of lavender and yellow. Even though she could have fit in a couple of her clients who she'd had to cancel on on Monday.

Even though she was feeling slightly blue because Ace Vance, for all his sincerity, had ended up not calling her after all. She knew that because she'd watched her phone like a pot of water on the stove. Not a peep. Not even a text.

After signing in, she put on her visitor's pass and walked the now-familiar path down to Emily's classroom. Emily was lecturing at the front of the room about mysteries. Meredith smiled at both her and the class before heading to the table on the side of the classroom.

But as soon as she took off her coat, a silence slipped over the room.

"What happened to you?" Bryan called out.

She lifted her head to find the entire class staring at her. She looked at Emily in confusion.

"I didn't tell anyone about what happened,

Meredith," Emily said. "I thought that was your story."

And just like that, she blushed like one of the freshman girls sitting in the front row. "It's no big deal. I just had a little accident on the bike trail."

"You've got a big bandage on your hand, Miss Hunt," Emily said. "And a good-size bruise on your cheek. It might just be me, but I think it might have been more than just a little accident."

"It isn't just you, Miss Springer," Bryan said. "Miss Hunt, you look like you got in a fight."

Courtney Pritchard, a cute freshman with a pixie cut, stared at her wide-eyed. "Did someone hit you, Miss Hunt?"

"I . . . well . . ." Then, to her shame, she locked eyes with Finn Vance. And that was when she knew she couldn't completely lie. Straightening her shoulders, she faced everyone. "The truth is, I was mugged."

And . . . those were the magic words to send the whole room into a frenzy. Emily—bless her heart—didn't do a darn thing to stop them.

A couple girls even got to their feet. "You were mugged? Where?"

"On the bike trail."

It turned out that was the wrong thing to say. "Mugged?" Courtney repeated. "Right here in Bridgeport?"

Feeling terrible that her appearance had set

Emily's whole lesson on its ear, Meredith tried to amend her explanation. "Mugged might be putting it a little strong. A man grabbed my backpack and knocked me down while I was out running."

"What did you do?"

Meredith's gaze darted from Emily's to Finn's. When she spied both Emily's look of concern and Finn's brief nod, she felt comfortable telling the whole story. "I'm happy to tell you that Finn and his father just happened to be on the trail, too. His father helped me to my feet and Finn ran after the guy and found my backpack."

Emily's eyebrows rose. "Finn, was that even a good idea? You could have gotten hurt."

Finn shrugged off his teacher's concern the same way he'd shrugged off her own. "It wasn't any big deal. I didn't see the guy. All I did was pick up Miss Hunt's backpack on the ground. That's all."

"That was really brave," one of the girls said.

"Cool of you," another boy uttered.

Finn shrugged again. "It's good we were there."

"What happened to your hand? How come it's so bandaged up?"

"When I landed, my hand hit some broken glass. I had to get seven stitches," she finished almost proudly as she held up her hand. Goodness! She wasn't any better than the kids, showing off her wound.

Valerie Jenkins' eyes grew wide. "I bet that hurt."

"I got a couple of shots first, so it wasn't too bad."

And just like that, she felt her face flame. There had been only one way that she'd been able to get through those shots, and it had a lot to do with a very big man in a black T-shirt, with a voice like gravel.

Afraid to see Finn's expression, she smiled brightly. "Obviously, I survived."

A couple of the students grinned. Still others called out questions. She had a feeling the students in Emily's other classes were going to act the same way, though probably not as exuberantly as these freshmen.

"Did you call the police?"

"I did call the police when I got home, but they weren't too hopeful about me getting my wallet back. But everything is fine now. I got a new driver's license and credit cards, so it's all good."

"We're all glad you're okay," Emily said. "You could have been really hurt."

One of the girls in the back of the room glanced at Finn again. "You were lucky Finn was there to help you."

"You're right. I was very lucky. They helped me out a lot." Knowing that her little adventure had taken up enough time, she lifted her chin. "You will all be happy to hear that having a hurt hand will not affect my ability to help Miss Springer."

Just like before, her declaration was met with good-natured complaints.

"So, can we go back to English now?" Meredith asked. "It looks like we're finally getting to the good books."

As she'd expected, Emily raised one eyebrow in scorn. "*Finally* getting to the good books?"

Winking at a couple of the kids, she said, "I'm sorry, but you know I only like books that are fun to read."

Emily sighed. "Like *And Then There Were None*?" she asked as she picked up the Agatha Christie paperback.

"Exactly. I love Agatha Christie."

Sounding a little put upon, she said, "Then you're in luck, I guess. We were just finishing up the notes."

"While y'all do that, I'll get settled." She walked back to her chair, picked up one of the books Emily had stacked on the table and tried to get comfortable.

As Emily went over the schedule for the novel, Meredith noticed Finn glance at her curiously. She supposed that was to be expected. After all, they'd helped her so much and she hadn't even texted his father to tell him thank you.

Realizing that she'd been so fixated on hoping that Ace had felt the same thing between them that she had, she hadn't even done the minimum of good manners. Finn was probably thinking she was really rude.

Feeling worse by the second, she continued to fret. She should have done something for the two of them.

Maybe invite them over for dinner as a thank-you? Most men would probably appreciate a home-cooked meal. Or . . . maybe not. She was a pretty good baker but not a great cook, so she probably shouldn't invite them over to dinner. Besides, that would probably be too much, anyway. Ace would probably think she was making a move on him, which would be really embarrassing.

"Miss Hunt? You ready for us?" Bryan asked.

She jerked her head up. "Hmm? Oh, yeah. Sorry. My mind drifted." Looking at the six freshmen who had decided to join her, Meredith felt a momentary flash of disappointment when she realized that Finn wasn't one of them. But how could she blame him? He was trying to make friends and fit into his new school. Hanging out with the lady volunteer in the classroom wasn't the way to do that.

"So, I'll have you know that y'all are in luck. I have actually read this book before."

"Really?" Amy said.

"Yes, really," she teased right back. "And yes, I'm also a little disappointed that you have so little faith in your volunteer."

"Sorry, but you usually think everything we're reading is boring."

"Not boring, exactly. More along the lines of a little dry."

One of the girls snickered. "You're the craziest volunteer, Miss Hunt. Don't you know you're supposed to lie and say you like everything?"

"Emily must have forgotten to send me that memo." Before Emily got annoyed with her, she picked up the book. "How about I read the first chapter out loud?"

"I say yes," Bryan said.

"Sit back and get prepared to be impressed with my fantastic reading skills. They're impressive."

Just as she was about to begin, she caught Finn watching her from the corner of her eye. It was obvious that he wasn't sure what to think about her.

But it seemed he was thinking about her. She hoped he was realizing that she could be a friend.

She spent the rest of the forty-five minutes reading with the kids, entering some grades into the computer for Emily, and chatting with a couple of the students she'd gotten close to. When the bell chimed, signaling it was time to change classes, she took a sip of water and realized that she'd probably have to fend off the same kind of questions in the next two classes.

"Hey, Miss Hunt?"

Startled, she looked up to find Finn standing awkwardly in front of her. "Yes?"

He swallowed, looked around like he was seeing who was standing nearby, then blurted, "I, um, well, I was just wondering how you were doing. Really."

"I'm okay." Lifting up her hand, she said, "I really am. My stitches are starting to itch, which people tell me is a good sign." Smiling at him, she added, "Thanks for checking on me."

He nodded, then turned back. "Hey, my dad was talking about you with Miss Springer's boyfriend."

"He knows Kurt?"

"Yeah. My dad and him have been friends forever. They played ball in high school together."

"Small world." She opened her mouth, wanting to know exactly what Ace had said about her to Kurt, but realized that would put Finn in an awkward position.

Finn shifted his weight. "I think he's been wondering how you've been doing."

"Really? Oh. Well, you can give him a report now." Boy, she really hoped she sounded far more cool and collected than she felt.

"I'll do that."

Later, after she had helped out in two more of Emily's classes, made plans to join her for dinner later in the month, and taught two classes at her studio, Meredith finally got home, showered, and collapsed on the couch.

She was tired and hungry. But, just as she was trying to summon the energy to heat up a Lean Cuisine, she found herself scooting back on the couch and replaying Finn's words for about the seventy-third time in her mind.

Ace wouldn't have been talking about her if he wasn't interested . . . would he?

And Finn wouldn't have shared that his dad was talking about her if he didn't think that everything he'd had to say had been good. Would he?

Hating that she felt so insecure, she went to the kitchen, opened the freezer, bypassed the frozen dinner, and went straight for the Graeter's ice cream. Cookies and cream was calling her name.

And since her phone had stayed conspicuously quiet all day, she grabbed a spoon and went to town.

8

From Les Larke's
Favorite Poker Quotations:

"It's not about the cards. It's how you play your hand."

Finn had been starting to worry that he'd gotten outside too late to catch a ride home when Sam Holland appeared in the parking lot. As usual, Kayla was walking by his side. The two of them hardly did anything apart.

When he'd first moved to Bridgeport, Finn had been pretty disappointed that Sam had such a serious girlfriend. Sam had been the only person he knew at Bridgeport High, and Finn had been counting on hanging out with him a lot. As soon as he'd gotten to school he'd realized that that had been a pretty stupid idea. Sam was a senior and Finn was a sophomore. Seniors and sophomores didn't hang out all that much at Bridgeport High.

They hadn't back in Spartan either, but the lines weren't quite as drawn as they were in Bridgeport. Probably because Spartan High School had been about a third of the size of

Bridgeport. Social groups seemed to mean a lot more here than they did there.

"Hey, Finn!" Sam called out as he approached, Kayla's hand secure in one of his and her backpack in his other. "Sorry you had to wait."

"No big deal."

"It was my fault," Kayla said. "I had a cheer-leading meeting."

Finn shrugged again. "Like I said, it wasn't any big deal."

Since Kayla still looked kind of worried, he added, "It wasn't like I had a lot of other stuff going on."

"It sucks being the new kid," Sam said as he clicked open his truck's locks.

Finn waited until Sam had helped Kayla into his truck and she'd slid into the middle before he hopped in. "Yeah, but it's all right. It could be worse."

After Sam started driving, Kayla smiled at him. "I have a feeling you're going to start being a lot more popular."

"Why's that?"

"I overheard some of the freshmen girls talking about you in the locker room. Did you really take down some mugger on the bike trail?"

"No. I just ran after the kid and picked up Miss Hunt's backpack when he dropped it."

Sam glanced his way. "What? What happened?"

"Miss Hunt got attacked on the bike trail

a few seconds before my dad and I found her."

"Was she okay?"

"Not really. She had a concussion and needed stitches in her hand. My dad and I took her to urgent care."

"I didn't hear that," Kayla said.

"I didn't share that. And neither did Miss Hunt."

Sam frowned. "How come her name sounds familiar?"

"Because she helps out in Miss Springer's freshman English classes."

"Wait a second. Does she have thick red hair?"

"Yep, though she calls it auburn." He couldn't help but smile about that. His dad had whispered to him that he wasn't sure about the difference between red and auburn.

Sam was still trying to place her. "She's real pretty and has blue eyes, right?"

"Yeah. I mean, I guess she is for an old lady."

"She's not that old."

"Oh, really? Just how young and pretty is she, Sam?" Kayla asked.

Finn bit back a smile.

Sam reached out and squeezed her knee. "Stop. You know I don't mean anything by that."

"I know. I'm just teasing you."

"I hope so, because you don't have anything to worry about."

Finn decided to save himself. If he didn't step

in quick, he was going to be subjected to a whole lot of hand-holding and too-sweet talk. "Miss Hunt is a Pilates teacher and volunteers in Miss Springer's room once a week. They're friends I guess." And . . . he was starting to sound like a girl.

"Oh! That's Meredith," Kayla said. "My mom knows her. She's really nice."

"She is nice, but I can't believe you had to go to urgent care with her," Sam said. "That had to be awkward."

Thinking about how his dad acted around her, Finn was thinking that it probably wasn't as big a surprise as Sam thought it was. He'd also felt kind of sorry for her, since she'd told them that she didn't have anyone else to take her to the hospital. It had felt awfully familiar.

But since he wasn't in any hurry to share that, he just shrugged.

He stared out the window as Sam continued to drive through the hilly, windy streets of Bridgeport. Being the end of January, the trees were bare and the clouds were gray. Snow wasn't expected anytime soon, just temperatures to stay in the twenties and thirties.

It was enough to make everyone talk about spring, and it seemed that Kayla was no exception. She started talking about spring break, prom, Sam's upcoming graduation, and the job she'd just gotten at a nearby golf course.

All of those things sounded so familiar but kind of foreign to him, too. Not that nobody did any of those things back in Spartan, but that it had been all so different from his life.

Back in West Virginia, especially over the last year, he'd been just trying to survive. His mother, who'd always acted erratic, had started acting even more distant that fall.

He'd never told his dad, but there had been more than a couple of nights when she hadn't even come home. He'd been stuck in their house, worried about her, and kind of scared to be alone.

She'd never left him without food or anything, but it wasn't much to speak of. Frozen meals and cans of soup. Cereal, ramen, boxes of mac and cheese. Easy food for him to fix by himself.

He'd spent a lot of time alone, which meant he'd started working out even more than usual. The coaches had been pleased, and the guys on the team were impressed. His efforts had won them a lot of games, but even those victories had felt hollow—especially since winning games seemed like the only thing his mom cared about.

Depending on what guy she was sleeping with, she'd take them to his games. After the game, she'd wait at the field house, wearing too little and fawning over him like she cared. It had been embarrassing as hell. At first a couple guys on the team had teased him about it, but he'd shut that down quick.

Sometimes though, Finn had gotten the feeling that the guys had stopped teasing him more because they felt sorry for him than because they were afraid he'd beat them up.

Boy, there had been times when he'd really hated his life.

It wasn't until Mom had told his dad that she wanted to move that things had started to get better. Dad had come over to see him. And, for the first time in months, instead of just waiting in his truck, he'd walked inside their apartment.

It had looked pretty bad.

Finn had tensed, sure that his father was about to blow. But instead of doing that, Dad had clenched his hands and told him to pack a couple of bags because he was coming to live with him right away.

A couple weeks after that, he'd sat Finn down and talked to him about Bridgeport, Ohio. The way he'd described it, the place had sounded too good to be true. People had money and weren't scraping by. The school was fancy, and all the kids had laptops—even the ones who couldn't afford their own.

And the football coaches were interested in meeting Finn . . . if Finn wanted to meet them.

Finn hadn't cared about laptops or football programs as much as he did about getting some distance from his mother. Well, that and not having every kid he knew look at him with pity.

That had been the driving factor. Because going through high school with a mom who cared more about her social life than her son sucked. He'd said yes to his dad right away.

Now he was here, living in some kind of TV world, sitting next to Sam Holland and his beautiful girlfriend and listening to them talk about prom.

It was about a thousand degrees away from his life back in October.

"Hey, Finn? You okay?"

He jerked, realizing he'd been gazing off into the past while Sam had pulled into his driveway. "Yeah. Sorry."

"Is, uh, everything going okay on campus? Is anybody bothering you?"

"Nah, I'm fine."

"You sure? Cause sometimes upperclassmen can be pricks."

"Everyone's been cool. Probably because Coach McCoy asked a couple of the guys on the team to start working out with me."

"He's also pretty big, Sam," Kayla said. "It's not like he's like some of the other underclassmen boys."

Sam grinned. "Sorry. I still think of you being eight and eating glue."

"Thanks for that." Finn wanted to thank him for caring, but he wasn't going to say anything like that in front of Kayla.

"And . . . are you okay with your dad?" Sam coughed. "I know we're not real close or anything, but if you want to talk, I can listen." When he noticed Finn glance at Kayla, he said, "I mean, just the two of us."

First, Finn wasn't good at talking about his shit with anybody. Second? He sure wasn't going to start whining like a baby in front of his only friend or his cheerleader girlfriend.

Besides, what would he say? Sam Holland didn't have a mom anymore, but the one he used to have had been great. A whole lot better than his own, anyway.

"Thanks, but I'm good." He opened the door and hopped out. "Thanks for the ride home."

"No problem. See ya."

"Yeah, see ya."

"See you tomorrow, Finn," Kayla said with a smile.

Finn smiled back, feeling his cheeks flush. He hoped Sam didn't notice. If he did, he would probably think that it was because he had some kind of weird crush on his girl. In reality, Finn was embarrassed about them both thinking he was needy.

Luckily, Sam didn't even look back at him. He just put the truck in reverse and backed out of the driveway.

As he watched them drive away, Sam's arm slipped around Kayla. Finn figured that he was already the last thing on either of their minds. They were really tight.

"Do you really know Kayla Everett?"

Finn turned in surprise at the voice, then barely stifled a groan. There stood Allison Peterson. Their neighbor. Allison was a junior, some kind of 4-H nerd, and annoying as all get-out. During the few times they'd seen each other, she'd gotten all in his business. The girl had no filter.

Case in point. Here he'd just gotten out of Sam's truck and was heading toward his front door when she'd called out her prying question. One that made it real obvious that she'd been lurking in her driveway watching him.

Who did that?

Now here she was, asking him about Kayla. Who he knew or didn't know wasn't any of her business.

Back home, he would've ignored her and walked inside his house. But his dad would chew him out good if Allison's mom shared that Finn had been rude to her daughter.

"Yeah, I know Kayla," he said at last.

So there. He'd answered. But it wasn't friendly, like at all.

But that was all it took for Allison to walk through the gap in the hedge that separated their properties. She was wearing a white turtleneck, black leggings, and Uggs. All of it fit her kind of tight. And that hair of hers? It was golden and wavy and hanging down the center of her back.

He took a closer look at her body and was surprised. She was a lot better looking than he'd thought.

"Is she nice?"

"Kayla? Yeah." Then, realizing that he sounded like a jerk, he added, "She's my friend's girlfriend."

"Oh, I know she's Sam Holland's girlfriend." She said Sam's name like it was a big deal.

Which kind of bugged him. He didn't like how she was talking about Sam and his girlfriend like characters in some TV show.

Ready to shut the conversation down, he stepped closer. Almost into her space. "You know Sam?"

As he'd hoped, she took a step back. "No! I mean, he's a senior." Her light-brown eyes kind of bugged out. "I wasn't gossiping. I mean, everyone knows that Kayla and Sam are really together. I mean, he beat up Garrett Condon for her."

Allison sounded kind of dreamy, which might have been kind of sweet if she hadn't been such an annoying person. "If you knew about Sam and Kayla, why are you asking me about her?"

"I don't know. I was just surprised. I mean, here you are, brand new to Bridgeport and you're already hanging out with two of the most popular upperclassmen."

"I know Sam from back home."

"You guys are from West Virginia, right?"

Jeez. It was like the girl had been spying on him nonstop. "Uh-huh. Listen, I've gotta—"

"Our shepherd had puppies," she interrupted.

"Your what?"

"We have an Australian shepherd named Maggie. She had puppies two nights ago. Five of them." She smiled. "Want to see? They're really cute."

He didn't really want to have anything to do with her. But, she *was* his neighbor. And she had mentioned the one thing that he'd always wanted but never had. A dog. "Where are they?"

Allison looked at him strangely. "In our laundry room."

He didn't want to be around her much more. But, she had puppies.

And he was even less eager to be in his empty house. Even though he knew his dad was just at work and hadn't skipped town, it still made him uncomfortable—an insecurity leftover from his mom's frequent disappearances.

"Yeah, sure."

Allison smiled at him, obviously pleased. "Come on, then. They're adorable."

After putting his backpack next to his front door, he followed her through the hedge, into her garage, and through her back door.

When they walked inside, he felt like he was

walking into a different world. Her brother and sister, who were freshmen at Bridgeport, were sitting at a kitchen table with a mess of books surrounding them. They were eating apple slices. Their mom was ironing next to them.

All three of them turned to him in surprise when they entered.

Mrs. Peterson smiled brightly. "Hi, Finn. Did you come over to see the puppies?"

"Yes, ma'am."

"I'm glad. Are you hungry? I made scotcheroos. Want one?"

"I don't know what that is, ma'am."

The twins at the table laughed. "Do you always talk like that?" the guy asked.

Finn stared at him. "Like what?"

Allison stepped closer to him. "Ignore Phillip. He thinks he's funny but he's just rude."

Phillip narrowed his eyes at Allison but didn't look at Finn again.

"Finn, scotcheroos are bars with Rice Krispies and peanut butter with chocolate on top," Mrs. Peterson said. "They're nothing special but taste pretty good. My kids have been eating them for years, since they were little."

Allison looked completely embarrassed, which for some odd reason, made Finn start to like her a whole lot more. "You don't have to have one," she said.

Finn felt a lump in his throat as he realized that

this was what these kids were used to. Their mom was around, making them treats, smiling to their neighbors.

"I'm starving. One of those things sounds great."

Mrs. Peterson looked delighted. "I'll put some in a baggie for you then. Maybe your dad would like a couple, too."

"Thanks." He knew he was mumbling, but he didn't know how to act.

Still looking embarrassed, Allison said, "Ready to go see Maggie's pups now?"

"Yeah, sure."

"Take off your shoes!" the girl called out.

Belatedly, he realized that Allison had slipped hers off when she'd entered the house. He immediately dropped to a knee and started untying one of his Timberlands.

Allison leaned toward him. "You don't have to take off your boots."

"I don't mind. I should've done it in the first place."

After he pulled his other boot off, he picked them up and set them next to the wall.

The twins grinned at each other, telling him that, yet again, he was doing something wrong.

"Come on," Allison said as she led him down the hall.

He followed, wishing that he'd never seen her in the driveway in the first place. He didn't know how to act around her mother. He didn't know how to act in a house like theirs.

He made up his mind then and there to see the dogs and then get out of there. He could tell Mrs. Peterson that he'd forgotten to do something.

"They're in here," Allison said, her voice all soft. Then she opened the door and led him inside.

The room was warm, and there was what looked like a cut-up washing machine box in the corner. And inside was a black-and-white Australian shepherd surrounded by five little balls of black-and-white fur. The room smelled like dog and warmth, old blankets . . . and, he supposed, puppies.

Something in his insides turned to mush as he stared at them. He got down on his knees next to Allison and looked closer. One of the pups was kind of toddling toward its mom, squeaking. "Its eyes are closed."

"Uh-huh. Their eyes won't open for about a week." Still staring at the puppies, she murmured, "Aren't they sweet?"

"Oh, yeah." Though he tried to come up with something better, he wasn't able to. Because right at that moment he was struck that, for most of his life, he hadn't been surrounded by sweet things.

Not at home, since his mom wasn't the kind who dwelled on innocence any more than she'd been the kind to personify it. He'd never acted that way around his dad, either. Instead, he'd tried to be the tough boy he wanted. Around his friends, he was big and tough. Most people probably thought that all he did was eat, sleep, and think football.

And maybe that *was* all he'd done. Football had given him confidence and approval from his father, a group of friends, and a sense of security that his mother never had.

But kneeling next to Allison—with her awkwardness, too-good figure, TV mom, and box full of brand-new puppies—Finn realized that sweet could feel good. "Yeah," he added, "They're real cute, Allison. Thanks for showing them to me."

She turned to look at him, her freckles fading into the blush that had bloomed across her cheeks.

And, for the first time since he'd met her, Allison Peterson didn't seem to have a single thing to say.

Instead, she turned back to the puppies and giggled as one of the puppies knocked over one of its littermates.

"Would you like to hold one?"

"That's allowed?"

Allison smiled softly. "Yeah. Have a seat and I'll give you one."

He sat and was immediately rewarded by a tiny squirming fur ball about the size of his hand. He brought it close to his chest, kind of like he held a football. When the pup stopped squirming and snuggled into the folds of his sweatshirt, Allison smiled again.

Finn thought, right then, that he could stay there all day.

9

From Les Larke's
Terms for Poker Success:

Check: To take a pass on betting.
This is a good tool if you want to last
in the game. Everyone needs to know
when they've bet enough.

"Allison, come sit down for dinner!" Mom called. "And I know you hear me, so get a move on!"

Looking at the sleeping puppy in her lap, Allison sighed before carefully picking him up and placing him back in the box. He stretched one tiny paw out before snuggling next to his brothers and sisters. For a moment, she thought about how lucky those puppies were, having such a close bond with their siblings.

Just as quickly, she realized that that had been a stupid thing to think. After all, they were going to sell all the puppies in a couple of weeks. They'd all go to different homes and they'd never see each other again. It was kind of heartbreaking, if she thought about it hard.

"Allison, now!"

"Coming!" Knowing that the twins would get involved if she didn't join them right away, she edged out of the laundry room, washed her hands, and hurried to the dining room.

Both of her parents and the twins were all standing around and impatiently waiting on her.

Mom had come up with some weird rules over the years. One was that they all ate together, even if it meant it was before Phillip's swim practice or after Dad's late meeting. Though it sometimes meant that they didn't eat until eight o'clock, Allison figured it was kind of a nice tradition.

The other rule drove her crazy. It was that nobody sat down in their chairs until everyone was present. It was beyond annoying, especially since Chloe seemed to thrive on making a grand entrance. Tonight, though, it was her turn to keep everyone waiting.

And maybe because it was kind of a rare thing, both of the twins and her parents looked irritated.

"About time you got here," Phillip said. "We've been waiting forever."

Allison looked at her watch. "I'm only a couple of minutes late."

"See? You even know you're late," Chloe said with a smirk.

"Whatever. I'm here now. Mom, can we sit?"

One arched brow rose. "Excuse me?"

Why did everything have to be such a production? "May we please sit down now?"

And just like that—and just like when Mom reminded her about her grammar when she was six—her mother's smile grew bright. "Of course, dear."

Another rule was that they had assigned seats. But maybe that wasn't a rule so much as a habit—they all liked sitting where they sat. They did the same thing at church every Sunday, with them sitting in order by age.

That meant that her seat was across from the twins while her parents each took a chair on the opposite ends of the table. Just like something out of *The Brady Bunch*. Thinking of what Finn must have thought about her house already, she took a second to be glad he wasn't witnessing this.

After she sat down, they all folded their hands and bent their heads. Dad looked around the table, then said, "May we be truly grateful for what we are about to receive."

"Amen," Allison said with the rest of her family.

"I'm grateful for stringy meat," Phillip said as he passed his plate over to Mom. "I'm starving."

Smiling at their mother, Chloe said, "It looks great, Mom. Thank you." She winked at Allison before passing a plate to their mother, then passed the serving dishes of mashed potatoes and vegetables around until everyone was served.

"How was your day, honey?" Dad asked her.

"Fine."

As she handed Allison a bowl of broccoli, Chloe giggled. "It's been better than that, I think. I know what Ally is grateful for, and it isn't food."

Dad glanced Allison's way and winked, something he usually did when dealing with her and the twins at the same time.

Usually, Allison would have grinned back, but something held her back. Maybe it was because she had a terrible premonition about what was about to come out of Chloe's mouth.

"Ally likes our neighbor."

"What?" Dad jerked his head back toward her. "When did this happen? And which neighbor?"

She tried not to take it personally that he looked shocked. "I don't *like* anyone, and Chloe knows it. She's just being a brat."

"Allison." Mom chided.

"It's true, Mom." After glaring at Chloe again, Allison turned back to her father. "Chloe's talking about our neighbor Finn. He came over today to look at the puppies."

"The new kid?"

Mom chuckled. "That kid probably weighs as much as you do, Dale."

"I haven't met him yet. Just Finn's dad. But he's a big kid?"

"Uh, yeah," Phillip corrected unhelpfully. "Everyone's already talking about him. Coach

McCoy says he's going to lead the team to state next year."

"That's a pretty tall order. He must be something else."

"I heard he moved here just to play football," Phillip continued, just like he had his pulse on the Tiger football program at Bridgeport High.

Their father looked confused, which was really no surprise, given the way the conversation was going. "Why was he over here? Did you give him a ride home or something, Ally?"

"No." Feeling everyone's attention on her, Allison said, "I was outside when he got home. I just asked him if he wanted to see Maggie's pups."

"You asked him over?"

Ignoring Chloe's knowing smirk across the table, she said, "It wasn't any big deal. I mean, everyone likes puppies."

Dad's expression eased as he picked up his fork. "That makes sense. You're right. Maggie's puppies are adorable."

"Not as adorable at Finn Vance," Chloe said. "You should hear how he talks to Mom. He calls her ma'am. And he has earrings and wears old concert T-shirts. All the girls have noticed him."

"Guess I'll have to meet him soon," Dad said.

Allison stuffed a carrot in her mouth. Why couldn't she have been an only child?

Mom cleared her throat. "Chloe, why don't you share what happened in choir?"

Allison shot her mother a grateful smile as Chloe launched into a long and convoluted story about show choir, solos, and some upcoming competition.

As the conversation drifted from that to Phillip's basketball team, Allison wondered yet again how she'd ended up in this family. All of them were good-looking. Both of her parents and the twins all had dark brown hair and matching eyes. They also were slim, on the tall side, and had the ability to get along with just about anyone.

She, on the other hand, had blond hair with those brown eyes. She wasn't fat, but she'd known from about the age of nine that she was never going to be built like her mother. But what had always been harder to get used to besides her looks was the way she just didn't seem to fit in with her high-achieving family.

She was completely average and nerdy. Though she did just fine in school, her As and Bs weren't going to get her any awards or scholarships.

The only place she excelled was 4-H, and that wasn't even available in Bridgeport. She was part of a club in another town, and that was where a lot of her friends were, too. It hadn't been too bad during her freshman and sophomore years. Phillip and Chloe had been busy in middle school and thought she was cool because she was in high school and they weren't.

But now that they were halfway through their freshman year, each seemed to have come to the conclusion that their older, junior sister was still nerdy and completely unpopular.

At last, the meal was over.

"You're on for dishes, Allison," Mom said.

"I know." They all took turns with the dinner dishes, even her parents. Because of that, there were lots of nights off. But on the other hand, when it was her turn, it took at least an hour, because she had to do them all by herself.

Tonight she was looking forward to it. At least then she knew she would have an hour's break from Chloe and Phillip. No one wanted to hang out in the kitchen after dinner when they didn't have to.

When she was halfway through, her mother came back in, a glass of white wine in her hand. "You okay?" she asked.

"Yep. I'm almost done."

"No, I meant with Chloe's teasing about Finn."

"I'm fine. It was no big deal."

Her mother looked doubtful. "I know your sister can seem rude. She doesn't mean to be."

Yes, she did. "It was fine."

"For what it's worth, I think Finn really liked coming over here. He might be a football star, but I think, underneath all those muscles, he seemed kind of sad."

She'd thought the same thing, though she

would've never admitted that out loud. "I feel bad for him. It's got to be hard, moving to a new school."

"I'm glad you reached out. That was the right thing to do."

"It wasn't anything, Mom," she said, hoping that they could finally stop talking about Finn. "It was just puppies. That's all. Besides, you saw what he looked like. He's not just some football prodigy, he's really cute. Plus, he's good friends with Sam Holland and Kayla Everett."

Her mother tilted her head. "And that is important because . . . "

"Because Sam is really cute and some kind of brainiac who everyone says is going to go to Harvard or something. Kayla's his girlfriend, and she's a varsity cheerleader."

"You know what? When I was in high school, I thought labels were everything. When I got out in the real world, I realized that they didn't matter all that much."

"I'll be glad when that happens." Because right now, labels were everything. At last, she wiped down the counters. "I'm done."

"Yes, you are. What are you going to do now?"

"Homework. Then I need to check on Maggie."

"Do you have a lot of homework? I think Chloe is going to watch *The Voice* with me. You could join us."

"Sorry. I really don't have time." The last

person she wanted to be around right now was her sister.

Some of the light faded from her mother's eyes. "Oh. All right."

After smiling at her mother, she lugged her backpack up the stairs to the third floor. When she turned thirteen, her parents converted the big space into her own bedroom and bathroom. She loved the privacy.

When she got inside and tossed her stuff on her bed, Allison finally let herself imagine what it would have been like if things had been different. If she'd been prettier, more talented . . . able to talk to other people without sounding stupid.

Popular.

Would Finn have been the one searching her out instead of her looking for him? And if that happened, what if she'd smiled right back, and after a while they became a couple?

For a moment, she imagined walking down the hall by his side, everyone looking at them enviously. Okay, *her* enviously.

But try as she might, she couldn't imagine such a thing at all. Feeling resigned, Allison pulled out her books.

It was a better idea concentrate on English instead of things that were never going to happen. At least then she would have a better grade to show for it.

10

From Les Larke's
Favorite Poker Quotations:

*"Poker takes a day to learn and
a lifetime to master."*
—ROBERT WILLIAMSON III

FRIDAY

The call came at 6:40, two hours after Meredith had gotten home, eaten the sandwich she'd picked up from the deli on the way home, and stretched out on the couch. After teaching four group classes and two privates at the studio, she usually wanted nothing more than to stretch out and enjoy the peace and quiet. She loved her clients but sometimes they were a little chatty. Okay, a lot chatty.

They might even be surprised to learn that they weren't any better behaved than some of Emily's freshmen.

Earlier today, she'd even been excited for her usual Friday night routine, which consisted of doing as little as possible. But instead of feeling gratifying, it felt a little lonely.

Feeling restless, she pulled out the vacuum and took a turn around the living room and bedroom. Next, she pulled out some spray cleaner and wiped down her bathroom countertops.

She sat back down on the couch again.

And still didn't know what to do with herself.

Looking out the window, she gazed at the street lights' glow glinting against the last of the stubborn snow still on her front lawn. "That's what's wrong, Meredith," she told herself. "You're sick and tired of the gray and cold."

After the unexpected gift of two days of sunshine, the twenty-degree temperatures and dull gray sky returned, reminding everyone that it was still the middle of winter.

Yep, that was it. She was suffering from a little bit of seasonal depression.

Sitting back on the couch, she picked up the remote for the television. Surely there was something that would catch her interest and take her mind off the fact that she was sitting home alone on a Friday night. That she always sat home alone on Friday nights.

When her cell phone rang, she couldn't pick it up fast enough. "Hello?"

"Hello, Meredith, it's Ace."

Ace! He had called her after all. "Oh, hi." And before she realized she was doing it, she sat up straighter and smoothed back her hair.

"I called to see how you were doing. How's your hand?"

Ace's voice sounded more gravelly over the phone than in person. "It's fine. Healing." She was so tired of talking about her hand. "How are you? How was your week?"

"I'm fine. It's been a good week."

"I'm glad." She opened her mouth to add something, but couldn't think of much to add.

After a second's pause, Ace spoke again. "So, I heard you volunteered at the high school yesterday."

"I did. Thursday is my volunteer day. I guess Finn told you he saw me?"

"He did."

"It was fun to see him again." She paused, unsure of how much to add or what else to say. Had Finn told his dad that she'd done something wrong?

"He liked seeing you, too." His voice warmed. "Sometimes I can't believe how I don't know too many people in Bridgeport, but my son is in my buddy's girlfriend's English class."

"You know what they say, we're all in each other's circles."

"I guess there's some truth to that." After another pause, his voice softening a bit, "Finn said you were hurting at the end of the day."

"I was mainly tired of talking about my little accident."

"You were mugged, Meredith."

Tired of talking about herself, she cleared her throat. "So, how was your day? What did you do?"

"It was good. In between some of my other jobs, I'm working on rebuilding the transmission on a '62 'Vette at the shop."

He sounded so pleased about that, like the proverbial kid in the candy store, Meredith realized that she probably should double-check what he was talking about. "Isn't that like a Corvette or something?"

"Yeah," he replied, his voice tinged with amusement. "It's *exactly* like a Corvette or something. And, just so you know, working on a 'Vette like that is kind of the reason guys like me become mechanics."

"Hmm." All she could think about was that there were a whole lot of small pieces and parts that had to fit together to work. She would rather work with the human body any day of the week. "So, how's it going?"

He laughed. "Do you really want to know?"

"I'm interested, but I should probably warn you that whatever you're doing probably won't make a lick of sense to me."

This time he laughed outright. "I take it that you're not much of a car person?"

"Does knowing how to fill up my gas tank count?"

"Not in my world."

This time she giggled. "Then you could say I'm not." Hating that she sounded so prissy, she said, "But honestly, my lack of knowledge isn't as much by choice as circumstance. I've never had a lot of time or money to care about cars, well, other than the fact that I needed them to get me where I needed to go." Looking around her house, which now seemed really, really feminine, she said, "I hope that doesn't drive you crazy."

"Not at all. Taking care of people like you is what my job usually entails. If everyone knew how to fix their transmissions, I wouldn't have much to do."

"Whew. I was worried there for a moment," she teased.

"I don't care what you say, as long as it's the truth," he replied, sounding completely forthright. "I'm not hard to get along with."

"That's good to know." She pulled in her bottom lip, wondering what else to say. Talking about her Pilates students or her time volunteering in Emily's classroom didn't sound all that interesting. "So, do you and Finn have any plans for the weekend?"

"Well, tonight is poker. I'm about to head over there."

"Where do you play? Downtown at the casino?"

"Hell, no," he replied, sounding mildly outraged. "My buddy Kurt runs a game once a month in his garage. I play there."

She tried to imagine that sounding fun, but couldn't. "Why in his garage? And is it just the two of you?"

He laughed again. "I guess you haven't heard of the Bridgeport Social Club?"

"Nope."

"It's basically about twenty-five guys who get together to play poker. Sometimes we do other stuff like fish and hike, and hunt, but more often than not, it's just a standing Texas Hold'em tournament."

"I've lived in Bridgeport all my life but I've never heard of it."

"That's likely because it only started a couple of months ago. It's new. Kurt put in a couple of tables in his garage, guys get together, drink beer, smoke cigars, talk about everything under the sun, and play cards."

"I'll be sure to stay far away from Kurt's house on Friday night," she joked. "Hope you have a good time."

"Thanks." He paused. "Hey, listen, Finn and I are just hanging out tomorrow night. Do you want to come over here for supper? I thought I'd make shepherd's pie. Do you like that?"

Now would be the perfect time to head him off and explain how she really wasn't up for dating anyone at this time. But when she opened her mouth, the opposite thing popped out. "I don't know if I've ever had shepherd's pie. It sounds great, though."

"You're in luck then, because I make a pretty awesome one."

"I can't wait to try it. Thank you."

"No prob. I'm glad you can make it."

"Can I bring anything? A salad? Dessert?"

"Either would be good. I can make a couple of things pretty well, but that's the extent of my talent. I don't make a lot of salads for Finn and me."

Smiling, she said, "I'll bring a salad and some cupcakes or something."

"Cupcakes?"

"They're small little cakes with frosting on top," she teased.

"Ha, ha. Any chance you could make them chocolate?"

"There's a very good chance I can do that," not even trying to keep the smile out of her voice.

"It's a plan, then. Listen, I better go."

"Okay. Have fun."

"You're sure you're going to be all right tonight?"

"Of course, Ace."

"All right then. I'll text you our address, and see you tomorrow night, say about six?"

His voice was so low and gravelly, she couldn't stop the little shiver that ran through her. "Six is good."

"Good. See you then. Bye."

"Bye, Ace," she replied softly.

So, she had a date. Kind of.

Curling back on the couch, she let the feeling of expectation wash over her. It felt good. Kind of exciting. Warm. Closing her eyes, she started planning out her Saturday morning. She was going to need to run to the store and get some fresh lettuce for the salad and some powdered sugar and cream cheese for the frosting. Thinking about Finn and Ace's fondness for chocolate, she wondered if she should make two kinds of cupcakes. It would be overkill, of course, but she could leave a bunch with them and take any extras to the studio.

Her Lunch Bunch class would love them.

And so would Ace.

She felt a little silly, but since she was all alone and there wasn't anyone to find out, she imagined what it would feel like to have his arms wrapped around her. He was so big. No, he was so built. She wasn't exactly small, but she had an idea she would feel petite in his arms.

Especially when he bent down to kiss her. Giving into the daydream, she sighed, wondering just where else he had those tattoos. She started wondering if there were any on his chest or shoulders—when she saw someone walking around the side of her house.

Caught off guard, she sat upright. Told herself

124

to not get too spun up. Maybe it was a teenager and he was cutting through her yard?

Getting to her feet, she moved off to the side, positioning herself so she could see out, but no one could really see her standing there.

And her heart started beating faster. The man in her yard was definitely not passing through. He was wandering slowly. And staring at her house.

Her anxiety rose up a notch. What was he doing? Who could it be? When she peeked out again, he was gone. Which, unfortunately, didn't make her feel any better. If she didn't see him in the distance, he could be somewhere else in her yard.

She took a step toward the front door. Then, at the last minute, ran to her bedroom window instead. She was just in time to see the back of a man walking around to the front. He was literally making a circle around her house!

She knew what she should do. She should call 911. But what if the police responded to her complaint like they had when she'd told them about her wallet? She wasn't in any hurry for another conversation like that.

Making the decision, she hustled back to the front door and opened it wide. Walked out on the stoop. "Hello?" she called.

All she heard was an answering rustle of wind.

She was cold now. Of course, she hadn't

taken the time to put on a coat or boots and the temperature had to be in the twenties. She shivered, but forged ahead. "What are you doing in my yard?"

Something crashed on her back patio before she saw a figure run off through the Carpenter's yard and down the street. Staring at the person intently, she realized it was definitely a man. He was wearing jeans and a black hoodie. But even in that oversize sweatshirt, it was easy to see that he wasn't very big.

Remembering how Ace and Finn had said that it had looked to them like an older teenager who'd grabbed her bag, she wondered if it could be the same person.

"Meredith?" Katie Carpenter called out from her front porch. "Is everything okay?"

"You know, I'm not sure," she said as she wrapped her arms around herself. Meeting her neighbor's eyes, she admitted, "I think someone was wandering around my yard."

Katie, who was dressed in an off-white stretchy outfit, complete with cute little fawn-colored suede booties, walked to her side. "Really?"

"I could be wrong, but I think he was looking in my windows."

"Goodness!" Looking worried now, she said, "Want me to go get Mike?"

"No, I saw the guy run off. I don't think there's anything your husband can do."

"I haven't heard of any robberies in the area, but I wouldn't be surprised. Sooner or later, our neighborhood is likely to be targeted."

Sooner or later. Targeted. "Katie, my wallet got taken the other day on the bike trail. I thought he only wanted my money, but maybe he found my address."

"What? You didn't tell us that in class."

Katie was part of Meredith's Lunch Bunch, a group of five older women who did Pilates twice a week at eleven and then stayed to eat lunch with her at noon. "I didn't want to broadcast what happened."

"Still, I wish I would have known. Mike and I would have done something."

"There was nothing you could have done," Meredith said, realizing just then that she probably could have called Katie when she had gotten hurt. Why was it so hard for her to reach out to people when she needed help?

Studying Meredith's front yard, she said, "Maybe you should call the police, dear."

"I don't know. I stopped by the day after I got my wallet stolen and they almost laughed at me. All they said was that they'd call if someone turned it in."

"This is different. He was in your yard."

"You've got a point."

"I know I do." Like a blond shepherd, Katie ushered Meredith to her front door. "Go on inside now before you freeze to death. Call up the police."

"I'll do that."

"I'll check on you tomorrow. Go on, now. Give them a call."

Closing the door and locking it, Meredith knew that Katie was right. Picking up the phone, she dialed 911 and told the dispatcher what had happened. When she promised that an officer would be by shortly, Meredith sat down to wait.

And wondered what could possibly happen next.

11

From Les Larke's
Terms for Poker Success:

Maniac: A very aggressive player. These guys just don't know when to stop.

FRIDAY NIGHT

"You're almost late, Vance! I'm about to make everybody sit down," Kurt Holland called out as Ace walked through the open doors into Kurt's garage-slash-monthly poker room.

"Sorry," he said. "Something came up."

"Like what?" Kurt asked as he walked over and clasped his hand. "Last time we talked, you said you were going to be here in time to have chili. I tried to save you a bowl."

Ace didn't even try to hold back his grimace at the thought of choking down a bowl of Cincinnati-style chili. "In that case, I'm glad I was running late." Looking around the room, he slapped Kurt on the back. "Glad I got here, though. You've got a good crowd tonight."

"Three full tables. Twenty-four guys," Kurt

said, looking really pleased. "I'm going to have to buy us another table come summer. Word's getting around about the game. Two guys showed up late and we had to turn them away."

Ace made a mental note to head on over to one of the big-box centers and buy the large circular table and chairs for Kurt. The guy was already hosting poker, he shouldn't have to pay for every single expense by himself.

After waving to a couple of guys he had sat next to the previous month, he said, "You got anything besides chili?"

"Saying you don't like Skyline is like calling someone's sister ugly," Troy said as he approached. Troy was another transplant from Spartan and a longtime friend of Ace's and Kurt's. Not only had he played ball in college, he was also one of the most successful men to come out of their Podunk town. He was now a successful financial advisor. "Everybody around here loves it."

"Not everybody, 'cause I sure don't." For some reason, he'd learned when he moved to Bridgeport that everyone loved a particular type of chili known only to Cincinnatians. The meat sauce was thin, had notes of cinnamon and chocolate in it, and was served over cooked spaghetti noodles and topped with diced raw onions and mounds of shredded cheese. Ace had hated it from the first bite.

Troy laughed. "Hey, at least you're here. Go buy in and grab a seat."

There were only two empty chairs left. He picked the one farther away from the space heater. It would get cold in the corner, but he preferred that to having heat blowing on his face. Besides, he was dressed warm enough with a hat and several layers of shirts and fleece.

After paying his forty dollars, getting chips, and finally popping the top of his can of Bud, he sat down and said hello to the men sitting around him.

Luckily, he knew a lot of the guys' names by now, and even remembered something about each one. At his table of eight, one was a coach at the high school, two were some kind of doctors, another guy worked at a plant closer to the city, and then there was him, Troy, and two men he'd only met once before.

Then a bell sounded and the games began. Immediately the buzz in the room settled down and conversation became more focused.

"Ante up," his table's dealer said. Ace tossed in his chips and stretched out one of his legs. With each hand being played, he could feel his sore muscles easing and his mood lifting.

"How's work?" Jeff asked.

"Good. I just hired another mechanic for Cliff. The guy is older and used to build Fords for a living. I think he's going to work out good."

"I saw Cliff's wife at the bank the other day. Wendy told me he thinks of you as a godsend."

"I don't know about that, but I'm glad to be there. It's a good fit," he said as he studied his cards before discarding two.

As the conversation continued around him, all the guys talking about work, skiing nearby at Perfect North, and the state of the high school basketball team, Ace glanced over at Kurt and grinned at him.

As much as he'd hated leaving his parents and Lana and Brennan and their families, he knew it had been the right decision. Actually, sometimes, late at night, he wondered if all of his talk about moving to Bridgeport for Finn's well-being was just that—all talk. Maybe he'd only really moved so he could play poker on Friday nights with Kurt, Troy, and the other guys in the club. He needed this, this connection to others as much as he suspected the country-club guys needed their five hours on the golf course.

An hour later, after a couple of guys got out and they moved tables, Ace found himself sitting next to Kurt. After they caught up on Kurt's newest account, landscaping a company headquarters close to downtown Cincinnati, they moved on to talking about Sam's latest scholarship offers and Emily.

When there was a break in the action, Kurt said, "Want to join Emily and me for dinner tomorrow night? That way the three of us can catch up. We're going out for Chinese."

"Thanks, but I can't."

Kurt lifted his eyebrows. "Really? Why not? You got plans with Finn?"

"Nope." Unable to hide his feeling of satisfaction, he said, "I've got plans with a woman."

"No way. You met someone already? Who?"

"Remember that woman Finn and I told y'all about? Meredith?"

"Meredith." He frowned. "Wait, is she the gal who got hurt on the bike trail and helps out in Em's class from time to time?"

"Uh-huh. That one. She's coming over to hang out with Finn and me."

The conversation was halted for a few minutes while everyone bet chips and picked up and discarded cards. Twenty minutes later, both he and Kurt had folded and were out.

They walked over to a metal container of bottled water on ice and each grabbed one. Then Kurt dove right back into their earlier conversation, just as if it hadn't taken a temporary hiatus.

"I'm thinking about you already putting Finn into the mix, Ace." He lowered his voice. "Are you sure that's a good idea? You and her need to get to know each other first, don't you think?"

"I've talked to her on the phone. Plus, I mean to keep things open with Finn. He's been hurt too much by his mother for me to keep things from him, make him feel abandoned."

Looking serious, Kurt nodded. "That's a good point. I hadn't thought about how Liz screwed with him."

"She screwed him around his whole life. I'm starting to learn that she treated him even worse than I thought."

"Damn."

"Yeah." He took a fortifying sip of water to cool his temper.

"So, is Meredith cooking or are you buying a pizza?"

"Neither. I'm cooking a shepherd's pie."

Kurt looked surprised, then smiled. "Shoot, I forgot that you actually know how to cook."

"Not all of us were spoiled by our mommas growing up."

"Don't even go there. Your momma would cook every meal if she was nearby and you let her."

"Maybe. She's all about Brennan's kids now. You need to figure out how to cook a couple of things, Holland."

"I suck at it." He winked. "Besides, I still have no shame. My Emily feels sorry for me and feeds me every now and then."

"You're pathetic. I'm surprised you don't have Sam cooking," he said sarcastically.

"I probably would get him to—if I thought he

was any better in the kitchen than I am. He's not." He grinned again. "In any case, good for you. I hope y'all have a good time—and that things progress."

"We'll see. For now, I'm just glad Meredith's giving me the time of day, though I'm not really sure why."

Kurt leaned toward him. "Why do you say that?"

"Because I'm a mechanic and have a kid. She has her own business, is bordering on beautiful, and actually has an accounting degree."

"She sounds too good to be true. Who are you talking about?" a guy on the other side of Kurt asked.

Ace's first inclination was to not answer the guy, but then he decided that seeing Meredith wasn't a secret. "Meredith Hunt. Do you know her?"

The guy leaned back. "Doesn't she have all that red hair and run a Pilates studio or something?"

"She owns that studio." Ace wasn't all that crazy about telling the guys what he was doing. He really wasn't into hearing another man's opinion, and this guy was already starting to sound disrespectful.

The guy looked around the room. "She's pretty hot. I've never been into gingers but I don't suppose that matters if the rest of her is that built—"

Ace lowered his voice. "Not real happy with you talking about her like that."

"Like what? All I said was that she was hot." He looked around at the other five men and grinned.

None of them grinned back.

Kurt cleared his throat. "Meredith is a good friend of Emily's. She wouldn't be real into you talking about her like that, either."

He raised his eyebrows. "And you're going to *tell* on me?"

Kurt shook his head. This time it was Ace who spoke. "What I'm trying to tell you is that it would be a real good idea not to talk about Meredith anymore."

Troy stood up, too. "Do you get the idea, Garrett, or do you need some more specific instructions?"

Garrett lifted up his hands mockingly. "I get it. Sheesh. I don't know when all of y'all got so touchy about your women."

Ace knew that tone. Garrett had had too much to drink and was now itching for a fight. Some guys got into that from time to time. At one time, he'd been the same way. Luckily, that wasn't him anymore. He had a lot more in his life besides a need to act like a jerk.

Troy clamped his hand on Garrett's shoulder. "Let me call you an Uber, buddy. You need to head on home."

"I can drive."

"No, you can't," Kurt said, his voice hard. "And believe me, you don't want to argue about this. You aren't going to win."

Garrett inhaled, obviously intent on saving his pride . . . until he looked at the three men facing him.

Ace, Kurt, and Troy were standing shoulder to shoulder, and even though they were now all in their early thirties, Ace was sure they could hold their own in a fight.

Garrett must have thought the same thing, because he glared at Troy but nodded. "Yeah. Call me an Uber. I'm ready to get out of here."

Ten minutes later, he'd been folded into a Honda and sent on his way. Ten minutes after that, the rest of the guys had gone, too, leaving just the three of them in the garage.

Though most of the guys had made decent use of the trash cans, the place was still a mess.

Kurt glanced at his cell phone. "It's barely one o'clock. Ya'll want to hang out a while?"

"Just a few," Ace said. "But I'll get up early and come over in the morning."

Kurt shrugged like he wasn't too worried about it. "Don't come over too early. Not before eight."

"Eight thirty then."

"I'll stop by, too," Troy said.

Kurt looked at the two of them, looking

pleased. "Bridgeport Social Club is doing good, don't you think?"

"Oh, yeah," Ace said. "It occurred to me earlier that I'd be lost without this group. It's helped me settle in."

"Me, too," Troy said. "And I hadn't even thought I needed it."

Still looking around the room, Kurt said, "We need to recruit some more guys from home."

"Not everyone wants to move to Ohio, buddy," Troy said.

"Yeah, but what we've got is a good thing."

Ace didn't disagree. Thinking about some of their old friends' reactions when he'd told them he was moving to Bridgeport, he said, "I think I might know of a couple of guys who don't necessarily want to stay back in Spartan."

Kurt looked at him curiously. "Like who?"

"Like Jackson Koch."

"What makes you think Cookie wants out of Spartan?" Kurt asked, using the nickname they'd all called him growing up.

"Since his wife died and he lost his job at the mine," Ace said. "I think he's been really struggling. He's got that little girl, too."

"You should call him up. Invite him to come out for the weekend," Troy suggested.

"I might." Thinking about it, he said, "Or maybe I'll ask my dad or my brother Brennan to stop by his house. Both of them know him better

138

than me. It's worth a shot, you know? Sometimes a person forgets that he has options."

Kurt slapped him on the shoulder. "That's a good point." Stifling a yawn, he turned off one of the lights. "Now, not to kick you out, but—"

"But, you're kicking us out," Troy said with a grin. "See y'all tomorrow."

"Yeah, see ya," Ace said as he walked out to his truck. Once he got it running, he pulled out his phone while the heater kicked in. He vaguely remembered getting a text while they were playing but he'd forgotten to check his screen.

Feeling guilty, hoping that Finn hadn't needed him for something, he was pleasantly surprised to see the text was from Meredith instead. He passed his thumb over the screen, half afraid she was canceling on him. Then felt as if he'd been kicked in the gut.

Someone had been walking around her yard and peeking in her windows, and she'd been scared enough to call the police.

And to reach out to him.

Now it was almost five hours later and in the middle of the night. Too late to call. No doubt she thought he was the biggest jerk she'd ever met.

Damn.

12

From Les Larke's
Terms for Poker Success:

Wildcard: A card that can be played as any other card. It keeps things hopping. If Jacks are wild, you're in for a wild ride, y'all.

SATURDAY

A little after eleven the next morning, Katie stopped by Meredith's house. "Hello? Mer, is now a good time?" she called out after knocking briefly on the door and letting herself inside.

"It's perfect," Meredith replied, even as she realized she should've locked the front door after going outside to get the mail. She needed to be better about that, especially when she considered how much she'd tossed and turned the night before. "Come on back to the kitchen."

"It smells like heaven in here," Katie exclaimed as she entered the room. Eyeing the countertops, she whistled low. "You've been busy."

Too restless to sleep, Meredith had gotten up early and gone to the store. Now she was in the process of frosting four dozen cupcakes, half plain chocolate with vanilla frosting, the other half chocolate with dark fudge filling and chocolate frosting. They had turned out really well, and almost made baking four dozen cupcakes for two men seem like a good idea.

Seeing Katie's expression, she chuckled. "Maybe a little too busy. I've kind of gone cupcake crazy."

"They look fabulous."

"I'll send some cupcakes home with you for Mike."

"He'll like that . . . if I feel like sharing them with him."

Meredith smiled at her, thinking once again how glad she was to have moved next to such a nice retired couple. Katie was dressed in her usual winter attire, a velour track suit. She seemed to have the same one in a dozen colors.

After hopping up on one of the stools, Katie looked at her directly. "I saw the police cruiser over here last night, Meredith, and two officers come to your door. What did they say?"

"Not too much, unfortunately." The two patrol officers—one a man and the other a woman—had been sympathetic and walked around and looked at her yard, doors, and windows, but they hadn't seen anything suspicious. And though they did listen and sounded more compassionate than the man she'd talked to when she'd visited the station after her wallet was stolen, Meredith had gotten the feeling that they thought she was overreacting a bit.

Actually, more than that. Like a whole lot.

Filling in Katie, she said, "So that's the story. I'm glad I called, and I'm glad they stopped by, but I don't think there's anything they can do." She picked up another cupcake and slathered a generous amount of frosting on the top. "I almost feel like I wasted their time."

"You didn't. Calling them was the right thing to do, Meredith. Don't second-guess yourself. You are a woman living on your own. You have to be vigilant."

As she frosted another cupcake, Meredith pressed her lips together so she wouldn't grin. Katie's point would have been driven home more if she didn't feel like she was a prized goldfish in a fish bowl. Everyone here kept tabs on each other.

As Katie watched her put the cupcake down and pick another one up, she said, "Who's the lucky recipient of all these yummy-looking treats? Besides me and Mike, that is."

"I'm bringing them over to a friend's house tonight," she explained, feeling proud of herself for sounding so at ease instead of nervous. "I said I'd bring salad and dessert."

Katie's face lit up. "Are you going over to Emily's? I do like her, and she's such a good cook, too. What's she making?"

"Um, actually, I'm not going over to Emily's house. This friend is a man." Boy, could she sound any more awkward?

"Meredith, do you finally have a date?"

Unable to help herself, Meredith started laughing. "You make me sound so desperate."

"Not desperate," Katie corrected as she crossed her velour-covered legs. "Just by yourself far too much. So, who is it? Anyone I know? I mean, if you don't mind me asking."

Meredith knew that if she told Katie her date was a secret that her neighbor wouldn't pry . . . for about thirty minutes. She'd learned over time that it was easier to simply share her information and not fight it. "His name is Ace Vance and he's new to Bridgeport. I don't think you know him. I actually met him when I got mugged. He saw it happen and helped me out."

"He saved you." Katie sounded a little dreamy.

"No. Well, kind of. He and his son, Finn, took me to urgent care and then made sure I got home safe."

"He has a son?"

"Yes," she said as she got out a plastic container and carefully arranged six cupcakes in it. "Finn's a teenager at the high school. Ace isn't married, though."

"So he's a hero, a dad, and helpful, to boot." Katie's voice turned even warmer. "This man sounds perfect for you."

"I don't know about that. I mean, we're only friends. I mean, we don't really know each other."

"But you will know each other better after you have dinner with him and bring him cupcakes."

"Katie, even Mike would say that you are being a little too optimistic about a romance happening."

"I suppose you're right. I do tend to get a little ahead of myself from time to time."

"Really?"

Katie rolled her eyes. "All right. A lot of the time." Hopping off the stool, she said, "But what's important is that you give this man a chance."

"Katie—"

"Just listen. I know I'm sticking my nose in where it doesn't belong, but I feel strongly about this. You are far too young to be sitting alone at home every night. Try and give this Ace a chance."

"It's just dinner and cupcakes."

"But what if it's the start of something more? You'll never know if you don't at least think about living your life differently."

Her neighbor's statement hit a little too close to home. Pasting on a fake bright smile, Meredith handed Katie the container. "Thanks for stopping by, but I better let you go. I've got a lot to do."

Katie took the carton. "I understand," she murmured, but it was obvious that she didn't feel good about ending their conversation.

Walking her to the door, Meredith said, "Be careful on the sidewalk. There's some slick spots."

"I'll be fine and leave you in peace. But, will you promise me that you'll tell this Ace about your visitor?"

Katie's gaze was piercing and serious. Meredith felt right then and there that the woman would see right through her if she attempted to evade the issue. "I will."

"Good. I know you like to be independent, but it's always better to ask for help. You'd be amazed at how many people will take your hands if you just hold them out there."

While she knew that could be true, she also knew that some people were only too happy to bite those fingers. "I'll keep that in mind."

"Thank you, dear. And thank you for the cupcakes, too. Mike and I will stop by tomorrow."

"You're the best, Katie."

"No, I'm just a friend." She smiled softly. "And your neighbor. Friends and neighbors help each other, you know."

She turned away and closed the door behind her before Meredith could comment on that.

But actually, maybe it was good that she didn't have time to comment on that after all. What

145

could she say, anyway? That she wasn't exactly sure how to rely on other people?

For some reason, she had an idea that Katie would find a way to make her think about that more than she wanted to.

Because she wasn't sure how to willingly lean on other people. All her life—with the exception of when Finn and Ace showed up—every time she'd fallen, there was no one around to help her get up.

In the past, all those stumbles had done was remind her that she shouldn't have been so clumsy in the first place.

13

From Les Larke's
Terms for Poker Success:

Three of a Kind: Three cards, all of the same value. If you have three of anything, you should be pleased. It doesn't come along as often as you'd think.

SATURDAY

Ace wasn't sure if he actually had a date, or if he and Finn were simply having a guest over for supper who happened to be a girl. Maybe what he called it didn't even matter. He couldn't keep up with what was politically correct these days.

Though, that was kind of a joke, he supposed. His mother had drilled so much advice into him about how to treat a woman that he wasn't sure how he should or shouldn't act anymore. He usually just did what felt right and hoped for the best.

And . . . that thought made him glance at his phone again. He'd woken up at seven and texted Meredith back. First, he'd apologized for not calling her the night before, then had let her know that they could either talk about the person she'd seen last night, or he could stop by her house this morning. Ace knew Kurt would be fine with him blowing off the cleanup once he told him about Meredith's call. But she'd texted right back and said that while she appreciated his concern, he didn't need to come over. She would tell him about it tonight.

Okay.

Feeling a little disappointed that she hadn't taken him up on the offer, he'd stewed on her message. Over and over, he tried to decipher hidden meanings in her text while he helped Kurt clean up his garage for an hour. He'd come close to talking about it with Kurt, but had decided against it. He didn't want to share Meredith's story until he knew exactly what had happened. Something inside him told him he needed to tread really carefully in the trust department with her.

Now that he was back home, he knew he needed to talk about their dinner guest with Finn. He'd meant to talk to Finn about her last night, but he wanted to give the conversation the time it deserved, not just throw it out there and then leave for poker.

Walking down the hall, he noticed Finn's door was closed. This was rare. The kid wasn't shy around him in the slightest. He slept with his door open and walked around the house in his boxers half the time. Heck, he was usually after the kid to close the bathroom door when he showered.

Feeling a little awkward, he rapped on the door. "Finn, you awake?"

"Yeah."

Still standing at the door, he cleared his throat. "Can I come in?"

"Huh? Oh, sure."

Ace was surprised to see Finn sitting at his desk. He realized then that he'd been half expecting him to be laying on his bed on his phone. "What are you doing?"

Finn closed his laptop. "Nothing."

"Really? Huh. Listen, you don't have to tell me, but if you need something, all you have to do is ask."

"I don't need anything."

"Okay . . . "

"I've been emailing some of my friends."

"Emailing?" Ace sat down on his boy's bed, the blue plaid comforter soft under his hand. "I thought y'all texted all the time."

"We do, but sometimes it's easier to email."

Ace figured it was also easier to call, but he kept that thought to himself. "What's up with everyone back in Spartan?"

"I don't know much. Everyone's still asleep after last night's basketball game."

"I reckon so," he said slowly. "I bet you miss everyone."

Finn nodded. "Do you?"

Ace realized then that he didn't miss his life back in West Virginia as much as he thought he would've. He'd been ready for a change, and more than ready to put some distance between himself and his ex. Not wanting to hurt his boy's feelings, he treaded carefully. "I miss your grandparents. I miss Lana and Brennan." He not only loved his siblings, he genuinely liked them. Both Lana and Brennan were married and had bought houses within a few miles of their parents. He'd seen them all the time.

"It feels weird never seeing them."

"I know. Being away from so many people we care about has been harder than I thought it would be." Hoping to lighten the conversation, he added, "It's a heck of a lot quieter though. I do like that." He winked. "And between you and me, I'm not missing your cousins all that much."

Finn grinned. "Casey's okay, but Kit? I don't know."

"I do. She's a handful." He chuckled, thinking about Brennan and Barbara's two kids. Their Casey was three and the spitting image of his daddy. Kit, all of eighteen months? She was a tiny hellion. "I figure we'll get to missing her eventually," he joked. "She is cute."

"Dad."

"I mean, she is when she's not tearing up everything she can get her hands on."

Finn grinned. "She's all right when she's asleep."

Taking a deep breath, he figured he better bring up the other person he might be thinking about, too. "So, speaking of people who you might miss . . . have you talked to your mom?"

Finn looked back at his laptop. "Yeah. She emailed me last week."

Though his first inclination was to wonder why the heck Liz couldn't pick up the damn phone, he kept his voice level. "That's good. I'm glad she's keeping in touch. So, is she okay?"

Finn looked down at his hands that were clenched in front of him. "I don't know. She didn't say much. All she did was ask how you were doing."

That caught him off guard . . . and pissed him off. Besides their son, there wasn't a whole lot of connection between him and Liz. Nothing beyond a couple of nights where he'd been too consumed with lust to be more careful. Usually, she didn't want to have anything to do with him . . . unless it was to ask for money. "What did you say?"

"I didn't answer her." Finn looked at him again. "Do you want me to?"

"Nope. You don't have to do anything that you don't want to." He paused, cautioning himself to take the high road, but he wasn't that kind of man. "As far as I'm concerned, your mother

151

made her choice when she took off with that guy."

Finn hesitated, then said, "All I could think when I read her email was that it felt like she was fishing for information. Not that she really cared how I was doing."

Ace took a deep breath, thinking of all the times he'd gone to pick Finn up and the kid had been at the door waiting for him, his mother too busy to do anything but yell goodbye when he left. He took another breath and held it. When he felt like he was no longer about to start spewing profanities, he continued. "You're not a little kid anymore. Sometimes I don't think you ever have been. That's why I want you to take this to heart, Finn Vance." He stared at him intently. "There's a lot that's special about you. You're great."

Finn shrugged. "I can play football."

"Hell, yeah, you can. You're great at it. And that's something to be proud of. But it's not *all* you are."

"The coaches here already want me to start training with a couple of the guys."

"I know. One of them called me, too. They want you to get settled and feel a part of the team, and for some of the upperclassmen to get to know you."

"That's cool."

"It is. But Finn, listen. If you got hurt or you suddenly decided you never wanted to pick up a ball again, you'd still be special."

He rolled his eyes. "To you, maybe."

Ace felt a bolt of pleasure, liking the fact

that Finn was assured of his love. But it wasn't enough. "To other people, too. There's a lot of good things about you. You're loyal, you're funny, and you've got a good heart. And that's just to start. All you've got to do is let people see the real you."

"I have been."

"If you have, that's good. But if you've been keeping yourself a little distant from the kids here, I want you to think about opening up to them a little more."

"So, you want me to go all in."

Ace heard the note of sarcasm in his kid's voice. On another day, he'd probably say that he wasn't a real fan of getting lip service. But he let it fly because what they were talking about was more important. "Yep. Even if it hurts, go all in. Just like in poker."

"Because you can't win otherwise."

"That's right," he said softly. "Sometimes you have to go all in in order to get something good."

Finn smiled at him.

Feeling like they'd just covered some pretty important ground, Ace smiled back. "Now, uh, there actually was a reason I came in here."

"Okay . . ."

"I invited Meredith Hunt to come over for supper."

Finn's eyebrows went straight up. "Miss Hunt's coming over here?"

"Yeah. I . . . well, I thought it would be a good idea to get to know her better."

"Why?"

Ace felt his palms start to sweat. "Why do you think, sport? Because I like her." There. It was out in the open.

"Oh." Doubt flickered in his expression. "Well, okay."

"That's all you have to say?"

His boy's eyes narrowed. "What do you want me to say?"

"Shoot, I don't know. I guess this is all new to you and me, isn't it? I'm not really sure what I'm supposed to share and what I'm supposed to keep to myself."

"I don't think there's a playbook for you and me, Dad."

His kid was smarter than he realized. "I suppose not. I just wanted to talk to you about me seeing her. See, I really just want to spend some time getting to know her better . . . unless you've got a problem with that?"

"I don't. I mean, I guess I don't."

Liking that they were talking about this even though it was awkward as hell, Ace said, "Here's the deal, when it comes to dating, I don't know what I'm doing."

Finn rolled his eyes. "I'm pretty sure you've dated a lot of women, Dad."

That wasn't a lie. But things with Meredith

were different. She was different. Classier. More tentative. More closed-off. And, maybe, if he was being completely honest, more off-the-charts gorgeous than he was used to. But that wasn't what concerned him the most. "I'm not sure if I'm supposed to be dating right now. Not here in Bridgeport. I don't want you to think I'm abandoning you or something."

Some of the light that had dimmed in his boy's eyes glinted again. "I don't think that."

"Will you do me a favor?" When Finn met his eyes, Ace said, "If I start doing something that makes you uncomfortable, will you tell me?"

"I'll try."

"Good enough." Though he hadn't done it in a long time, Ace bent down and brushed Finn's forehead with his lips. Then he walked out, closing the door firmly behind him.

After he got himself a Coke, he sat down in front of the fireplace and thought about things.

Huh. Maybe he'd finally gone all in into fatherhood. It was moments like this that made him a dad. Not the football games, not even the driving around and paying for stuff.

It was caring enough to say the stuff that was hard.

14

From Les Larke's
Favorite Poker Quotations:

"I must complain the cards are ill shuffled,
until I have a good hand."
—JONATHAN SWIFT

SATURDAY NIGHT

Though he reckoned it bordered on creepy, Ace had been imagining what Meredith would look like when she came over that evening. He figured she'd be wearing jeans and a sweater, both items fitting her like a glove. Would probably have her hair up in a ponytail again. Maybe she'd even be wearing a little more makeup than when he'd seen her on the bike trail or when he stopped by her house.

He knew she'd look pretty because she *was* pretty.

But then she knocked on his door.

Right off the bat, he realized his imagination needed a lot of work. Meredith did have on jeans and a sweater, but she didn't just look pretty. She was downright *gorgeous*.

Her dark red hair was hanging down around her shoulders, looking soft and touchable. The ivory sweater she had on over a pair of skinny jeans and boots made her skin look even more perfect. And those blue eyes he couldn't stop thinking about? They were just as clear and translucent as he'd remembered.

Just as he was about to spout off some kind of compliment that would make him sound like the hick he was, he took a better look at her expression.

And realized that she was stressed out and worried.

"Oh, sweetheart. Come on, let's go sit down," he said as he took a big canvas bag out of her hands and set it on the counter.

"Wait." She looked around. "Where's Finn?"

"He's out with a buddy of his. There's a girls' volleyball game or something at the high school. He'll be back in time for supper."

Not wanting to give her another moment to hesitate, he got them two glasses of water out of the tap and led her over to the couch.

She sank down next to him on the couch, then immediately took a sip to calm herself. "Thanks."

Even that small motion looked stiff and wooden.

Which made him even more worried. "Meredith, baby, talk to me. What's got you so upset? Is it about that guy you saw in your yard?"

"Yes." She shifted, looking even more agitated.

Damn. "I'm sorry. I should've had my phone out last night or stopped over this morning."

"No, it's okay. I mean, you did ask, and I told you no."

Next time she called and sounded upset, he wasn't going to ask if he could see her. He was going to get in his truck and drive on over. "Tell me what happened."

"It's probably nothing. I mean, I promised my neighbor that I'd tell you, but maybe I've let my imagination get the best of me."

Her answer wasn't making him feel better. "Rewind, baby," he said, just as he realized that calling a grown woman "baby" probably wasn't a real good idea. "Start from the beginning. What happened? What did the police say?"

She lifted her eyes to his, and in that moment, he felt as if everything in his life had brought him to this point. Meredith was gazing at him with complete trust. Maybe not to solve her problems, but with trust that she could tell him anything without fear of not being taken seriously.

He loved that. Liz had never looked at him so honestly. Come to think of it, he wasn't even sure if Finn had. He was close with Finn, but there were gaps in their relationship, the kind of gaps that stemmed from his being only a part-time dad.

She exhaled. "All right. Here goes. I think

the man who took my backpack was in my yard yesterday."

Reaching for one of her clenched hands, he smoothed it between his own. "What did you see?"

"I was sitting in my living room after we talked on the phone. That's when I thought I saw a man cross by one of the windows. I got up, sure it was just a shadow or something, but then I saw him peering in another one."

Struggling to keep his expression neutral and his voice easy, he said, "Did he see you looking at him?"

"No. I mean, I don't think so. But maybe. I mean, I ran outside and called out to him."

"You called out to a strange man wandering around your house?" The knot of worry that had settled in his stomach was getting bigger and bigger.

She pulled her hand from his and wrapped her arms around her middle. "I guess that was pretty stupid, huh?"

If he'd been sitting here with his sister or even his momma, he would have agreed that it was. No, he probably wouldn't have just agreed. He would've added his own spin on things, probably going so far as to say it was *really freakin' stupid*.

But he was beginning to get the idea that Meredith didn't just live alone. She *was* alone.

"I'm sorry, Meredith. I should have called you the minute I got your text."

She blinked. "No need to apologize. You had plans last night. I didn't expect you to check your phone right away."

"Meredith, I would have broken my plans if I would have known that happened."

"I'm really glad you didn't get my message then. It was probably nothing, anyway."

Her voice sounded small. And the way she was holding herself instead of allowing him to keep her hand? Well, it kind of killed him.

But Meredith brought out something tender inside of him. Something that until that moment he hadn't realized he'd possessed. "I'm sorry, but I've got to do this," he murmured as he pulled her into his arms.

She stiffened. "Ace?"

He ran a hand down her spine. Lightly, attempting to soothe her. "I know we need to talk more. But do me a favor and let me just hold you for a sec first, 'kay?"

Gradually, she settled against him. Maybe a minute later, she snaked a hand up his body and pressed her palm flat against his chest. "Thank you," she said after a while.

"For what?"

"For this," she said against his chest. "For holding me close and not lecturing me. For giving me something I didn't even know I needed."

He closed his eyes, sending up a prayer of thanks that he had shown some restraint for once. "Don't ever thank me for giving you a hug." After rubbing her back for another minute or so, he pulled back and tilted down his chin so he could see her face. "I could hold you all night . . . but I think we still need to talk."

She sighed. "I know."

"So, did you talk to the cops?"

She scooted away from him. "I did. They were nice enough and came right over. They even checked for fingerprints, but they didn't find anything."

"It's a start, at least."

She nodded. "They said for me to keep my eyes and ears open and to let them know if I see that man again."

"And if you do, you call me right away, okay?"

"Okay." Her expression cleared a little bit, looking a bit wry. "I promise that I'm not that kind of woman who needs a man to do everything for her. I'm not helpless."

"I don't think you're helpless at all. You have your own business, you have your own house. Just because I want to be there for you doesn't mean I don't think you can't handle a lot of things. Don't twist things around in your mind, 'kay?"

She exhaled. "Okay."

Still feeling like he needed to hit the point home, he continued. "Seeing weirdos peering in your windows isn't something you should have to deal with, baby. That crap ain't right."

Suddenly, she looked like she was struggling not to giggle.

"What did I say?"

"Nothing. I was just wondering if you call all your girls *baby*."

Though he knew she was teasing, he didn't like the way that sounded. "I don't have lots of girls. I'm not a player, Meredith."

"I see."

"Do you?" He knew they'd really only just met, but he had hoped that she had felt the same connection that he did. "Look, I don't want to offend you or anything. If you don't want me calling you baby, just tell me."

She waited a beat, then shook her head. "You know what? There's a part of me that says I shouldn't want to be anyone's baby . . . but I don't mind it."

"Promise?"

She nodded. "Maybe I shouldn't, I've been alone for so long, held myself back from other people for so long, I kind of like the idea of getting a pet name."

She was killing him. Ruining him for another girl. "How about I don't call you baby in front of other people? I mean, I'll try not to."

"I'm good with that . . . unless I discover that you call other women that, too."

"I won't be doing that." Getting to his feet, he said, "Let's get going on dinner. Finn will be back soon."

"Ace, your shepherd's pie smells fantastic."

He winked. "I promise it tastes even better."

15

From Les Larke's
Terms for Poker Success:

*Pot: Money or chips in the center of the table.
Your goal is to get as much of that prize
as you can . . . without making
stupid mistakes in the process.*

It was after eleven.

Finn had come home, eaten supper with them, and after teasing Meredith a little bit about her "girlie" exercises, she'd challenged him—right there on the living room floor—to a plank competition. Ace knew his boy found planking a whole lot harder than it looked. As Meredith serenely planked next to him, looking like she could stay that way for half the night, Finn's eyes had gotten wide, then scrunched up, then, with a sigh of defeat, he had collapsed on the floor.

And Meredith? She'd laughed and laughed, the girlish sound flowing through the room and filling in gaps in their lives that Ace hadn't even realized had existed.

Finn had glanced his way and smiled. Ace had smiled back as he'd knelt on the floor to give

Meredith a hand up. She'd taken it gracefully, even though it was obvious to all of them that she didn't need the help. Then, that gal had turned to Finn and offered the boy a hand—which he'd taken, much to Ace's surprise.

The whole episode had been almost as sweet as those cupcakes she'd brought. Finn had placed four of them on a plate and retreated to his room. Meredith had looked surprised that he hadn't joined them but had taken Ace up on his offer to sit on the couch and watch TV.

That had been almost two hours ago.

"It's getting pretty late," she murmured. "I should go home."

"All right." He didn't move, though. And to his delight, neither did she. For the last hour, Meredith had been curled up by his side. Her sock-covered feet were curled up under his thigh and one of her hands was resting on top of his stomach.

After flipping through the choices, they'd settled on watching old episodes of *The Big Bang Theory*—a show he'd never had any interest in watching before, thinking every one of the characters had little to do with an auto mechanic from a small town in West Virginia.

He hadn't been wrong. Sheldon, Amy, and the rest of the characters couldn't have been more different than him. But their awkwardness and humor had been unexpectedly compelling.

He found Meredith's enjoyment of it even better. She'd filled him in on eight seasons of *Big Bang* drama and even started singing some kind of "Soft Kitty" lullaby. Her voice was sharp as nails, and the words were ludicrous. So, of course, he'd laughed until tears formed in his eyes.

She'd seemed pleased by that and had snuggled closer. And though his arm was getting a little numb, he'd have been content to hold her on that couch all night long.

All of that was going through his mind when she stood up. Well, all that, and the fear that had been in her eyes when she'd first arrived.

"I really do need to go home," she said around a yawn, belatedly covering her mouth. "Sorry. I guess I'm more tired than I thought."

"It's late for me, too. But I had a good time."

"I did, too." She smiled at him. "And your shepherd's pie was great. I think it might be the best thing I've had in ages."

"That's too bad. Though I might say the same thing about those chocolate cupcakes you brought."

The corners of her eyes crinkled. He'd learned tonight that that was a sure sign that she was happy about something. Unable to help himself, he reached for a couple fingers of her left hand as he walked her toward the back door where he'd hung her coat. After helping her into it, he thought about how stressed-out she'd looked when she'd first arrived. "How about I follow you home and help you get inside?"

"There's no need for that."

"I know, but I hate the idea of you going back to an empty house by yourself."

She pulled in her bottom lip as she nodded. "I'll be fine."

Because he had a feeling she said that to just about everyone, he made an offer he hadn't even known was in his head. "You could stay here, if you'd like. You could have my bed."

Blue eyes widened. "What?"

"I mean without me in it." He sounded like a moron. "I mean, I'll sleep on the couch while you take my bed."

She smiled slowly. "You would do that, wouldn't you?"

"Of course I would. I don't want you being scared."

"I'll be all right. All the windows are locked and the doors will be, too."

"You need a burglar alarm system."

"I never thought I did, but maybe I do. One day."

"You have my phone number. Text me when you get home."

"Okay."

"And, if you get scared, don't text, just call."

She looked like she was about to protest, but instead just nodded. "Okay, Ace."

"Or even if you can't sleep or something. I keep my phone by my bed. I'll hear it."

"You really mean all this, don't you?"

"Every word."

She shook her head, like she could hardly believe it. "I've never met another man like you."

"I'm nothing special, baby." She was beautiful and sweet, educated, and had her own business. He was a mechanic whose edges were so rough they bordered on jagged.

She put one finger to his mouth. "That's where you're wrong, Ace."

He couldn't wait another second. He leaned down and pressed his lips to hers. He let his mouth glide against hers softly, testing her response. Ready to pull back if she wasn't ready for anything more.

But instead of pulling away, Meredith leaned closer.

That was all the incentive he needed. He slid one of his hands under her hair, stroked the soft skin behind her neck. Ran his palm along her spine. Keeping her close, deepening the kiss. Tasting her.

She lifted her arms with a sigh and looped her hands around his neck.

She was so pretty, so delicate, so feminine. He felt his body respond. Not wanting to push things further, he stepped back and finally released her.

When her eyes fluttered open, he didn't know

if he'd ever seen a prettier sight. She looked sleepy and surprised. The romantic tension that had been floating between them strengthened and flared. Almost shocking him with its intensity. He needed her to leave before he forgot about Finn and all his reasons for taking things slow with her.

Kissing her brow, he murmured, "Good night. Don't forget to text me."

"I won't." She smiled as she dug in her purse and pulled out her keys.

"I'll call you tomorrow. Try not to worry."

"Okay. Night, Ace."

Unable to resist, he kissed her brow again. "Good night, baby." He stood at the door, watching as she got in her car, started it, and buckled up. Remained there as she backed up, gave him a small wave, then finally drove down the street.

Knowing she'd get home in less than ten minutes, he walked into the kitchen to grab his phone. Taking off his shoes, he padded along the kitchen floor. For some reason, the dark cherry wood caught his attention and he found himself staring at it. He was thinking about those planks—how he was taking polished wooden floors for granted, when his mother had always coveted them—when he noticed Finn had come out of his room and was leaning against the kitchen counter and watching him with an amused expression.

Feeling like their situations should be reversed,

Ace put his phone in his back pocket and got himself a glass of water. "How come you're still up?"

"Because it's not even midnight. And I got hungry." He opened the fridge and pulled out the casserole dish.

Ace watched him put the whole thing in the microwave and grab a fork out of the drawer. "Looks like I won't be eating that for lunch tomorrow."

"Sorry, Dad."

Figuring he might as well join him, Ace pulled out a fork, too. Just as the microwave dinged, his phone buzzed.

Home safe. Doors R locked, 2.

> **Good. Sleep well, and
> I'll call you tomorrow.**

K

Smiling at her texting shorthand, he set the phone on the counter. Then noticed that Finn was grinning at him.

Ace knew why, too. Here he was, texting and grinning at his phone like a teenager. "Is the pie hot enough?"

Finn held up his fork, which was piled high with mashed potatoes. "Yeah. It's great."

Ace speared a bite and nodded. For some reason, late-night leftovers always tasted even better.

Finn smirked. "Was that Miss Hunt?"

"Yeah. I wanted to make sure she got home and inside okay."

"Dad, she lives like five minutes away."

Remembering that Finn had missed Meredith's arrival, Ace said, "She was pretty worried when she first got here. She thinks she saw whoever grabbed her backpack through her windows yesterday."

Finn put down his fork. "Do you think she really did?"

"Oh, yeah. She's not the kind of woman to make up something out of nothing. Besides, she called the police."

"Did they find him?"

"No. He was already long gone and didn't leave any fingerprints. There wasn't much they could do but tell her to keep her eyes and ears open."

"What can we do to help her?"

"We, huh?" Ace smiled in spite of the gravity of the conversation. His boy was a good kid.

"Don't forget, I was right there, too. Plus I found her backpack."

"I haven't forgotten that," he said as he put the empty casserole dish into the sink to soak. "The truth is that I don't think there's much we can do. Meredith called the police and said she'd do what they said and keep an eye out. I think that's the most she can do. It's not like we got a good look at the guy."

"But Miss Hunt did, right?"

"A little bit. She was pretty shaken up and scared."

"You think she'll be all right?"

"She said she would. She said her windows were locked and she was going to lock the door good."

Finn just stared at him, making Ace realize that he wasn't the only one who was still worried. "I told her she could stay here," he blurted.

Finn's eyes lit up. "You invited her over for a sleepover, Dad?"

"I offered her my bed."

"Sure you did." Finn grinned wide, messing with him.

"Without me in it," he clarified for the second time that night. "I mean, I said I'd take the couch."

"She didn't want to do that?"

"No. And I don't blame her. I mean, it isn't like she knows me from Adam."

"From who?"

"It's an expression." He scooted out his chair a couple more inches so he could kick his feet out. "Anyway, I think I'm going to call Troy in the morning. He knows just about everyone around here. Maybe he can talk to a couple of cops for me." Thinking out loud, he continued. "You know, just to make sure they took her concerns seriously."

"You really like Miss Hunt, don't you, Dad?"

The question hit him hard. Not because he didn't like Meredith, but more that he wasn't used to explaining himself to anyone. The Vance men hunted, fished, played cards, and hiked. They didn't sit around a lot and discuss their feelings about girls. "I'm just trying to help her out," he said, feeling awkward.

And, almost, like a liar.

"Dad."

Ace rubbed a hand across his brow. "Yeah. I guess I do like her. Do you have a problem with that?" When his boy gaped at him, he continued, "I mean, are you still okay with me dating someone seriously?"

After pouring himself a glass of water, Finn turned back to him. A kind of odd expression was on his face. "Dad, no offense, but what does it really matter?"

Out of all the things Finn could have said, Ace hadn't seen that coming. "Of course it matters."

"Right. Because if I say no, you're going to stop seeing her," he said sarcastically.

A punch rolled through him as he contemplated telling Meredith that he couldn't see her again. It would be hard, but he'd do it if it mattered that much to Finn. He would do just about anything to help his kid—even move to Ohio.

"If you have a real problem with me seeing her, with me seeing anyone, yeah, I would hold off."

Finn started to smirk, then stilled. "You're serious, aren't you?"

"Of course. Why are you having such a hard time believing that?"

"Because you never really dated anyone back home. And Mom . . . " He took a deep breath. "You know what Mom was like."

Ace knew. Liz had craved attention, especially men's attention. He'd known that it had affected Finn, but he hadn't expected her actions would have made their son so closed off.

"I know," he said at last. "But I'm not her."

Finn stared at him for a long minute then nodded. "I don't care if you start dating Miss Hunt seriously, Dad. I like her a lot."

"Okay." He got to his feet. "I'm pretty tired. I'm going to go to bed."

"Me, too."

For a moment, he was tempted to cross the room and give him a hug. He didn't, sensing that Finn would think Ace was coddling him. He made do with smiling slightly before going to his room. Ten minutes later, when he was drifting off to sleep, he found himself thinking about Meredith again. About her auburn hair. About those blue eyes, always so filled with doubt.

The way she tried so hard to not need anyone when it was so obvious that she needed him. The way she'd slipped her hands around his neck and kissed him so sweetly.

He drifted off thinking that few things had ever felt so right.

16

From Meredith Hunt's
Guidebook to SHINE Pilates:

Tip #9: Don't Overcomplicate Pilates.
Pilates wasn't designed to be difficult.
Yes, it can be challenging, but everything
can be modified to suit you. The important
thing is that you showed up.

TUESDAY

"Did you bring your lunch today, Meredith?" Jane asked as she walked into Meredith's studio, Shine Pilates.

Watching Jane hang up her fleece jacket on the coatrack by the door, Meredith answered, "I did. It's nothing special though. Just half a roast beef sandwich, pretzels, and an apple. What about you?"

Jane pointed to a snazzy-looking soft-sided emerald-green cooler she'd placed against the wall. "As a matter of fact, I brought poppy seed chicken casserole."

"I'm impressed. Is that from your dinner last night?"

"Nope." The smile that had been playing on her lips broadened. "I baked it this morning and brought it in to share."

"Wow." Meredith was impressed. Though they usually ate lunch together, it was rare for anyone to have anything fancier than a sandwich or a carton of yogurt and a granola bar.

Jane's eyes lit up as two other ladies from their Lunch Bunch walked through the door and got settled. "We girls decided to have a potluck today. It's going to be grand."

Meredith smiled hesitantly. "We're having a potluck? All of us?"

Jane nodded. "Yep. Surprise!"

"I brought a fruit salad," her neighbor Katie announced. "And I might be mistaken, but I do believe that Vanni's been baking."

Vanni grinned as she held up her plastic cake holder like she was Vanna White. "Behold—a chocolate pound cake, full of sugar, cream, and Ghirardelli goodness. I made it from scratch last night."

Meredith shook her head in wonder. "I can't believe all of you went to so much trouble. This isn't just a potluck lunch, it's a party."

"We were hoping you'd think of it that way, honey," Katie said. "We wanted to do something nice for you."

"For me? Why?"

"Why? Because you hurt your hand and had to

stay home and cancel class. We missed you last week."

Thinking about how she hadn't thought about her hand much at all during the last few days, she held it out. "See, it's fine now. Just a small bandage covering some itchy stitches."

"Don't spoil our fun, Meredith," Katie said. "We had a good time planning this."

"I'm excited, and everything looks and sounds fantastic. Thank you."

The three ladies looked at each other and smiled. "You're very welcome," Vanni said.

"Now, we better get started. Go get settled," she said as she gestured to the four Pilates reformers in a row, all set up and ready for them.

"I suppose we have to exercise before we eat like pigs," Vanni said with a sigh.

"Yep. If you come to Pilates, you actually have to do Pilates."

The three women groaned good-naturedly as each went to her usual machine and laid down.

"All right. Foot centers one and two. Breathe in . . . and exhale . . . and press out," Meredith began, calling out the instructions to the warm-up.

The ladies quieted right down and dutifully started following her lead.

As she continued to give instructions that she called out at least a dozen times a week, Meredith thought about how much these ladies had come to mean to her. She told people that she'd started the Lunch Bunch—the group of women over fifty who came twice a week—in order to help them retain strength and endurance. She sometimes even told her younger students that the older group enjoyed going at a slower pace and that she liked being able to pay attention to their various specific needs.

But that wasn't actually true. Instead, the women had each kind of discovered Pilates at the same time and started taking private classes. Eventually, they'd all gravitated toward the eleven o'clock spot. What had happened in the group had been magic. It turned out that they weren't just the same ability level, they had the same temperament. They'd become good friends. Then, when they discovered that Meredith usually ate lunch by herself after their class, they started bringing their lunches and eating with her.

Jane had been the one to give their little group a name, saying her granddaughter was part of a Lunch Bunch in her preschool class.

It was funny, but Meredith had always felt kind of special that they included her. They were caring women and seemed to genuinely like her.

And, for someone who rarely confided in anyone or allowed herself to get too close to anyone for fear that they'd stab her in the back, it was a pretty big deal.

As she directed the ladies through the next series of movements, warning them all to pay special attention to their core muscles, Meredith found herself eyeing the front door. "I know Gwen is on vacation, but where's Pam today? She left a message that she wasn't coming in but didn't say why. Is her daughter in town?"

Katie and Jane looked at each other. "Beth is, but that isn't the reason Pam isn't here," Jane said, her expression somber. "She got some news from the doctor and didn't feel like exercising."

Meredith felt her stomach roll into a knot. "What's wrong? Did the cancer come back?"

"No, honey," Katie said. "Pam's just feeling pretty poorly. Her doctor decided to change the dosage of her cancer pill, and her body doesn't care for that one bit."

"She's been sick as a dog," Vanni added.

"I wish I would have known. I would have stopped by her house or something."

"Beth's there. There was no need for you to do that."

"But still, I would've gone by or at least called."

Katie smiled. "You still can." As she picked up her hand straps and began another series of movements that Meredith directed, she murmured, "Pam knows you care about her but she didn't want you to worry."

"Oh." In spite of the kindness, Meredith felt a little left out. She thought that she and Pam had become friends.

"Don't fret, Meredith," Jane murmured after Meredith directed them through another ten minutes of movements. "You know how it is. When you're feeling poorly, it's nice to have some people in your life who don't badger you with questions."

"I guess that's true."

"I know it is." After Jane finished the next session of bicep curls, she looked over at Vanni. "Now, you know what Pam is going to ask me about when I call her tonight. She's going to want to know if Vanni's crush has come by yet."

And just like that, all the tension in the room dissipated.

Vanni winced. "Stop, Jane. Meredith don't tell her."

As she adjusted Katie's form, Meredith couldn't resist playing along. "I would tell her if Mr. April has come by. But he hasn't yet." Winking at Jane, she said, "We're in luck. My mailman started a new route. Rick now comes here just before twelve."

"Now, isn't that interesting?" Jane asked. "It's at such a good time, too. Very close to when our class is done."

"I think you should talk to him today, Vanni," Meredith said. "Put him out of his misery."

"It would put all of us out of our misery!" Katie called out. "The waiting is killing me."

After directing everyone to put on their long

181

box, which was a fancy Pilates term for a three-foot-long padded box that they sat on to do crunches, Vanni's face flamed. "I doubt Rick even knows who I am."

"Now you're lying," Katie said around a hoot of laughter. "Every time Mr. April walks in here he looks directly at you. He's smitten."

"He's also unmarried and very single," Jane said. "Just like you."

That was actually how they'd ended up calling Rick "Mr. April." One day last April, after they'd all watched Meredith's very hunky mailman slip mail through the slot on her door for weeks, he'd come inside to deliver a package. The room had gone silent as they all craned their necks to get a better look at him.

Then, to everyone's shock, Vanni had asked if he was married.

When Rick had looked at her directly in the eye and said he was not, Vanni had blushed like a schoolgirl. Meredith had thought it was just about the cutest thing she'd ever seen.

After he'd gone on his way, all of them had hooted and hollered. Meredith had been so proud of Vanni for even speaking to Rick. Her husband had left her two years before for a trophy wife, doing a lot of damage to her ego in the process.

Since then, Rick had always come inside to drop the mail on Meredith's desk instead of just dropping it through the slot in the door. He usually paused to speak to them for a few minutes, but it had been obvious to all of them—except maybe Vanni—that he usually only had eyes for the fifty-two-year-old brunette.

"Even if he was interested in me, I don't know what I'd say to him," Vanni fretted.

"You could say hello," Katie said.

"Or say something about the weather. Like, 'Nice weather we're having,'" Jane added.

"It's gray and thirty degrees outside, Jane," Vanni muttered. "If I say that, he's going to think I'm an idiot."

"You could always ask him to join you for lunch," Katie said as she wiggled her eyebrows. "Mr. April does look like he gets a lot of exercise. I bet he gets hungry."

Meredith chuckled. "Katie! What would Mike say?"

"That I'm married but not dead."

After Meredith directed them to lay back down and put on foot straps, she said, "I think you should make it simple. Hand him a piece of paper and say here's my phone number."

Vanni sputtered. "I would never do that, Meredith. And don't tell me you would, either."

"You're right, I wouldn't. But you should."

Vanni groaned. "Oh, you all. You're terrible."

"You're too shy, that's what you are," Jane said.

"Maybe. I don't know. It's just that dating in

this day and age is harder than you would think. All of you gals are married. Only Meredith and I are the single ladies."

"Maybe we should see if Meredith wants to flirt with Rick," Jane said. "She could use some male companionship."

"As a matter of fact, I had a date last week. On Saturday night."

All three women stared at her. "Really?"

"Yes, really. It was with the man who helped me when I was robbed on the bike trail."

As the room buzzed with questions, Meredith succinctly told them the story, with Katie adding more information about the police visits—and how cute and manly Ace was.

All the women looked impressed by Meredith's toughness, Ace's description, and how sweet Finn sounded. Meredith fended off the comments but as she remembered just how much she'd enjoyed being at his house, eating dinner with Finn, and cuddling on the couch, she couldn't resist smiling. Maybe she, like Vanni, had been making progress in the dating game, too.

"Ladies, we're done. Good class," she said . . . just as the door opened.

In came Rick. He was wearing dark wool pants, a black sweater, and some kind of blue postal uniform coat. He also had a black knit cap on his head and a perfect smile and dimple for all of them. "Hello ladies," he said.

"Hi, Rick," Meredith said. "I hope you're staying warm today."

"Warm enough," he replied . . . as his gaze darted toward Vanni, who was now on her feet. After an awkwardly silent moment, Rick kind of gave them all a salute. "Well, I better get on my way. You ladies have a nice day."

Just as he started walking toward the door, Vanni darted forward. "Let me get the door for you," she said brightly.

And even though Rick had both of his hands free, he let her! "My name's Vanni," she said as she pulled open the door, her voice breathless. "Vanni Fuller."

Then, right in front of all of them, he smiled at Vanni and touched her arm. "Vanni, I'm real glad to meet you," he said before walking down the steps.

The moment the door closed, Meredith was pretty sure that half of Bridgeport heard their collective squeal. It was followed by lots of laughter and teasing as they sat on the wood floor and shared the casserole, fruit salad, and excellent chocolate cake.

"You are all terrible," Vanni said when they finally started cleaning up and putting on coats. "But I wouldn't trade you ladies for anyone else in the world."

Hugging her goodbye, Meredith realized she felt the same exact way.

17

From Les Larke's
Terms for Poker Success:

Rake: Chips taken in by the cardroom as compensation for hosting the game. The rake is a necessary but not necessarily pleasant obligation. Kind of like your mother-in-law.

FRIDAY

Later that week, Meredith got a call out of the blue, just five minutes after she'd dismissed her last class of the day.

Maybe that was why she'd picked up her cell without a second thought. The group of ladies who'd just left were some of her favorites. They were young moms of preschoolers. Once a week six of them blew in, each looking like they'd accomplished something pretty amazing just because they'd been able to sneak away for two hours. While Meredith took them through their paces, they chatted about babies and holidays and their smitten husbands.

Even though she wasn't much older than the majority, Meredith found them adorable.

They laughed and joked so much that they always put Meredith in a good mood, even when they sometimes made her feel as if she were corralling a group of preschoolers herself.

Still smiling about the news that two of them were pregnant again, she was more than a little distracted when she heard her mother's voice on the other end of the line. "Meredith."

"Hi, Mom," she said as she walked to the door of her studio and flipped the sign over from OPEN to CLOSED.

"You sound like you're in a good mood. What are you up to today?"

"I just finished my last class. It was a good one." She paused, half expecting her mother to ask why it had been so special. It would be fun to tell someone about those gals.

"You are referring to your Pilates classes."

Feeling some of the wind fly out of her sails, Meredith cleared her throat. "Yes, Mom. I was talking about one of my Pilates classes. One of the ones I teach at Shine." When her mother didn't respond, she added, "You know, my Pilates studio."

"Ah."

Gritting her teeth, Meredith reminded herself that there were lots of reasons that she shouldn't hang up. Honestly, they went through this every time. Her mother pretended she didn't have a real business while Meredith pretended her mother's insistence on putting down her livelihood didn't bug the hell out of her.

"I take it that you still enjoy it."

Her mother's tone was so brittle, it was as if she was asking if Meredith still liked being an ax murderer. "I do. I absolutely do still enjoy it. Very much." Okay, that was a bit redundant, but she didn't care. Maybe one day, if she said it enough, her mother might even pay attention to what she was saying.

But her mother remained silent as Meredith noisily shifted the phone from one ear to the other.

Tired of this game they were playing, Meredith cleared her throat. "Um, is there a reason you called?" Because her mother didn't ever call to simply say hello.

"As a matter of fact, I did call for a specific reason. Your birthday is coming up."

It was on February twenty-eighth, several weeks away. "Yes, it is."

"I can't believe you're going to be thirty-one."

"I'm having a hard time realizing that, too," she replied. It wasn't a lie, either. Sometimes the fact that she was out of her twenties did catch her off guard. Time really did move by so fast.

But then on its heels, Meredith recalled how miserable she'd been in her twenties. She'd dated a string of losers, ending with Scott, who'd been the worst of them all. She'd attempted to start a career in banking, and then had spent months recuperating from a motor vehicle accident. Each one of those things had been extremely hard in its own way. Combined, it practically made her shudder. She now knew that she wouldn't turn the clock back even if she could.

Her mother's formal tone tore through the memories and brought her back to the present. "What do you want? Is there anything specific? If you know, I could take care of it right now."

They'd played this game before, too. Her mother, after remarrying about twelve years ago, now considered herself in high society, which was pretty laughable, since they'd been barely middle class all while Meredith was growing up. Mom was now busy. Very busy.

So busy that she wasn't shy about considering Meredith's birthday present a chore that needed to be taken care of as quickly as possible. Mom had even told her once that she wasn't all that thrilled about having a daughter who was not only in her thirties, but wasn't married, didn't have any children, and had a job that her mother didn't understand.

Meredith knew that saying she didn't care wouldn't do anything but make her mother annoyed. She thought quickly. "You know, Mom, I would love a massage or a facial." That gift would give them both what they wanted. Her mother would consider either of those things to be activities she could relate to, and Meredith would totally enjoy either treatment.

"At Mitchells?"

"Yes, I would love to go there."

"I'll get you a gift certificate then."

"Thanks." Only with her mom did receiving such a nice gift feel like a verbal slap.

"You're welcome, dear. I'm glad I asked what you wanted. Now, do you have the same email address?"

She sat down on the metal bench by the door and leaned back. "I do."

"All right then. I've got a dinner to go to, so I better get off the phone. Oh, did you ever go out with Monroe?"

Monroe worked at her stepfather's company. She'd met him for drinks three days before she'd met Ace. She'd had once glass of wine. He'd had three bourbons, which had sent up a bright red flag for her. "I did," she replied, realizing that she hadn't thought of him since.

"You did? That's wonderful." Her voice warmed for the first time in the conversation. "I'll tell Ken. He and I will be seeing Monroe's dad next weekend. I'll pass on that news. Jeff and Kara will be so happy. When will you see Monroe again?"

Bracing herself for the wave of disappointment that was about to come, Meredith said, "I'm not going to see him again, Mom."

"Why not?"

"Monroe turned out to be a jerk." She paused, half hoping that her mother would leap on that statement and ask for the full story.

But just like with her Pilates job, her mother ignored the opportunity. Instead, she let out an impatient sigh. "No man is perfect, Meredith."

"I know that, but I wasn't looking for perfect. Just someone I clicked with. He wasn't it. Besides, Mom, he drank three bourbons in under an hour. You know that was too much for me."

"No, dear. Of course you don't want to put up with a man doing something like that," she said softly. "If he behaved that way, I'm glad you won't be seeing him again. I would have been wary, as well."

That was probably the only reference her mother was ever going to make to Meredith's father, who'd been a drunken wife abuser.

Funny, that little bit of vulnerability in her mom's voice had been all Meredith needed to feel like maybe everything between her and her mother wasn't over for good.

"I'm glad you found someone better than my dad, Mom."

She let out a surprised laugh. "I am, too. Though if I had been smarter, I would have never given Jeff the time of day."

Meredith felt herself lean forward, half hoping her mom would tell her more about her mysterious terrible father, whom she hadn't seen since she was five.

But with a clearing of her throat again, her mother changed tactics. "Even though Monroe wasn't the man for you, I hope you will try dating again."

"I actually have. I met a nice guy on the bike trail here in Bridgeport."

"Really? Well, tell me all about him."

"There's not a lot to say yet. We're just getting to know each other." Realizing that she was sounding just as distant as her mother often did, Meredith forced herself to add some more details. "His name is Ace and he has a teenaged boy named Finn. He . . . well, so far, I think he's pretty special."

"Ace? Is that his real name?"

"I think so." She giggled. Giggled! "Come to think of it, I should probably ask."

"You sound different when you talk about him."

"I guess I do." She realized then that she probably did sound different because she felt differently about Ace.

"He sounds intriguing. What does he do?"

"He's a mechanic."

"Of what?"

"Of cars, Mom."

"Ah. So he works in a garage or something." Her voice had turned flat again.

Which made Meredith jump to his defense, even though she had a feeling that Ace never needed anyone talking him up. She already knew that he was the type of man who faced the world head-on, letting people take him or leave him. "He works in a garage, absolutely. He's a nice guy, Mom. He's a single dad. His kid Finn? He's amazing."

"What happened to his wife?"

"He never married her." She braced herself then, waiting to hear the recriminations and warnings.

Her mother did not disappoint. "Meredith, you can do better than that."

"I don't know about that. Ace is pretty great." He had his act together a whole lot better than she did. That was for certain.

"Did he even go to college?"

"He didn't." And neither had her mother.

"Maybe that doesn't even matter to you. After all, you got your degree but threw it away."

She'd almost had an anxiety attack by doing something she hated while recovering from her accident. Through all of which her mother had never done much to help her, on account of the fact that she'd been on an extended vacation in Europe.

All of a sudden, Meredith realized that she couldn't do it anymore.

She couldn't pretend any longer that she didn't

need support. That she didn't care that her mother didn't want to see her. Didn't even want to spend more time on her birthday than she absolutely had to.

Couldn't pretend that she didn't wish that things were different between them.

But since things weren't going to change, it was better to let it go. Feeling as if she'd just lost something vital inside of her, she said, "I need to get off the phone, Mom. Thanks for the phone call."

"Ah. Yes. I need to go, too. I've got that—"

"Dinner. I know."

"I'll send you that gift certificate. It will be good for you to treat yourself. You deserve it. I'll call on your birthday, too."

"Thanks, Mom. I'll talk to you then."

After another couple of meaningless promises, they disconnected.

Sitting on one of the comfy couches in the waiting area, Meredith leaned her head back and breathed deep. She needed to bite back the disappointment. Swallow the wishes that there had been something more of substance between them.

Well, do that instead of doing what the mean part of her wanted to do, which was throw her cell phone across the room or jump up and down in the room and scream out her frustration.

One minute passed. Then two.

She'd just calmed herself down when she heard someone knock on the glass.

She turned in annoyance. "We're—" She stopped herself just in time.

Because there was Ace himself.

He was wearing a well-worn green-and-black checked flannel shirt over a black T-shirt, cowboy boots, those velvet-soft Wranglers, and a ball cap advertising some kind of power tool on his head.

His earrings were in his ears, his cheeks had a layer of scruff on them, and his dark-brown eyes were staring at her intently.

As she walked to let him inside, Meredith decided that Ace Vance looked like everything she thought he was—gorgeous, Southern, a little rough around the edges, and all man.

He was kind, he was terrific, And yes, he just happened to be there to see her.

Her mood suddenly got a whole lot brighter.

18

From Meredith Hunt's
Guidebook to SHINE Pilates:

Tip #1: Find a Qualified Pilates Instructor.
There is no better way to learn something than
to have quality, individualized instruction.

FRIDAY

"Hey, you. This is a surprise," Meredith said as she opened the door for Ace.

"A good one, I hope."

Thinking about the phone conversation she'd just had with her mother, she grinned. "It's a really good one. Come on in. I was just cleaning up. And for future reference, you don't need to knock. Just open the door."

Walking in, he scanned the large room, with its couches near the front, her old wooden desk off to the side, and the grouping of reformer machines off toward the back. "This is real pretty, Mer."

"Thank you." Scanning the room again, she tried to imagine how it would look to an outsider. The walls were a pale gray, the woodwork was shiny white, and the wood floor had been stained a muted grayish-brown color. There were accents in steel and lavender and even deep purple. She'd tried hard to make it look comfortable and professional, feminine but not too girlie. "I'm pretty proud of Shine, getting it to this stage has been a lot of work."

"I'm glad you have those windows near the front door. I looked in before I knocked." Looking a little embarrassed, he said, "I worried I was going to walk in a bunch of women in yoga positions or something."

She patted his arm. "Those would be *Pilates* positions, buddy." Pointing to the Keurig machine by her desk, she said, "Would you like a cup of coffee or tea?"

"No thanks, I'm good." He studied her more closely. "Are you okay? I saw you speaking on the phone. It looked kind of intense."

She bet it did. "I guess you noticed my frown?"

A wry expression settled in his dark eyes. "You mean did I notice that you looked pissed? Yeah." Reaching out, he brushed back a strand of hair that had fallen over her cheek. "So, I'm gonna ask again. Are you okay? Did it have something to do with that guy in your yard?"

"Him? Oh, no." She paused for a moment, both surprised that she hadn't even thought about that guy in two days and wondering just how much about her relationship with her and her mom she wanted to reveal.

On its heels was the realization that she needed to be open and honest with Ace. That was the only way for the two of them to develop a deeper relationship. "What you saw was how I usually look when I talk to my mother."

"I see."

"Yep. For some reason, no matter how much I coax myself into thinking differently, by the time I've been talking to my mother for five minutes, I'm looking for ways to get off the phone. Any chance your mother does the same thing to you?"

A smile played on his lips as he shook his head slowly. "I'm sorry, I can't help you there. My mother's great. Well, unless she shows up at my door without asking, but that's kind of hard to do now that I'm here in Ohio." Looking a little self-conscious, he added, "And even then, I can't complain all that much. She and my dad have done so much for me and Finn. I'd be lost without them."

Meredith felt her insides turn to mush. There was something about hearing a tough-looking guy like Ace talk so earnestly about his parents. She smiled softly. "Your parents sound amazing."

"They are. Me and my whole family are close."

"You miss them, don't you?"

He nodded. "Finn and I both do. Hopefully they'll come out soon."

"Maybe I'll get to meet them if they do."

"I know you'll get to meet them if they do."

Looking more serious, he said, "I'm sorry you can't say the same about your mom. Or, maybe you can and y'all were just having a bad conversation?"

"Unfortunately, our conversation was pretty typical. My mother isn't evil or anything, but I don't think I'd ever classify her as sweet."

"Speaking of coming by uninvited, I just realized that I must be my mother's son after all, because here I am. Stopping by without getting an invite."

"Don't apologize. I'm glad you stopped by." Wanting—no, *needing*—to get the focus off her problems, she turned and waved a hand. "So, this is my Pilates studio."

"It's impressive."

"Do you think so?"

"Yeah. I mean, I would, if I knew what all those contraptions were called."

"Those are called reformers."

"And that's what you work out on?"

"Sometimes. I do mat classes, too. But most of the time, each of my students is on one of these things."

He was still looking at the six reformers in the room like he was afraid one of them was about to blow up. "How do you get on them?"

"You lay down on them, silly. Most of the time, anyway."

He walked to the one closest to them and

tapped the foot bar at the end of it. "So everyone comes in here and lays down for an hour and calls it working out."

She knew he was razzing her, but she couldn't help but take the bait. "You put your hands and feet in the straps. You concentrate on your form and your abdominal muscles, among other things. It's harder than it looks."

"I'll take your word for it."

"No reason to do that. You want to give it a try?"

"Like, right now?"

She waved her hand toward one of the reformers. It was a Balanced Body Allegro 2, her most expensive model. That machine was so fancy, when it had first arrived, she'd joked to some of her students that it could practically fly a plane. "No time like the present," she said with a grin.

He backed up from the machine like he feared it was going to grow teeth and bite him. "Thanks, but no."

"Please? Just for five minutes?"

He stopped in midshake of his head. Looking at her more closely, he murmured, "You're serious, aren't you?"

"I guess I am," she admitted with a trace of embarrassment. She knew she was only asking him to look at her work because her mother had flat-out refused to ever visit her studio.

"I'd have to take my boots off."

He was sounding like that was a surprise. She grinned. "Most of my clients have to take their shoes off, too."

"Are you being a smartass?"

"Maybe. So, what do you say? Want to give it a try?" She knew she probably shouldn't be pushing Ace to fill that gap.

But maybe she wasn't. Maybe she was simply attracted to him and wanted him to feel that way about her. And because she was kind of on the awkward side in most social situations, she wanted him to see her in this setting, where she shined brightest.

But because that seemed so needy, she attempted to keep her voice light. "I don't want to hurt you, I only want you to see what I do all day. That is, if you don't mind giving it a try in your jeans."

As she'd hoped, he looked all manly and offended. "Honey, getting on this thingamabob ain't going to hurt me. I played football for twelve years. I wrestled for six of them, too. Now I spend half my days under cars. I'm used to getting contorted."

"I'm sure you've done all kinds of very impressive things, Ace Vance. But that doesn't mean you can't try something new every once in a while, does it?"

"No. I mean, fine. I'll give it a try." Walking

over to the reformer closest to them, he sat down on the carriage and looked up at her. "All right, Miss Pilates Instructor. What would you like me to do?"

Seeing him sitting there, looking up at her? She should probably be embarrassed about all the things she was suddenly thinking about asking him to do, none of which had anything to do with exercising or Pilates.

First, she would ask him to hold her close in his arms. She'd run her fingers up his chest until she had them looped them around his neck, just like she'd done on Saturday night.

Then, well, her next thoughts involved a lot of kissing, quite a bit of touching, and a whole lot less clothes on.

And speaking of removing clothes . . . Feeling her cheeks heat, she said, "Like I said, you're going to have to take off those boots."

A new, darker glint appeared in his eyes as he did as she asked. "Is that it, sugar?"

She bit her bottom lip and felt gratified when his gaze followed that motion. "Actually, I'm going to need you to take off something else, too."

His voice deepened. "What is that?"

She smiled. "Your socks, too."

Sitting on the frame of the machine, he gripped one of his boots and pulled it off. Then pulled off a thick gray sock with something that looked like reindeer printed all over them.

"Do you have on reindeer socks, Ace?"

"Maybe." Grinning a little wickedly, his voice deepened. "Just you wait, sugar. I'm a man of many surprises."

Her mouth went dry as she realized that she might have a few ideas about flirting but he was a master at it.

She might be in big trouble.

Ace was realizing real fast that he might have had more experience than Meredith Hunt in the dating and flirting department, but she was a master of manipulation.

There was no other way he could think to describe how his innocent visit to her studio had ended up with him flat on his back on a wooden and metal contraption that was full of springs, hand and foot stirrups, and moved.

She was currently standing over him and smiling. "You're doing good. Are you comfortable?"

He was wearing jeans, a belt, two shirts, and she was wearing only a small pair of shorts and some kind of sports bra. Because of that, he was trying hard, make that *real* hard, not to embarrass them both by letting her see just how much he was appreciating her outfit and all that gorgeous fair skin.

"I'm doing real fine," he said.

She looked doubtful, but nodded. "All right,

then. Now, I want you to lift up your legs." She walked to the machine next to him, laid right down on it, and lifted her knees up. "Make your legs look like mine. It's called putting them in a tabletop."

Half because his tight jeans were actively protesting the movement, and half because he was starting to realize he'd had no idea was he was getting himself in for, he winked. "I don't think there's a real good chance that my legs are ever going to look as fine as yours in this position, Meredith."

"Oh, brother. Just hold onto the sides of the machine and tighten your stomach muscles."

Focusing on her directions, he did as she asked—and a couple of muscles he'd plumb forgotten were in his body twinged in alarm.

"Good job, Ace," she said she stood close to him again. "Are you tight?"

She had no idea. "Yes, ma'am," he murmured, just as she reached out and pressed a hand to his stomach.

"Good job," she said, smiling down at him. "Your stomach is, um, really hard."

She was going to kill him. Thinking two could play this game, he smiled right back at her. "Glad you approve."

Just when he thought she might move that hand, she reached over and took hold of two black spongy-looking straps. "Now were going to do some simple movements, just for you to get the hang of things."

"I'm not going to be able to do a whole lot right now."

"Oh, I know." She smiled.

He was suddenly feeling like he needed to explain himself. "Because I'm dressed like this." He shook one of his legs. "These jeans weren't made for moving and stretching this way and that."

"Next time you can wear something else."

Lord, he hoped there wasn't a next time. He wasn't as flexible as he remembered, and he was having a really hard time pretending that lying down with her bending over him wasn't affecting him the way it was.

But because saying that would make her think he couldn't hack it, he explained himself. "I'm sure I'd be able to move around a lot better if I was in sweats or something."

"You're right. Being comfortable is very important." She leaned forward, giving him a good whiff of her perfume. And a good look at her cleavage—which he tried his best to pretend he didn't see. Her voice turned soft. "Ace, I want you to feel like you can move around easily."

He blinked, feeling like he'd just been given a one-two punch in the gut. The soft voice, the perfume, the creamy expanse of her skin. The image of them moving around easily. In unison.

His mouth went a little dry . . . until he remembered himself. "Yeah. Me, too."

She straightened. "Are you okay? Did you pull something?"

"No." He cleared his throat and attempted to laugh. Boy, for a minute there, he'd been half sure she was talking about something far different than him wearing jeans while attempting to stretch.

Looking relieved, she leaned close again. Reached out and touched his thigh. "Let's move your leg a little."

There was no way he was going to last with her hands on his thigh. Abruptly, he sat up and planted his bare feet on the wooden floor. "Thanks for showing me what you do, Meredith."

Her eyes widened. "You don't want to do anymore movements?"

Oh, hell no. "Not like this." Getting to his feet, he kind of kicked out a foot. "Like I said, these jeans weren't really made for moving around on my back."

If Meredith was surprised by his comment, she didn't remark on it. "You're welcome. I'm glad you wanted to give it a try."

"Next time, when I'm dressed more appropriately, I'll give it a try again."

Her eyes lit up. "It's a date."

Finally. A segue to the real reason he'd stopped by. "Believe it or not, I didn't stop by just to try out your machines."

"Oh?"

Her expression was full of mischief again. He loved seeing that smile and glint in her eyes. "I wanted to see your studio . . . and see if you were free on Saturday night."

"I think I am."

"When you know for sure, would you like to go out to dinner? Just the two of us?"

"Actually, I do know for sure." Her smile got bigger. "I'd love to go to dinner. Thank you, Ace."

"I'll pick you up at seven at your place."

"I'll be ready."

Unable to help himself, he stepped closer, leaned down and pressed his lips to her forehead. "See you then, and I'll call you soon."

"Okay."

He nodded, feeling satisfied. "Okay then. Bye, baby."

He walked out the door before she could say a word about him calling her that.

Though, if he was a betting man, he would guess that she didn't mind it too much at all.

19

From Les Larke's
Terms for Poker Success:

Cardroom: The space where all the action is. Make sure you're comfortable. If all goes well, you might be there for a while.

Though Allison never said a word to him at school, every couple of days over the last two weeks, Finn would see her standing in her driveway. Sometimes it was early in the morning, when she was warming up her car and waiting on her brother and sister and he was waiting on Sam to pick him up. Or, if it was in the afternoon, he saw her taking something out of her car when Sam dropped him off.

If she'd acted stalker-like, he would've put a stop to it. No matter what his dad said, he wasn't a fan of people watching what he did. He'd been burned too badly when he was younger by a couple of his neighbors in the apartment complex. The adults had loved to gossip about his mom and their kids had loved to give him crap about the many different men his mother spent time with.

Allison, though? She just usually wandered over and said hey. Always looking awkward. Always looking kind of flustered, like she was waiting for him to make fun of her or something.

He wouldn't do that. He might not want to be her new best friend, but he would never make fun of her or try to be mean. Again, he knew what it was like to be different.

The last time she was outside when Sam dropped him off, his buddy had said something. "What's up with your neighbor?" he'd asked. "She always watches you but never says anything."

"Nothing's with her. I think she's kind of shy."

"I've never seen her at school. What year is she? Sophomore like you?"

"She's a junior. Her name's Allison."

"Huh." Turning to his girlfriend, Sam had said, "Do you know her, Kayla?"

"Not really. I think we had a chemistry class together last year. She's pretty quiet."

"Allison is into dogs," Finn said, realizing as he said it that he wasn't helping make his goofy neighbor sound cool.

Sam blinked. "Dogs?"

"She has an Australian shepherd that just had puppies," Finn had explained. "She's raising them."

Kayla's eyes had lit up. "She has puppies?"

"Six of them. They're really cute. If you ever

want to see them, I bet she'd show them to you."

Kayla had looked like he'd given her a million dollars. "Thanks, Finn."

He shrugged. "It's nothing. Plus, I think she'd be happy to show them off."

Kayla turned to Sam. "Let's go over there soon."

Sam had rolled his eyes like he didn't get it, but Finn knew he was just playing around.

Hopping out of the truck, he grinned at both of them. "Thanks for the ride."

Sam had given him a little salute before backing out and driving off. Just like he always did.

Today, though, it wasn't Sam who took him home but his dad. As he saw her peeking over at them when his dad pulled into his driveway, Finn realized that his days of avoidance were about to change.

Dad looked over at her after he parked. "That's our neighbor girl, right?" Dad asked.

"Yes."

Still studying her, he said, "What's her name? Do you know?"

"Her name's Allison."

"She's a cute little thing, ain't she?"

"Allison?"

Dad turned back at him. Gave him an impatient look. "Well, yeah."

Looking at Allison a little more closely, he noticed something more than her awkwardness.

Noticed her dark-blond wavy hair. How she wasn't all skinny but looked soft and girlie. "I guess she's okay."

"Okay? Huh. I guess boys these days are harder to please," he murmured as he got out.

Now what was that supposed to mean? And what did his father see in her that he didn't? Stifling a groan as he got out of the truck, he watched his father stop and smile at their neighbor girl. "Afternoon," he called out. Just like they were back in Spartan at the Piggly Wiggly.

Finn tried to mentally prepare himself for what was about to happen.

"Um, afternoon, Mr. Vance," Allison said as she started walking toward them. "Hey, Finn."

"Hey, Allison." Today, she was wearing skinny jeans and a blue zip-up. All that curly hair was up in one of those buns girls put up at the top of their heads. Finn turned. "Dad, you ready?"

His father looked at him sharply before smiling at Allison like she was as sweet as all get out. "I'm sorry, I don't think we've officially met. Finn tells me your name is Allison?"

"Yes." She glanced at Finn again before looking down at her suede loafers.

Dad grinned. "It's good to meet you officially. I'm Ace."

Her head popped back up. "You mean Mr. Vance."

"No, he means Ace, Allison," Finn said. "You don't need to go around correcting my father."

"I don't need you speaking for me, son," Dad said sharply. Softening his tone, he turned to Allison again. "I take it you and Finn here know each other?"

"Yeah. I mean, yes, we do." She looked flustered. "I mean sometimes we say hi to each other and, um, he came over once to see the pups."

Dad glanced over at him again, this time looking more confused than irritated with his poor manners. Then his voice gentled again. "You have puppies?"

"I do."

"What kind?"

"Australian shepherd." Smiling slightly, she added, "Our dog, Maggie, had six pups. They're really cute."

"I bet. I love dogs."

"Their eyes just opened. Would you like to see them?"

Finn inhaled as he waited for his dad to tell her that they were way too busy. But instead, he stepped forward and kept talking to her in that gentle tone of voice. "That's real kind of you to ask. You know what? I'd love to see those pups."

Allison smiled. "They're just inside."

Finn didn't even try to stifle the groan that came out of his mouth.

His father turned. "Boy, you comin'?"

Finn knew that tone of voice. It had nothing to do with answering the question and everything to do with Finn getting his act together real fast. "Yes, sir."

Allison opened the back door. "Come on in. My mom's in the kitchen." She paused after she looked Finn's way. "You don't need to take off your shoes this time."

Dad raised his eyebrows as he closed the door behind them. "I'm guessing you did that when you were here?"

"Yes, sir."

Dad didn't have any time to respond to that because Mrs. Peterson met them at the doorway with a smile. "Hi, Finn. And hello, Ace. It's Sharon. It's good to see you again."

"Good to see you, too," he said as he shook her hand. "I hope you don't mind Finn and me barging in like this. Allison invited us over to see the puppies."

Mrs. Peterson smiled. "They're hard to resist. Messy, but cute."

Dad turned and grinned at Allison, looking like he did when he was around Aunt Barbara, who was kind of quiet and shy. "I could be wrong, but I'm guessing that's how they're supposed to be."

Allison's cheeks turned pink. "They're down this way." She started down the hall, his father right on her heels. When Finn lagged, she paused. "Finn, do you want to see them again?"

"Yeah, sure."

But when Allison opened the door to the laundry room, Finn forgot all about how he hadn't wanted to be come over.

Once again, the room was uncomfortably warm and smelled like old newspaper and puppies. But instead of seeing some slow-moving furry lumps like last time, all six puppies were staring at the three of them in wonder, their black eyes round and curious.

Then, out of the blue, one barked.

That seemed to be the signal the other five needed. All of a sudden, the room was filled with yipping and whines.

Maggie hopped out of the box and looked up at Allison. "Hey, girl," she whispered as she rubbed the dog's neck. "I bet you're ready for a break. Go on out, I've got them."

When Maggie trotted out, the puppies started yipping even louder.

"It's all right. Your momma'll be back," Dad whispered as he approached the large cardboard box. Kneeling down, he reached out and gently rubbed the scruff on the neck of one of the dogs.

Looking ecstatic, all six scrambled toward him, their little paws scraping the sides of the large cardboard box.

Chuckling, Allison turned and closed the door. "Now they can't escape. Let's get them out."

Finn moved forward, wanting to reach for them but being afraid to. "It's okay?"

"Oh, yeah. It's just fine," she said as she pulled one out. "They're sturdy now."

Pulling two puppies out and setting them gently on the floor, his dad sat down on the floor, too. Finally, Finn did the same thing. When all six were free, they started scampering around, their paws sometimes sliding on the linoleum.

"They're as cute as all get-out," Ace said, a pleased smile on his face.

Allison laughed. "I think so, too. My mom's right. They're noisy and make a huge mess, but I'm going to miss them when they're gone."

"I bet," Finn said as one of the puppies toddled over to him. He picked it up and held it in his lap.

"Do you already have homes for all of them?" Dad asked.

Allison shook her head. "I'm going to start posting news about them next week. They'll go fast, though. This is Maggie's third litter. Last year they were all spoken for in a couple of days."

Dad was holding one and letting it chew on his pinkie. "I'm not surprised. They're good-looking dogs. You should be real proud."

"Thank you."

Watching them all, Finn said, "Do you hate having to give them up?"

"Kind of. But they're a lot of work. And it's not like we can have seven dogs."

"You're right about that." Dad laughed as one of the puppies yipped and then knocked over another one. "Boy, are they cute. This made my day, honey," he said as he got to his feet. "Thanks for inviting us over."

Finn stood up too, belatedly realizing he was holding one like a baby in his arms. "Do you want me to help you get them back in the box?"

"No. I'm going to stay in here with them. I've got to clean up the shredded newspaper anyway."

Finn tensed, half expecting his father to volunteer him for that duty. Luckily, though, his dad just nodded and led the way out of the room.

Finn squeezed through the opening and walked by his side back into the kitchen, where Mrs. Peterson was sipping coffee or something and sitting with the twins.

"That's a fine litter of pups you've got there, Sharon."

Mrs. Peterson smiled as she stood up. "I think so, too. Ace, this is Phillip and Chloe."

His dad walked over and shook their hands. "Hey."

"Hi," Phillip said.

"Hi, Mr. Vance."

Finn couldn't help but smirk as the freshmen kind of gaped at his dad. Dad, who was a six-foot-four, 260-pound former linebacker with earrings and tattoos on one arm looked a lot different than a lot of other kids' fathers. He'd always secretly loved that about his dad.

Stepping back, Dad pressed a hand on his shoulder. "We better get on home. Thanks again for letting us stop by, Sharon."

"Anytime," Mrs. Peterson said. "Let me know if you know someone who wants a new puppy."

"Will do."

She walked over and pressed a paper plate covered in plastic wrap into his hands. "I made some brownies yesterday. I thought maybe you men might like a couple."

"Thanks, Mrs. Peterson."

"That's real kind of you, Sharon. Thanks again."

Finn's dad was quiet as they walked out through the garage and down the Peterson's driveway. He didn't say a word while they gathered their things out of the cab of the truck and he locked it.

In fact, it wasn't until they'd gotten inside and Finn was headed to his room when his father spoke.

"Not so fast, son. I'm thinking we need to have a little talk."

Maybe he was getting smarter, because he didn't even try to act like he didn't know what his father wanted to talk about.

20

From Les Larke's
Terms for Poker Success:

Blind Bets: The bets that start the action. A Blind Bet is one that is made in the dark without looking at your cards. Take my advice and don't do this — it can lead to confusion and heartbreak.

FRIDAY

As Ace watched his son silently turn around and head back into their sparsely furnished living room, he realized his mother had been exactly right. Sooner or later, everyone got a taste of their own medicine. He was getting a good taste of the attitude he used to display to his parents.

Of course, he had to admit that he'd been more of a pill than Finn ever was. Ace remembered his mouth getting him in trouble over and over again. Had he ever simply turned on his heel when he'd known his parents had been about to give him what for? He doubted it.

After Finn sat down, he stared up at him, his expression carefully bored. Waiting for Ace to get to the point.

Sitting down on the corner of the coffee table, Ace silently said a little prayer, hoping he wasn't about to say the wrong thing. "So, want to tell me what is going on with you and Allison?"

"I would, if I knew what you were talking about."

"I meant that it's pretty obvious you're barely tolerating that girl."

"Dad—"

Ace interrupted. "It was obvious to her, too, and I want to know what your reasoning is."

Finn's lips pursed. "I haven't been mean to Allison. And I've been just fine with her parents."

"That isn't what I meant. It's apparent that she wants to be your friend—just as it was apparent that you'd be fine if you never had to see her again."

"Dad, don't you think it's a little late for us to be talking about me playing nicely with the neighbor girl?"

Oh, that teenage attitude, loud and proud. Barely holding onto his temper, Ace said, "No . . . I'm thinking it's a little late for me to have to chat with you about being nice to a girl who obviously needs a friend."

"I went over there, didn't I?"

"You did. Practically kicking and screaming."

"So what's your point?"

Ace felt his jaw clench. He took a deep breath, needing to calm down. "I don't want to go round and round with you about Allison Peterson, boy. Instead, I want to know what is going on with you. I've never known you to be so rude to someone for no reason. What is it about being around her that bothers you so much?"

Finn clenched his hands. Opened his mouth. Shut it. It was obvious that he was trying like hell to rein in his emotions. Ace got to his feet, ready to let his bigger size intimidate the kid— willing to do just about anything to force Finn to lay whatever was weighing on his chest down at his feet.

"I don't like going over there, okay?" Finn finally said.

"How come?"

"Because it's . . . it's perfect in that house."

Well. He sure hadn't seen that coming. "I'm sure it ain't perfect, son."

"It's close, Dad." Finn waved a hand. "Mrs. Peterson is like a mother on television. She bakes cookies all the time. They have puppies that pee and poop everywhere, and she isn't yelling at Allison about it," he continued. "And then there are the twins."

"What about them?" Ace asked softly.

"Both times I've been over there, they sit at the table and do their homework and eat apples." His voice cracked. "Mrs. Peterson cooks them supper. And cookies. The first time I went over, she even offered me some. It . . . it was like she knew."

Ace sat back down and stared at him, poleaxed. "What does she know?"

"That I didn't have that." One lone tear slipped down his cheek. Finn impatiently swiped it away. Voice hardening, he continued. "But you know what the problem is?"

Feeling choked up himself, Ace shook his head.

"What's crazy is they don't even get it. Allison and her brother and sister? They've got everything and they don't even care. They think it's normal. They think everyone has moms who—" He stopped abruptly. "Never mind."

Watching Finn struggle, Ace felt like crying, too. His boy was hurting. Worse, he'd been hurting and Ace hadn't even realized it.

Holy hell. He'd misread the situation. He'd been thinking Finn had been acting full of himself when instead it had been something else entirely. He'd been intimidated.

Damn. How could he have been so wrong? Maybe he'd even misread everything about Finn and his mother and himself and the move.

"This is about your mother and me," he said quietly. "It's about us."

Finn averted his eyes. "Maybe it is. I don't know."

Before he realized he was doing it, Ace pulled him into his arms. "I'm sorry," he said. And he was. He was sorry he'd assumed that Liz wanted Finn enough to take care of him. He was sorry

221

he'd had some kind of notion that little boys needed to be with their mothers instead of fathers.

He was sorry that he'd taken Finn's easygoing manner for granted and never questioned him more about his life with his mother. Never doubted that he actually had been fine. Never assumed that there was ever anything darker lurking underneath his compliance.

Looking limp, Finn leaned back. "Nothing to be sorry about."

"I think there is. But because I can't go back in time, I'm not going to try. All I can promise is that things are gonna be better."

"I don't like being around Allison and her family because I don't know how to act. It's not like on the football field, when all I've got to do is get the ball and run. Over there, I don't know what to do when they're all looking at me, expecting me to say or do things that I don't know shit about."

"But one day you will," Ace promised. "Sooner or later, you're gonna get used to being here and used to ladies next door offering you macaroni and cheese and shy, sweet girls like Allison wanting a couple minutes of your time."

After letting out a ragged sigh, Finn stepped away. "Maybe. I don't know."

"I'm not great at it either, but we'll figure it out," Ace promised.

"You really think that, don't you?"

"I do. Because we don't have a choice. We're stuck here and settled."

"But Mom says—"

Ace decided to cut that off in the bud. "Your mother was a woman I slept with, Finn. That's it. I slept with her, I wasn't careful, and we got you. Now I'm going to tell you something, and I want you to take it to heart, okay?" When Finn tilted his head, he continued. "I will never regret that night because *I got you*. I will never regret knowing Liz, because she had you and you are everything to me. *Everything*. You always have been, and you always will be."

Finn's cheeks flushed. "But—"

Ace knew he probably needed to let his kid speak more about his mom. And he would let him. But not right at that moment. Right now, he wanted Finn to get it in his head that he was wanted and valued.

"No buts, kid. You made my life better. You made me into someone decent and someone I could be proud of, and someone my parents could be proud of. I know I'm a shit mom, but I'm trying to be a good dad. I want to be worthy of you, okay?"

"You already are a good dad."

"I could be better. I'll keep working on it, 'kay?"

"Okay. And . . . and I'll try to be nicer to Allison."

Ace smiled. "It's okay if you don't want to be her new best friend," he said gently. "But son, don't make her be afraid to seek you out."

"Dad, she's not afraid of me."

"But she could be. You're a big guy, kid. And if you play football, you're going to get even bigger and all the kids are going to give you a wide berth. That girl is never going to have that. And since she's the oldest, Allison doesn't have an older brother looking out for her. You could be that person."

"She's older than me, Dad."

"Even though that's the case, I still think she might need a protector every now and then. Who knows? Maybe one day she's going to need a friend like you. You could be that friend."

Finn studied his face. "You did that, didn't you? When you were in high school, did you look out for a neighbor girl?"

"Let's just say that kids in high school are cruel and some of the people they pick on can't fight back. I didn't have a problem rectifying that."

For the first time all afternoon, Finn smiled. "I understand."

Ace put his hand on the back of Finn's neck. "We good now?"

"Yessir."

"Good. Because there's something else I needed to talk to you about."

"What?"

"I've got a date with Miss Hunt tomorrow night."

"Is she coming over here again?"

"Nope. This time, I'm taking her out on a real date."

"Dinner and everything?"

Thinking of all that he hoped *everything* would entail, Ace nodded. "She's a pretty fancy girl. I thought I'd take her out for a steak dinner or something."

Finn grinned like he'd just won the Powerball lotto. "You made your move, huh?"

"Kind of." Thinking of how he'd looked like an idiot, all sprawled out on that Pilates reformer machine, he rolled his eyes. "I really like her. I know I already asked you, but I'll probably be asking this a lot. Are you still okay with me dating her?"

"I think I'm gonna be just fine with you dating Miss Hunt, Dad." After a second, he laughed. "I'm not sure how you're going to do, though. You're not used to dating much."

Thinking about how he was already feeling nervous, Ace nodded with a wry shake of his head. "To tell you the truth, I was just thinking the same thing. I'm beginning to think that Meredith Hunt is going to have me twisted in knots, trying to not make a fool of myself."

21

From Les Larke's
Terms for Poker Success:

*Buy-In: The cost to enter a tournament.
Consider the buy-in carefully. You don't
want to put out more than you have to give.*

FRIDAY

Allison was almost sure she hated Finn Vance.
The twins had teased her and her mother had
almost started planning their prom night. Like he
was ever going to take her anywhere.

And when she mentioned that, just to get her
mother off her back? Mom had just smiled and
said that there was nothing wrong with a junior
asking a sophomore to the prom.

Which, of course, had made Chloe snicker
again.

After very firmly cutting down her mother's
further attempts at matchmaking, Allison had run
up to her room. Maybe she could stay there the
rest of the weekend. And if she hoped and prayed
that Finn got amnesia or something, he might not

ever look at her like she was the plague again.

It wasn't meant to be. Her mother knocked on her door and asked her to come down and have a sandwich with her. Allison agreed after she'd learned that Dad was out on some poker night and both Phillip and Chloe were out with friends.

"I made you a grilled ham and cheese," Mom said. "I'm sitting in the living room watching old reruns of *Law & Order*. Want to bring it over here and sit with me?"

"I don't have to sit at the table?" she joked.

"Ha, ha. I know you think all my little traditions are ridiculous, but one day you're going to appreciate them."

Thinking her mother was probably right, she took her plate and sat down on the couch. "Thanks for the sandwich."

"I'm glad you came downstairs."

Feeling guilty about leaving the dogs alone for so long, she said, "Have the puppies been a lot of trouble?"

"Not at all. I made the twins clean the shredded paper on the floor and asked them to give Maggie some attention."

"They were okay with that?"

"Yes. They love Maggie, too. And no one can deny how much fun those little puppies are." She chuckled. "They're a mess and loud and are a ton a work, but there are few things cuter."

Allison grinned. "I feel the same way."

"Do you want to talk about you and Finn?"

"No." She took another bite of her sandwich, mentally bracing herself for her mother to chide her for being so closed-off.

Instead, her mother crossed her legs and looked like she was happy to settle in for a long discussion. "You might be surprised to know this, but I've actually learned some things about our new neighbors."

"How is that?"

"My friend Beverly is married to Coach McCoy."

When Allison stared at her, waiting to see what that meant, her mother grinned. "Coach McCoy is the head football coach, Al."

"I'm still not sure what you're getting at."

"Finn Vance came here to go to school, but he also came to play football for Bridgeport. He's already been working out with the varsity team."

"Really? He's that good? I mean, he's just a sophomore."

"Oh, yes. People are saying that he's not just that good, he's an incredible running back. If he's even half as good as people say, Finn could get the team to finally win district, maybe even get to state."

"Wow." She felt even more uncomfortable. Unfortunately for her mother, her news was making Allison feel even more intimidated by her new neighbor.

Her mother turned so she had both feet curled up on the couch. "Last time Beverly and I went out walking, she confided in me that her husband really likes Finn and wants to look out for him."

"That's nice of him."

"Coach McCoy doesn't want to do that just because he's going to help the team, but because he's kind of had a hard life."

"What do you mean?"

"Normally, I wouldn't share this, but I think you need to know." After a pause, her mother said, "It seems Finn's mother kind of left him to his own devices. Actually, I don't think she was around much at all."

"Really?"

"Really. I think that might be why he sometimes looks like he doesn't know what to do when he's here. I don't think he's had a lot of structure."

"That's too bad about his mom," Allison said, just as she remembered that her mother hadn't had a lot of structure, either. Her parents hadn't been too interested in raising kids. Instead, they'd been focused on their jobs and hired nannies and babysitters. Then, when her mother was ten or eleven, her father took a job overseas and she had to move in with her grandparents. "I guess you think I need to be more understanding toward him."

"I think you need to remember that he might be cute and a star football player . . . but he hasn't had a charmed life, Allison."

As if on cue, Allison's cell phone buzzed, signaling that she got a text. As she ate another bite of her sandwich, she clicked on it, and just about choked when she saw who it was.

"Mom, Finn just texted me. He wants me to go outside to talk to him."

"What are you going to do?"

"You aren't going to tell me no?"

Looking bemused, her mother shook her head. "You're sixteen, honey. I think you're a little old for me to be telling you that you can't go outside to talk to a friend."

"What do you think he wants?"

Gently pulling the plate from her hands, her mother stood up. "I guess you're about to find out."

Too afraid to take the time to go upstairs and try to fix her hair or put on something different, Allison texted him that she'd be right out.

"Have fun, Al," her mother called out softly.

She didn't say anything back, thinking that it was more likely she was about to be in another awkward situation with her neighbor. But even if that was the case, she supposed it didn't make much of a difference.

Where he was concerned, it seemed that she didn't have a lot of barriers.

Finn was standing next to her car when she came out. He'd changed from what he'd had on earlier. Now he was wearing gray sweatpants and a gray-and-green zip-up, too.

As usual, her gaze first went to his eyes, which were looking straight at her and not giving anything away. Then to his earrings, which glinted against the glare from the streetlights.

"Hi," she said.

"Hey." He pushed back from her car and walked toward her. "I wasn't sure if you'd be home."

Like she had an amazing social life. "I'm going over to a friend's tomorrow night, so I decided to stay home with Maggie and the pups."

"My dad liked them a lot."

"I'm glad. Your dad seems great."

Finn's chin went up. "He is."

"How did you get my phone number?"

"Oh." Looking a little uncomfortable, he said, "I asked Kayla to ask around. She got it for me."

"Why did you want it?"

He kind of smiled, like the answer was obvious. "So I could text you."

"Why did you ask me to come outside to talk to you?"

"So I wouldn't have to text you all night."

Of course, she wanted to push that answer. Ask him why he wanted to text her in the first place. But that seemed kind of rude. And, well, what if she didn't want to know the answers?

Looking for something to say, she ventured, "I'm surprised you're home, too."

"Yeah. Well, I don't know a lot of guys yet." He

frowned. "And most of the guys I'm starting to know the best are all upperclassmen. They don't want to hang around a sophomore at night."

"My mom heard Coach McCoy has had you practicing with the varsity team."

"Yeah. I'm good at football."

He said that the way most kids would say they liked to read or liked to go to movies. "Do you like it?"

"Football?"

She lifted a shoulder. "Well, yeah."

"Love it."

"Oh. I mean, that's good."

He grinned. "I think so, too."

"I haven't seen you wear that sweatshirt before," she said, just as she realized that she probably shouldn't mention it. No doubt he would think that meant that she paid too much attention to what he wore.

"It's from my old high school. The Spartan Eagles."

"Your colors were gray and green?"

"Uh-huh." He pulled at the sweatshirt. "It's not like I can wear it around Bridgeport."

Thinking about how hard it would be to move and lose everything you were used to, she said, "I bet you miss your old school."

"I do. I miss it a lot."

"It's too bad you had to leave."

He nodded as he stuffed his hands in the front

pockets of his zip-up. "You know, what's funny is that when my dad first mentioned us moving, I couldn't wait to go. Now, though . . ." He shrugged.

"Are you going to go back and visit soon?"

He shook his head. "No. It's better if I don't."

Realizing that it probably had something to do with his mom, she just nodded.

His dark eyes studied her. "You aren't going to ask why?"

"No. I figured if you want to tell me something, you will."

He stepped closer. "I can't figure you out, Allison Peterson."

She stared at him in confusion. "I don't know why. It's not like there's a lot to figure out. I'm just your typical nerdy junior."

He looked at her closely. Then, to her surprise, he grinned. "Nah. I don't think that's who you are at all."

Maybe she should have asked him what he meant by that, but she started thinking that she didn't want to know.

Thinking about her mother's past and now Finn's secrets, she started thinking that maybe it was okay to not be an open book with everyone.

Sometimes it was better to just simply be.

22

From Meredith Hunt's
Guidebook to SHINE Pilates:

Tip #8: Focus. If your mind is drifting,
you aren't going to appreciate the full
benefits of this activity.

SATURDAY NIGHT

Meredith was pretty certain this date of theirs
was going to be a disaster. Correction. More of a
disaster than it already was.

For someone who prided herself on usually
being reasonably well put together, she'd been
doing an abysmal job.

First, she hadn't been ready when Ace came to
the door. She'd gotten herself so agitated every
time she'd thought about how she'd acted with
him in her studio, she'd decided to do another
work out. Then she'd managed to lose track of
time and had stayed at the studio far too long.

Then she'd needed gas, which had taken
another fifteen minutes at the gas station.

After she'd finally gotten home and showered,
she couldn't decide what to wear. While she'd
been trying on outfits, she'd realized that it

had been hours and hours from when she'd had anything to eat. When she heard her stomach growl, she'd grabbed half a sandwich so he wouldn't see her shove most of her dinner in her mouth before he'd even taken his first bite.

Which, unfortunately, had wasted more precious time.

But all of her poor planning wouldn't have ruined the night. Ace hadn't blinked when she had invited him to sit down while she finished getting ready. If anything, he'd seemed amused.

Their drive to the lovely steak restaurant had gone just fine, too. As had the first twenty minutes after they'd sat down at a linen-covered table and placed their order.

Yep, everything had been almost going okay . . . until she'd asked him about West Virginia and Finn's mom.

Like a dust cloud in the desert, something had come over his features and Ace's calm expression turned dark.

She'd known right then and there that she hadn't just made him uncomfortable—she'd pissed him off.

That was over ten minutes ago.

Now she was looking at a plate holding an eight-ounce filet, grilled vegetables, and baked potato and wondering how she was ever going to do justice to the expensive meal. She was both kind of full and also kind of nervous. This was the nicest dinner she'd had in months yet it felt like it was lasting seven hours and the tension between the two of them was getting awful.

Ace was now only speaking in monosyllables.

She needed to fix things and fast.

But how?

After racking her brain, Meredith decided that she could only be honest. "I'm sorry if I made you uncomfortable by bringing up Finn's mom. I didn't mean to do that."

Ace blinked slowly, like her words had just freed him from a trance. "Don't worry about it."

"I kind of can't help but worry about it, seeing as that was the most you've said to me in fifteen minutes."

His eyebrows snapped together. "I haven't been that bad."

This time she was the one who gave him the incredulous look. He lifted his chin and closed his eyes. "Okay, maybe I have been. Sorry."

She knew good manners dictated that she should shrug off the apology, but honestly, she still wasn't sure what had been wrong about her asking about Ace's ex. She took a sip from her glass of cabernet instead.

Ace shifted in his chair and sighed. "It's just that Liz has been on my mind a lot this weekend. I'm starting to realize that Finn had an even worse time with her than I'd realized. It's pretty much killing me."

Concern for both of them filled her heart. She was tempted to reach out to him but she wasn't sure how he'd take that gesture. She thought he might take it as a sign that she thought he was weak, which couldn't be further from the truth.

Instead, she kept things simple and direct. "Ace, did Liz hurt him?"

"You mean, do I think she abused him?"

"Well, yes."

"Nah. I mean, not physically." His voice lowered. "She didn't make him feel wanted, though. Like, not ever." Staring at the table, he continued. "I think it messed him up."

"How, so?"

"We have neighbors next door who have a litter of puppies. The girl who lives there took us over yesterday afternoon . . . "

"I bet they were cute."

His eyes warmed. "They really were. So cute." He sipped his beer before continuing. "But the whole time we were in the Petersons' house, Finn wasn't acting like his usual self." He waved a hand. "He was being rude to Allison and acting strange around her mother." He shook his head. "I'm not describing it right, but trust me, it wasn't like him."

"You're right. Acting rude and distant doesn't sound like Finn."

"At first I thought he was just practicing a little teenage attitude . . . but then I realized that there was something else going on. When we got home I made him talk to me." He sighed. "That's when he told me that he was uncomfortable going over to the neighbors' house because Mrs. Peterson makes everything so nice. Finn called her a television mom. He doesn't know how to act and worries about what to say."

Thinking of Finn, who usually looked so tough—like no one in the world could intimidate him—turn so tentative made tears form in her eyes. "Poor Finn."

Ace stiffened. "Oh, no. Don't you start crying on me."

"I don't mean to. It's just so sad."

"Yeah. It is." He stared at her a moment longer then leaned back with a sigh. "So, that's why I've been crappy company and haven't been saying much. It's on my mind, I don't know how to make things better, and I didn't want to bring it up and bring you down. But it looks like that happened anyway."

"I've begun to realize that sometimes things happen whether we try to make them go away or not. Sometimes it's inevitable."

Ace nodded slowly. "My grandma used to call that Jesus having a plan."

"Maybe it is." She shrugged. "I'd like to believe that's true."

His gaze warmed. "Have I messed up everything?"

"No." Looking at him, thinking about how much he'd entrusted her with, Meredith knew it was time to share something of her own. Even if they never went on another date, she realized that her story might help him. And if that was the case, then it would be worth the awkwardness she might feel sharing it. "Can I tell you something?"

"Of course."

"Well, um, do you remember when we first met and I didn't want to accept your help?"

"Yeah."

"And how I said I didn't have any other family here in Bridgeport?"

"I remember."

"Well, my situation wasn't the same as Finn's, but my situation when I was growing up wasn't very traditional, either." Hearing how she was describing it, she rolled her eyes. "Sorry. What I meant to say, is that it was hard. My father left my mom when I was five."

"So they divorced?"

"No, they'd never married." She was almost whispering now, and she hated that. Hated that she could be in her thirties, feel so accomplished in so many ways . . . yet still felt ashamed about something that she had nothing to do with.

Gathering herself together, she continued. "I honestly don't think either of them ever thought they were *meant* to be together. They just had me, didn't hate each other, so they decided to give living together a try."

"I'm guessing it didn't work out."

She liked how Ace had injected a little humor in his voice. Not enough for her to feel like he was making fun of her, but just enough for her to realize that he was still there, still by her side.

It was suddenly easier to breathe. She wasn't alone in this. She smiled back at him. "You're right. Their experiment didn't work out. Not at all. So he left."

His dark eyes flickered as he examined her closely. "Do you still see your dad from time to time?"

"What? Oh, no. I haven't seen him since he left."

That dose of warmth that had infused his voice vanished. "Not after all this time? He didn't keep in touch?"

She shook her head, letting her adult mind wrap itself around her father's actions. As a child, she'd longed for something different, something better. She'd wanted to fit in, to feel like she was just like everyone else. She'd known her mother had been frazzled and overwhelmed by motherhood. She'd dealt with it in her own way.

But now, Meredith realized that she couldn't relate to any of it. Not her father's actions. Not her mother's way of coping.

She would have done so many things differently.

Ace sat up straight, bringing her back to the present. "Did he ever pay child support or anything?"

"Nope."

"Did your mom go after him? You know, try to track him down so he could help y'all out?"

"I don't think so. Though, to be honest, he could have offered and my mom could have thrown that back in his face. I could see that happening." She smiled, hoping to show him that she wasn't as bitter about it as her words might have sounded.

"He sounds like an ass." Looking sheepish, he said, "Sorry, I mean a jerk."

She chuckled. "I think he sounds like an ass-jerk, too." Thinking of her mother's other stories, about his drinking and abuse, she added quietly, "He was a lot of things, I'm afraid." Clearing her throat, she continued. "But that isn't my point. It's that after all that, my mom wasn't happy. She wasn't abusive or anything really terrible, but she wasn't attentive."

"She wasn't the mother who came up to school for parties?"

Meredith chuckled, trying to imagine her mom serving cupcakes or ice cream with the other moms in the room. "That would be no. She didn't go to class parties or parent conferences, though to be fair, she was trying to make a living at the bank. She worked as much as she could, which meant she didn't have a whole lot of extra time for me."

Thinking back to it, it seemed like her mother had mentally allocated a certain percentage of her time, energy, and money for Meredith. She didn't go over that amount willingly. "Because of how she was, we were almost more roommates than mother and daughter. Then, when I was sixteen or seventeen, she met Ken."

"Your stepfather?"

Meredith nodded. "Ken was older, thought she was great and smart, and for some reason had a whole lot of money he was dying to spend on her."

"I bet, after being on her own for so long, she jumped at that."

"Jumped like a bullfrog." Realizing how judgmental she sounded, she said, "Though, I can't say I blame her. My birth father wasn't the type of man to count on and she'd been alone for a long time."

Looking at her closely, Ace asked, "What was he like? Was he okay? Was he mean to you?"

"He wasn't mean. He was, and he is, fine. But he was never interested in a single mom with a teenaged daughter."

"He only wanted your mother."

"Yeah. He only wanted Amy Hunt. Not Amy

and Meredith," she agreed softly, hating that she still felt the pinch of rejection. "My mother moved to Florida the day after my eighteenth birthday."

"Where were you?"

"I was finishing up my senior year in high school. She and Ken moved me into a small apartment, paid a six-month lease, which would get me through the summer until I went to college, then took off for Tampa."

"At least they did that much for you." A line formed in between his brows. "But you went to college, didn't you?"

"Oh, I did. I got scholarships. Majored in accounting. I put myself through school by working in a bank, not the one my mother worked at, but it was close. Mom was really pleased with me . . . until I quit."

"And she hasn't jumped back on your bandwagon, has she?"

"No." She lifted her chin. "I try not to let it bother me, but it does. I'm really proud of Shine Pilates. It would be nice if she was, too."

"So you really don't have anyone in your life?"

"No, I do. I have good friends. Just not family."

Ace looked down at his plate. "I'm real sorry about that."

"It's okay."

"Mer—"

"No, listen. Ace, I didn't tell you all this so you

would feel sorry for me. I told you my story so you'd realize that Finn is going to be okay. He's got you. Even better, he's always had you. And even if he wasn't in an ideal situation with his mom, he has something special with his dad."

"I hope he feels that way one day."

"I don't think you have to worry about how he'll be feeling one day. You already know how he feels now."

"And that's enough?" he asked softly.

Her heart melted when she saw the vulnerability in his eyes. "I think it's more than enough."

Reaching out, he gently squeezed her hand. "Thanks for telling me all that, sweetheart. Now, how about we try to put a dent in this dinner?"

Picking up her fork, Meredith smiled at him. "I'm game if you are."

"Always, baby," he murmured as he stabbed a piece of broccoli. "Always."

23

From Les Larke's
Terms for Poker Success:

Bring It In: When a player starts the betting in the first round. Hey, you've got to start somewhere, right?

WEDNESDAY

Now that Finn had gotten settled into school, he was beginning to do more and more with the football team. Coach McCoy had welcomed him with open arms and invited him to start working out with the team. He'd also explained that he liked to have his players run and do weight training four days a week. He said all of his players needed to stay in top shape, especially the ones who weren't involved in wrestling or spring track and field.

Finn soon learned that most of the JV and varsity players hated running and weren't real into February workouts. He actually didn't mind it. The workouts gave him something to do. He hadn't liked coming straight home from school and didn't like mooching a ride off Sam every day, either.

Plus, he was making some decent friends in the weight room. Keaton Taft in particular. Keaton was a sophomore, just like he was, and was super easygoing. He was also pretty popular and had no problem introducing Finn to everyone he knew.

Today they were running side by side. They'd just reached the halfway mark, and like clockwork, Keaton was starting to slow down.

"I don't know how you do it, Vance. Every day, you just keep running like your life depends on it."

"Not hardly."

"Close enough."

"You better be careful. Coach is going to make you run track or something."

"Hell no."

"How come?"

A conversation flashed in his head, one where his mother was telling him that she wasn't made of money and that he shouldn't expect her to pay for all of his extracurriculars. Though his dad had paid without complaint, ever since then, he hadn't wanted to do more than one sport. "Football is enough for me."

"Yeah, it's enough for me, too," Baron, another one of his new friends, said from behind him.

All the guys laughed. "You playing one sport is enough for all of us, B," Keaton said. Finn knew what they were talking about. Baron was the type of guy who everyone liked having on the team because he got along well with everyone and helped smooth things when the coach got everyone riled up.

But he wasn't really all that good of a player. Fact was, he wasn't great at all.

Baron shrugged as he caught up, just as the rest of them all slowed to a walk. "Just 'cause I'm not some football prodigy like Finn here doesn't mean I suck at everything."

"You run a decent mile," Finn said.

Baron grinned. "Thanks, Vance. I'll take decent." He rolled his shoulders. "It doesn't matter anyway, since Bridget likes me no matter what."

Keaton rolled his eyes but didn't say anything about that.

Baron glanced at Finn. "What about you?"

"What about me what?"

"All the girls have been flirting and following you around like you're their new favorite designer. Are you ever going to give any of 'em the time of day?"

Finn felt his cheeks heat up. "They ain't following me around."

Keaton and another two guys who Finn didn't know very well grinned as they joined them on the final lap around the field. "Janie is. And she's hot."

He wasn't even sure who Janie was. "I don't have time for girls."

"What else do you have to do? I mean, it ain't like you have to get into shape for August."

"I'm in shape, but I haven't made the team yet."

Baron coughed. "You go be Mr. Modest with somebody else. We know better. Coach practically starts drooling every time he comes within five feet of you."

Finn looked behind him. "Don't talk like that."

Baron laughed louder. "What's wrong, Finn? You afraid one of Coach's pets or spies is going to find out that we're talking trash?"

Finn saw no reason to lie. His old coach had no problem assigning suicides to anyone who gossiped about him. "Maybe."

"Wow. You got game, but you're really just a—"

"Shut up, Baron," one of the guys called out before Baron could finish his sentence, which was good, since Finn knew he would have laid one on the kid if he'd said what he was about to.

"Just 'cause you don't take the game seriously, it doesn't mean the rest of us don't," Keaton said. "Besides, I know what Finn's been doing in his extra time. He's been hanging out with Allison Peterson."

Baron raised his eyebrows. "Who's that?"

"You know," Jackson interjected. "She's that goofy junior who has blond hair almost to her butt."

Baron raised his eyebrows. "Her? Why are you hanging out with her, Vance?"

"She's my neighbor." Finn was starting to feel weird, almost pissed off about the other guys' words. He didn't get it, either. It wasn't like he knew Allison that well . . . and hadn't he just recently been thinking about how much he hadn't liked her watching him?

"No offense, Vance, but you ought to stay away from her," Keaton said as they headed back to the locker room in the field house. "Everyone gives her kind of a wide berth."

"She's not bad."

"She's not good," Baron said. "She's odd. Like crazy-odd. If word gets out that you're spending time with her, the rest of the girls won't give you the time of day."

Finn shrugged. "I don't care about that."

Baron looked like Finn had just said that he didn't care about touchdowns in the fourth quarter. "How come?"

Finn shrugged again, figuring if he had to explain that, he was going to have explain most of his life—which he was in no hurry to do. It was actually pretty nice to not feel like everyone he met knew his story—including that his mother wasn't anything to be proud of.

"You ain't going to listen, are you?" Keaton said.

"Nope."

"Even if it's for your own good?"

"Nope." Realizing he sounded like an asshole, Finn explained himself. "Look, I know where you're coming from, and I appreciate it. But I don't really care about how what I do or who I'm friends with affects the rest of Bridgeport High."

Keaton stepped back. "You don't mess around—or is that how they do things back in West Virginia?"

"Hell, I don't know. Probably a little bit of both, I guess. Besides, Allison is all right. She's not as odd as you're making her sound, either. You should give her a chance."

"If you say so."

"I do." Tired of the conversation, he started messing with his combination lock. "I gotta go. See you later."

For a moment, nobody said anything. And though Finn told himself he didn't care, there was a part of him that was bummed. He hadn't meant to piss his new teammates off. Maybe he should have just kept his mouth shut.

Just as he was pulling off his sweatshirt, he heard his name being called. "Hey, Vance!"

He turned around. "Yeah?"

Keaton raised a hand. "See you later."

Finn grinned. Maybe he hadn't messed everything up after all.

Fifteen minutes later, just as he was looking at his phone to see if it was late enough to risk asking his dad to pick him up, he saw Miss Hunt walking toward the parking lot. As she was checking something on her phone, she caught sight of him.

Looking relieved, she waved. "Finn! I'm so relieved to see you."

"Why's that?"

"Because I was looking for you."

"You were?"

"I stayed late in Emily's classroom and was just texting your dad to see how his day was, and he said that you were at school. I thought maybe I could give you a ride home."

"That would be great, thanks."

"Yay. Want to text your dad and let him know, or should I?"

"I will, cause I'm still trying to wrap my head around the fact that my dad's texting you."

Her steps slowed. "Does he not usually text you?"

"No, he does. But, um, not a lot."

"He doesn't usually text the women he dates?" She held up a hand. "Scratch that. Forget I asked."

"I don't remember him dating anyone seriously. Like ever."

"Like ever," she murmured. "Huh." When they stopped next to her car, she clicked a button on her key fob. "It's open, hop on in."

When he got in, he noticed that it looked as new and spotless as it had when he and his dad had picked it up and taken it to her house. "I meant to tell you the other day that I think your car's great."

"Thanks. I got it about six months ago but it still feels like it's brand new."

"Six months is new for a vehicle."

She brightened. "You know what? I bet you're right."

He shook his head. Miss Hunt was something else. She had all her shit together, but she still acted like it was a surprise that anyone would think she did something that was good. "Did my dad say he was working late?"

"Yep. I'm sorry about that. I guess he's got some kind of classic car that he's rebuilding."

"It's an old 1968 MG. He's met some man who collects old cars but hasn't liked anyone working on them. For some reason he likes how my dad does things. He's working on the transmission."

"I bet you're proud of him."

"I guess. He's happy, which is good."

As they pulled out of the parking lot, she said, "I'm sure you're starving. What do you want to eat?"

He gaped at her. "What?"

"I'm going to run you through a drive-through."

"You don't have to do that."

"Of course I do. You're hungry, aren't you? I mean, weren't you just working out?"

"Yes, ma'am. But I can grab something at home." Mentally, he cringed, half waiting for her to get mad at him for calling her ma'am.

But instead, she just kept driving toward Bridgeport's main drag. "So, what do you want?" she asked, just as if he hadn't just told her that he'd eat at home. "Arby's? Wendy's? McDonald's?" She paused. "Skyline?"

"McDonald's?"

"You sure about that?" she teased.

"Yes, ma'am." As she took a turn and headed toward Main Street, he decided to tease her a little. "I'm surprised you even know where McDonald's is."

"Why do you say that?"

"Cause you're all healthy, Miss Pilates Instructor."

"Ha, ha. You're right. I haven't had a Big Mac in ages, but I've eaten my share of fast food over the years."

"Uh-huh."

"What's that supposed to mean?"

"I means I heard that you like tofu and veggie Chinese food."

"I might . . . but I had a steak with your father on Saturday night. I do eat meat."

Realizing that he was acting kind of rude, Finn said, "Sorry. I don't know why I brought that up."

"I know. Because I don't really seem like that. Besides, I didn't say I was going to get anything for myself. Anyway, we're here. What do you want? A number four?"

"A whole Big Mac meal?"

"Is that a yes?"

"Yeah. That's fine." He fished in his pocket.

"If you're getting out money, you better put that away. This is my treat."

"Thanks." He sat quietly while she placed the order, drove up, paid, then drove up again and got his sack, Coke, and a Diet Coke for herself. When she handed him his drink and food, he said thanks again.

"It's nothing, Finn. Just a burger."

He guessed it actually wasn't any big deal. So, why did it feel like one? He pulled out his burger, opened the cardboard box, and took a bite.

Miss Hunt drove quietly. He soon learned that she wasn't a fussy driver. She didn't fuss with the air or the radio or check her phone. She just kind of drove in a type of contented silence.

He couldn't help but compare it with his mom, who would have never *just happened* to be at school to pick him up. And even if she would've been, she wouldn't have been spending her money on a whole meal for him.

She would have been fussing with her hair and

her phone, the radio, and talking to him nonstop about nothing that mattered. He would have been trying hard to act like he didn't wish she was different.

So, this silence was odd, but good.

Almost peaceful.

24

From Meredith Hunt's
Guidebook to SHINE Pilates:

*"The acquirement and enjoyment of physical
well-being, mental calm, and spiritual peace
are priceless to their possessors."*
— JOSEPH PILATES

THURSDAY

Just as Meredith was about to have the Lunch Bunch plank for twelve seconds, she noticed that one of the members looked to be near tears.

Concerned, she rushed over to Vanni's side. "Hey, are you okay? Did you pull something when we did that last set of bicep curls? Are you hurt?"

"Hmm? Oh, no. It's nothing like that." Swiping one of her eyes with the back of her hand, Vanni gave Meredith a watery smile. "I'm just feeling a little emotional today."

Meredith paused, waiting for the other woman to expand. When Vanni only looked away, she felt a little foolish. Feeling like she'd just overstepped her bounds but not really sure why,

256

Meredith stepped back. "Oh. Well, okay then. I guess we should get back to work. Ladies, it's time to plank."

Giving Vanni a worried look, Katie dutifully rested her knees on the seat of the reformer. "How long are we going to hold the position today, Mer?"

"Um, I thought twelve seconds." Looking over at Jane and Gwen, who'd just returned from vacation, she said, "That sound okay?"

"It's fine," Gwen said, which Meredith knew was a flat-out lie. Gwen hated planking and would do just about anything to avoid it.

As soon as Vanni got into position, too, Meredith called out the directions that none of them needed, since they planked in the middle of every session. "Okay, ladies, push out your arms and get—"

"I just don't understand what I did wrong," Vanni interrupted. "I mean, all I did was smile and give him my name. And now? I haven't heard a word. Not even one. What do you all think? Is he mad at me?" she continued in a rush, each word a little louder than the last. "Did I turn him off or something? Was that really too forward?"

While Meredith tried to figure out how to get everyone back on track, Katie sat down in the middle of her machine and faced Vanni. "Oh, honey, don't start imagining the worst. I promise, you didn't do a thing wrong."

Vanni sniffed. "I don't know, Katie."

"I do," Katie replied. "I think he's just shy."

"No one's *that* shy," Vanni said. "Rick said he would text me. He hasn't."

"You mean our Rick? Postman Rick?" Meredith interrupted.

Vanni nodded before closing her eyes. "All this stress has kind of given me a headache."

"You poor dear," Gwen murmured. "You want some ibuprofen? I have a bottle in my purse."

Meredith sighed. If there was anything that bothered her more than losing control of her class, it was feeling left out while she lost control of them. "Ladies . . . "

"Hasn't it only been one day?" Katie asked, talking right over her.

"Maybe you need to be even more assertive," Jane suggested. "Some men simply need to be told what to do."

"So, what should she do? Ask him out?" Gwen asked. "Some men don't mind women making the first move."

"It couldn't hurt," Katie said with a shrug. "I asked Mike out. It worked for me."

"No offense, but that was a long time ago," Vanni said. "I don't think the same rules apply anymore."

Meredith looked at her bunch. All of them were now lounging on the reformer machines like it was a living room instead of her studio. Though the professional part of her knew she should try to get everyone back on track, the rest of her just wanted to sit down and be part of the group.

Figuring that no one was going to do anything worthwhile until the conversation finished, she decided to join them. Perching on a stool next to the wall, she said, "What happened with Mr. April? Can someone fill me in? And, um, does anyone care that we haven't actually planked yet?"

"I care," Vanni said. "Come on, Meredith. Let's go."

Feeling a little like the ogre, Meredith gave directions again and waited for everyone to get into position. Then she counted down the seconds for them to plank.

Gwen grunted. "Oh, Meredith. You know I hate planking. Besides, it's pretty obvious that we've got some bigger problems brewing than our abdominal muscles."

"I might agree with you . . . if I knew what the heck was going on."

Katie looked at Vanni meaningfully. "Vanni talked to Rick yesterday."

Just as Meredith was about to point out that Rick talks to her every Tuesday and Thursday, she realized that yesterday was Wednesday. "Wait—how did that happen?"

Vanni stretched out her legs. "I saw Rick in the frozen-food aisle at the grocery store and walked right up to him. At first, he seemed really surprised to see me, but then he warmed right up."

"That's good, right?"

"I thought so, especially when he asked me for my number."

"I'm proud of you for giving it to him." Two years ago, Vanni had felt so bad about herself, Meredith knew she wouldn't have believed that Rick would have actually wanted to call her.

Vanni, nodded. "That was yesterday around noon. Since then, I've been carrying my phone around with me, practically staring at it nonstop. But he hasn't even texted. Now my stomach is in knots. I feel worse than a seventh-grade girl."

"I'm sorry," Meredith said. "I bet he will text or call soon though."

"I hope so." Looking at the clock, she moaned. "Oh, gosh. It's almost the end of our class. Let's plank, Meredith."

Looking at the other ladies, she nodded. "Okay, gals. You heard Vanni. Let's plank for twelve seconds."

Immediately everyone rested on their elbows and toes and held the position.

Watching them all as she walked down the center of the room, Meredith counted down slowly.

Just as she got to one, Gwen called out, "Is it ever going to get easier?"

"I think so. You just need to give yourself some time and take things at your own pace. Don't you remember how hard a time you had when you first started coming here, Gwen? You could barely hold a plank for five seconds."

"I can barely hold it now."

"But it's twelve seconds, not five," she said, encouragingly. "Give yourself a break."

Katie grinned. "Meredith, I think you just gave the right advice to our Vanni, too. Don't you think, Van? Look how far you've come."

Vanni's blue eyes brightened. "You know what? That's true. I would never have approached Rick in the grocery store two months ago."

"If he doesn't want to get on the phone, that's his loss," Meredith said, just as the door opened and their man of the hour entered the building. Today he was wearing sunglasses and jeans with his usual uniform shirt and jacket. "Hi, Rick!" she called out.

Rick, all six feet, two inches of him, paused. "Hey, Meredith. I've got your mail."

"Thank you. Have a nice day," she began, just as she realized that she'd lost her class again.

Rick had walked right over to Vanni's side and was whispering to her.

Then, right in front of all of them, he crouched down and took hold of her hand. Next to her, Jane gave a little squeal.

After they saw Vanni smile and whisper something back to Rick, all the women froze as they watched Rick walk out.

As soon as the door closed, Gwen said, "Vanni, don't keep us in suspense! What happened? What did he say?"

Vanni turned to look at all of them, a look of such beauty on her face it took Meredith's breath away. "He said his nephew tossed his phone in the toilet and ruined it. Isn't that just the best news ever?"

Giggles erupted, then changed to a roar as Katie gave her a hug and announced, "Absolutely, honey. That's great news, indeed."

25

From Les Larke's
Terms for Poker Success:

Community Cards: Cards that are dealt faceup and can be used by everyone. They're like those rare people you meet who can be taken at face value. What you see is what you get.

"Thank you, Allison," Mrs. Chen said as she cuddled Sport closer to her chest. "I promise that we'll take good care of him."

Though she knew her parents would've wanted her to say something encouraging or at least grateful-sounding, all Allison could do was nod and grip the check the lady's husband had handed her.

As if she could read her mind, the woman smiled sympathetically again before getting into her car. Nestled in her arms, Sport looked a little alarmed but seemed contented enough.

Allison knew she was supposed to be happy about that. Too bad she felt kind of betrayed.

"See you," Mr. Chen said with a careless wave.

Allison raised her hand in a half-hearted wave

as he backed out of the drive and then drove off. Taking yet another of Maggie's puppies with them.

After carefully folding the check and stuffing it in her pocket, she sat down on the front step and told herself not to cry. But it didn't do any good. The tears had started coming hard and fast. She was really going to miss that pup. Oh, who was she kidding? She was going to miss all of them when they were gone.

"You crying?"

Startled, she looked up. Then didn't know whether she was glad it was Finn and not one of the twins or not. Figuring the evidence was kind of hard to ignore, she nodded.

Finn approached, walking around the pile of snow that was piled high in between their houses. "Did that couple buy one of your dogs?"

"Yeah. They bought Sport."

"Sport?" Finn grunted. "That's what they're calling him?"

"No. It's what I called him when no one was around," she admitted sheepishly.

"Why only when you were alone?"

"Because Mom told me that the more you do stuff like that, the harder it is to give them away."

Finn frowned. "Do you think that's true?"

"No. I was going to become attached to those puppies no matter what."

He sat down next to her, bringing with him

the faint scent of soap and cologne. "I'd feel the same way."

The statement was so surprising, she almost didn't notice how good he smelled and how big he felt sitting right next to her. "You'd have become attached to them, too? For real?"

"Heck, yeah. They were really cute. Plus, I've always wanted a dog."

She almost smiled. Finn didn't know it, but his dad had already talked to her about maybe getting a dog. He said he'd make the final decision after he finished up some project at work.

Glad she knew how to keep a secret, she looked over at him. Finn had kicked out his legs in front of him. He was wearing jeans, some kind of sweatshirt, and a black Patagonia coat over it. He had on boots, too. Like Bean boots or something. Once again, she thought he looked way too hot.

She, on the other hand, was wearing old leggings and an oversize T-shirt. She'd been too upset to try to put on anything else. Which, of course, now had been a bad idea. She looked like she'd just raided the sale section of Goodwill— and probably even more gangly than she usually did. When was she ever going to remember to actually take time to put a decent outfit together?

Trying not to notice the differences between herself and him, she sniffed and swiped at her eyes.

"Did you just get home?"

"Yep."

"It's kind of late. What have you been doing?"

He smiled. "Practice."

"Really? For what?"

"Football."

"What do you do for it in February?"

"Lift weights. Run." He shrugged. "Whatever the coach wants us to do, I guess."

"You sound like you don't mind running in February."

"I don't. I like working out."

Looking up at him, she studied his face. His dark-brown eyes looked kind of pleased, like he was in a really good mood. "I guess you really like football, huh?"

"Yeah. I've always liked sports." He shrugged again. "Probably because I've always been pretty good at them."

"How come you're not playing basketball now?"

"Years ago my mom told me to pick a sport because she didn't have time to take me to a bunch of practices all year long. I talked to my dad and we decided on football."

She smiled. "Since you're huge, I guess that was the right choice."

Finn laughed. "I ain't huge, Allison. I'm just glad I'm good at something, you know? I suck at math."

She realized then that she was good at school

and good with animals. Good with dogs. But what had that really gotten her besides a broken heart? She was really going to miss the puppies.

She sniffed again. Swiped her eyes again.

"Why did you start crying again?"

"Don't worry about it. I just started thinking about how much I liked those puppies." And with that, the tears started coming out faster.

He stiffened up next to her. "Crap."

Sure she now looked even worse and he probably thought she was acting stupid, Allison mumbled, "Look, thanks for coming over here, but you don't have to stay."

He turned so he could see her. "Why do you say that?"

She swiped at her eyes again. "I mean, it's not like we're really friends or anything."

"Yeah, we are."

"Come on, Finn. I've seen you at school. You've already got more friends than I do and you've only lived here a month."

"I don't know if that's true or not. But it doesn't matter, anyway. I like that we're friends."

She heard the sincerity in his voice and against her will, she fell a little more in love with him. He really was just, well, everything. Handsome and confident, a little dangerous with his black T-shirts, earrings, and dark hair and eyes. And that voice! His West Virginia drawl was awesome. It wasn't a surprise that a lot of the girls were already flirting with him. And one day—if it hadn't happened already—someone was going to tell him that being friends with Allison Peterson wasn't really a good idea.

"Okay, but if you change your mind, it's okay."

"Shut up, Al."

She gaped at him. And then closed her eyes, because he'd thrown an arm around her shoulders.

It wasn't a real hug, but it was close.

Her body shivered in response.

He looked down at her and frowned. "You're cold." Standing up, he held out a hand. "Come on, let's go inside your house and get warm."

Feeling awkward, Allison slipped her hand in his and let him pull her up. He squeezed it once before letting go. "Ready to go see Maggie and that last puppy?"

"Yep."

Remembering how he seemed to be always hungry, she said, "We have caramel brownies. Would you like one?"

"Oh yeah. I can't believe how much your mother bakes."

"Actually, it was me."

He stared down at her like she'd just admitted something amazing. "I didn't know you knew how to cook."

"Maybe you don't know everything about me yet, Finn Vance," she said, surprising herself.

When he just shook his head and smiled, she realized that maybe she'd been talking to herself as much as him. Maybe there was more to her than she'd ever realized.

26

From Les Larke's
Favorite Poker Quotations:

*"It's not gambling if you know
you're going to win."*

FRIDAY

He'd made it to the final table, had a pile of chips, and by his reckoning, was currently the most sober guy in the room. When he was dealt two tens, Ace figured he had a pretty good chance of winning the hand and knocking Troy out.

So, all told, he should be feeling pretty good. Great, even. So how come all he wanted to do was get out of Kurt's garage, take a shower to wash the stink off, and go see Meredith?

Was he whipped or what?

"Vance," Troy muttered, sounding irritated. "Call or fold."

"Sorry." After giving a cursory look at the other five guys there, he called. The dealer flipped over another ten. As the other guys showed their hands, he grinned like the lucky son of a gun he was, and collected his winnings.

He took a sip of his now lukewarm Bud Light and tried to be real pleased that he was now one of four.

But all he could think about was how it was looking at midnight now. Most likely too late to even give Meredith a call. Damn, he'd really wanted to hear her voice, too.

As the dealer shuffled, and one of the guys got up to grab a bottle of water, Troy leaned closer. "What's up with you tonight?"

Ace didn't even try to pretend he wasn't acting stupid. "I don't know. I keep thinking about Meredith."

Troy smirked. "That was quick."

"What? That I'm whipped?"

"Uh-huh."

Since another of the guys was texting something on his phone, Ace spoke again. "To tell you the truth, it's taken me off guard. One minute, I was only thinking about working on cars and getting Finn settled, and the next? I'm thinking of her all the time. I don't know how it happened."

"Don't knock it. Meredith's a great woman. Shoot, better than you deserve."

"For sure." Thinking of Campbell, the teacher friend of Emily's who Troy had been spending time with, he said, "Are you and Campbell exclusive yet?"

Troy laughed as the dealer announced everyone had one more minute to sit down. "I think we were exclusive from the moment I took her out for ice cream on our first date."

"You really did know that fast?"

"No. I didn't know what was going on. All I did know was that I was already trying to figure out how to ask her out again and get something on the calendar before I took her home."

He'd been thinking about stuff like that, too. "What did she say when you pushed to see her again?"

Troy grinned. "She said yes, Vance."

After playing another round and adding his chips to the pile, he murmured, "Meredith has been kind of skittish."

"You'll figure it out."

"Hope so. Glad you and Campbell are happy, though."

"Thanks. I've been looking at rings." He shook his head. "Go figure."

"Congrats."

"Don't be congratulating me yet. I still got to get down on a knee and convince her to have me."

Ace smiled, not wanting to inflate the guy's ego any more than it probably already was. But Troy had been a star college football player and an academic scholar to boot. Now he headed a successful financial firm. In addition, most women thought he could model if he wanted to. In spite of all of those gifts, he was actually fairly down-to-earth. Campbell wasn't going to turn him down.

As they started playing another hand, Ace's mind kept drifting. He was happy for Troy. He really was. And Kurt and Emily were no doubt on the way to the altar, if the way the two of them were constantly together was any indication.

So, were he and Meredith on the same path? He sure liked her enough to head that way. But did a girl like her really end up with a mechanic who didn't go to college and became a father at eighteen?

He sure didn't know.

"Damn, buddy. I thought you had it," Troy said.

Confused, he looked down at his cards. He had a two of hearts, a four of clubs, a king, and an eight. Nothing.

"Remind me to never take you at face value, Vance," Conrad, the Realtor sitting across from him called out good-naturedly. "You looked so smug, I thought you had a full house."

Ace forced a laugh. "Wish I had." After wishing Troy good luck, he grabbed his coat and went to go find Kurt, who he knew had been knocked out about an hour earlier.

Kurt was sitting out by his newly built firepit, smoking a cigar and talking with his little brother Sam and one of Sam's buddies.

"Hey," he said, smiling at the boys. "Kind of surprised to see y'all here. I didn't spend too much time at home on Friday nights when I was a senior in high school."

"We're designated drivers for tonight," Sam said.

Kurt nodded. "The kid needs some serious money. Winter dance is in two weeks, and someone has a girl to take out."

"Do y'all still buy corsages?" Ace said with a wink in Kurt's direction.

"Yep," Sam's buddy said, sounding put-upon. "And dinner."

"Sounds expensive."

"It is," Sam replied, but his eyes were sparkling, even in the firelight.

Ace stuffed his hands in his pockets. "Well, good luck getting all the drunk guys home."

"It's only a couple, and they pay good."

Kurt tossed the rest of his cigar in the fire and got to his feet. "You getting out of here?"

"Yep."

"What did you come in?"

"Fifth."

"Sorry you didn't win tonight."

Since he was thinking he did pretty good, especially when he'd hardly been able to keep his head in the game at all, he shrugged. "Can't win them all."

Kurt grinned. "True that. Hey, did Troy come out ahead?"

"Yeah. He's still in there."

Kurt walked with him to the top of his driveway. "I've been meaning to touch base with you this week. "How are you doing? Everything okay with Finn?"

"Finn? He's fine." Figuring he might as well say what was on his mind, he said, "I kept thinking about Meredith."

"I like her. Emily does, too."

"I like her, too. Maybe too much. It's happened fast, you know?"

He laughed. "I absolutely know about that. Emily and me were a couple before I knew what had happened. I wanted that, though."

"I think I do, too. Meredith's pretty close-mouthed though."

"You should probably talk to her about it then."

Ace nodded. "I was thinking the same thing."

Hearing a couple guys hollering in the garage, Kurt stepped back. "I better go make sure no one is getting too rowdy. See you later."

"Yeah. See you."

As he walked back to his truck, he checked his phone for the first time in an hour. He stopped when he realized he had two texts from Meredith.

Hey. Know you're @ poker.
Just wanted 2 say hi.

Then, five minutes after that:

Do I sound like a stalker? Hope not.

Though he had already promised himself that he wouldn't text her after midnight, he went ahead and texted her back.

Glad you texted. Finn's out Thursday night. Want to come over for steaks?

There. He did it. He'd taken it to the next level. If she said yes, she was saying yes to a night alone with him in his house.

And maybe even a whole lot more than that.

27

From Meredith Hunt's
Guidebook to SHINE Pilates:

*Tip #12: Start Slow. Just because Pilates
is low-impact doesn't mean it's easy!
There's a time to move forward, and there's
a time to wait. Be Patient.*

THURSDAY

"Any specific reason you're trying to slowly kill us today?" Katie called out about halfway through class.

Meredith laughed, just as she realized that she was the only one in the room laughing. The other four women—Gwen, Vanni, Jane, and Katie—all looked like they were simply trying to hold on for dear life.

She inwardly winced. "Uh oh. Has class been that hard today?"

"Umm . . . yes?" Jane said around a half smile. "I know I'm old, but this session has been a doozy."

"I'm sorry. How about everyone put on your

foot straps and we'll do some leg work?" When she noticed Katie and Gwen exchange tired glances, Meredith added, "Some slow legwork."

"Can I get a sip of water first?" Vanni asked hesitantly.

"Of course." Thinking that was a good idea, Meredith took a swig of her own water as Vanni and two other women picked up their bottles and gulped down some water before switching out the hand and foot straps on their machines.

After they got settled once again, Meredith instructed them to do some simple stretches while making sure everyone was settling in and not overworking themselves. "Sorry, guys. I guess my mind drifted off . . . "

"Instead of apologies, I'd love to know what has gotten you so worked up," Jane said. "Because I think it has to be your man."

"What makes you think it's him? I mean, Ace?"

"Because there's a rumor going around that someone saw the two of you in here a couple of days ago," Jane said.

Meredith felt her cheeks heat. "Oh?"

Jane nodded. "Oh, yes. And though I could be wrong, I think it had something to do with him on a reformer."

Katie smiled at her. "Were you giving your guy a private lesson, Meredith?"

"No. I mean, we um, I was just showing him what I did all day."

While all the women laughed again, Meredith began leading them through a series of simple leg exercises. The class was almost over, and she wanted to end the class on a good note . . . but since none of the women could seem to stop smirking at her, she was seriously contemplating ending the class early.

"I also heard that you two have been spotted around town together," Vanni said. "I think y'all were seen at Tony's."

Thinking of that steak dinner, Meredith sighed. "Boy, no secret is safe in a small town."

"Were you trying to keep it a secret?" Jane asked.

Each of her Lunch Bunch students was old enough to be her mother. But unlike her mom, these ladies didn't have years of ammunition to bring up whenever the idea suited them. Instead, they simply had good hearts.

Which made Meredith speak more frankly than she usually would have. "I haven't wanted to keep Ace a secret, but I guess I haven't wanted to jinx anything either. Things have been going really well."

"What do you mean by jinx?" Katie asked.

"Well, you know. I might do something to mess it up," she said as she adjusted Gwen's leg placement, then had everyone switch positions again.

As each woman easily moved and began the next set, Meredith gave an inward sigh of relief.

Everyone was back on track and no one looked to be exhibiting any strain or trouble. Now, they just had to get through the last five minutes.

"Meredith, you know that isn't how relationships work, don't you?"

"Maybe not for you all, but for me . . . "

Gwen shook her head. "Not for anyone, dear. All relationships have highs and lows. That's to be expected."

"I hope one day I can have the kind of relationship that you have. How long have all of you been married?"

Jane smiled. "Eighteen years."

"We're at twenty-six," Gwen said.

"We're at thirty-two," Katie announced proudly. "Mike and I have been blessed."

"You really have."

As she followed Meredith's directions, Katie continued to talk. "But it hasn't been easy. Even the best marriages have tough days."

"Adjust your hip, Katie," Meredith murmured before looking at the whole group. "So all of you are telling me that even good marriages have tough days."

All the women in the room laughed. "Absolutely," Vanni said to Meredith's surprise. "Of course, my marriage ended badly, but for a while there, things were really good." Smiling softly, she continued. "I guess I'm trying to tell you that all relationships experience growing pains from time to time. Just like kids have them during growth spurts, marriages have them every couple of years. Growing pains are part of it."

"Growing pains," Meredith repeated, thinking that the words almost felt reassuring, like nothing that happened with her and Ace was set in stone. Like maybe there wasn't one "right" way to start a relationship. "I like the sound of that."

"Me, too," Vanni said. "Now, girl, put us all out of our misery. What has got you so spun up today?"

"Dinner tonight. Ace invited me over to his house again."

"But you've already been over there. What's different this time?"

She had a feeling that this dinner was a sign that Ace was ready to take things to the next level. She might be ready for that, too. But what if they did go to bed? Would that change everything between them?

And what if he backed off after they went to bed together? What would that mean? Just thinking about all the eventualities made her stomach knot up. But how did she tell all these ladies that? She was a grown woman! Wasn't she too old to be feeling so insecure?

Therefore, her answer to Vanni was beyond lame. "It's different because it's for steaks."

Katie, who had been gamely following Meredith's hand signals, froze. "What the devil does that mean?"

"Katie!"

"We're all grown-ups here, dear. Just say what you think."

Feeling like her entire body was breaking out into a sweat, Meredith groaned. "Boy, talk about being direct."

"Y'all are making me flirt with the postman in front of everyone," Vanni said. "I promise, this is nothing."

She kind of had a point. Gathering her courage, Meredith said, "All right. Here goes . . . We're going to have steaks at his house because Ace said he wanted a *private dinner,* just the two of us. Finn won't be there. He might even spend the night at one of his friends' houses. If he does that we'll be alone . . . all night." Feeling completely ridiculous, she exhaled. "And by the way, we're done."

Gwen smiled as she stood up. "I'm not sure what is wrong with your plans, honey. It sounds romantic to me."

"It does," Katie agreed as she smoothed out the leg of her powder-blue jog set. "It also sounds like he aims to get you into his bed, honey."

Glad that was out in the open, Meredith nodded. "Yeah, I was thinking that, too." She braced herself, half expecting them to start asking about her nonexistent sex life.

But instead, the ladies just smiled. "What are you going to wear?" Vanni asked.

Finally, a question that didn't carry with it an emotional minefield! "I have a new dress that I found on sale at the mall. It's dark red."

"Red! Now won't that brighten up Ace's day! And it will go so nicely with your red hair, too."

She laughed. "Redheads usually shy away from anything red but I like the color, and it's a great shade, like a true crimson."

"I like crimson."

Grinning at her, Jane said, "Hope you got some new underthings, too."

"I did. Black lace," she admitted before she remembered she was trying to be more circumspect.

The women all laughed. "Next class is going to be so good!" Vanni exclaimed. "Now, are you making anything to bring?"

"He said I could bring dessert."

"What are you going to make?"

"A black forest cake."

Katie sighed. "Oh, I haven't had that in forever. Tell me where you got the recipe."

Luckily, they only discussed favorite cake recipes while they ate their lunches together. As they compared types of cake flour, Meredith ate her turkey sandwich and felt herself relax.

Thirty minutes later, she was walking the ladies to the door. "Thanks for putting up with me today," she said. "I hope you all won't be too sore."

"Don't you worry about us. We're tough old broads," Jane teased. "Also, I might only be speaking for myself, but I have to tell you that I enjoyed this class a lot."

"Really? Because it was so hard?"

"Because I felt like I got to know you a little better. No offense, but sometimes it feels like you keep yourself a little distant. I know we're just your students and not your friends, but—"

"You are more than just my students!" Meredith protested. "I really like each one of you."

"Then let us be your friends, too," Vanni said softly. "You aren't alone, Meredith."

"That's right," Jane said. "We've got your back."

"Thank you."

"Now, speaking of backs, I better get mine out of here. I'm a sweaty mess!"

Waving them off, Meredith knew that she'd needed their support and advice more than she had imagined. They were exactly right. She wasn't alone and she did have friends.

And good relationships really weren't perfect. They ebbed and flowed. She shouldn't expect perfection, or worry when she wasn't going to be perfect enough for Ace.

She sure didn't expect him to be perfect for her! Why had she thought she could disappoint him so easily?

For the rest of the afternoon, she focused on the conversation with her Lunch Bunch. Gradually, all of her worries about her future with Ace turned into an excitement about simply getting dressed up and sharing an intimate dinner with a man she really liked. As she gazed at herself in the mirror before walking out the door, she decided she had a pretty good chance of impressing him. Though he'd seen her in nice jeans and a sweater, her usual attire was her workout clothes.

And while they didn't hide her figure, they also didn't exactly make her look like the pretty girl she wanted to be for him. This dress, with its formfitting jersey fabric, low V-neck, and vibrant color made her feel feminine and sexy.

Now she just had to hope that Ace liked this version of her as much as he seemed to like her sporty side.

Her confidence lasted while she drove to his house and parked in his drive. It even carried over as she picked up her cake, which really was a masterpiece of chocolate, cherries, and whipped cream. Though she felt like she could gain three pounds just by looking at it, she knew it was going to taste great.

But when he answered his door and she saw that he was in faded jeans, thick ski socks, and a black Henley—pretty much his usual uniform—all of her doubts returned. What had possessed her to get so dressed up?

He paused as he took in her long black wool coat, black purse, and black patent-leather sling-back pumps. It might have been her imagination, but he seemed to stare at her heels for a moment longer than necessary.

"Come on in, honey, before you freeze out there," he said as he shuttled her inside and closed the door behind her. "And let me take that," he said, reaching for the cake.

"How are you?" she asked as he set the cake down on a kitchen counter.

"I'm better now." He smiled at her for a moment before turning to a closet. "I'm sorry. I promise, my father taught me better. Let me have your coat, baby." He moved behind her to help her remove it from her shoulders.

Feeling suddenly shy, she unfastened the thick wool belt, then unwrapped the coat, sliding it off of her shoulders and into his hands.

"Lord have mercy," he breathed.

"What?" She turned to look at him.

His eyes widened as he took in the rest of her. "What? You know what. You look absolutely stunning. Beautiful."

Warmth engulfed her as all of her insecurities faded away. She'd been so silly! Everything between them was great, and this night was going to be fantastic. She just had to relax and go with the flow.

And hope nothing went wrong.

28

From Les Larke's
Favorite Poker Quotations:

"Poker is like sex — everyone thinks they're the best, but most people don't have a clue what they're doing."
— DUTCH BOYD

THURSDAY NIGHT

It had been an amazing night. Ace had been attentive and sweet. After letting her know how much he liked her outfit, he'd kept things easy and relaxed while they'd sipped wine, eaten salad and steak, and talked about movies, sports, and their jobs. Just as she was starting to wonder what he'd planned for the second half of the evening, Finn walked in the door.

For a second, Ace had looked as surprised as she had been, but she watched him take care to cover up his initial reaction.

"Glad you got to see Miss Hunt before I took her on home, son," he said as he stood up.

Since she'd driven there, Meredith wasn't sure

what Ace was getting at, but she went with it. "Did you have a good evening?" she asked while Ace retrieved her coat.

"Yes, ma'am." Finn eyed her dress and heels, glanced at his father, then met her eyes again. "I hung out with some of the team."

"I'm glad you're making friends," she said, meaning it.

"Me, too."

"I saved you some steak and a potato, boy," Ace murmured as he held out her coat for her. "It's in the fridge."

"Thanks."

"I'll be back later," he murmured as he leaned closer to her. "Ready?"

She nodded before remembering that she was going to ask him what his exact plans were.

As soon as they walked outside, he smiled at her. "Are you mad? I just invited myself over to your place. We don't have to do that, if you don't want to, though. I want you happy."

She realized right then that he wasn't just saying words. He really did want her to be happy with him. "I'm not mad. Would you like to follow me to my house?"

His smile widened. "I would."

"I'll see you there, then."

Anticipation flowed through her as she drove the short distance home. She couldn't wait to kiss Ace again, to feel his arms around her. To do a whole lot more than that. This felt right. Though she felt a little fluttery, it was a good nervousness.

As Ace helped her unlock the door, he stepped in and then paused, obviously not sure how quickly to push her.

She solved his dilemma by pulling him in and wrapping her arms around his neck. Ace Vance obviously didn't need more instruction than that. With a groan, he pulled her closer, kissing her, deepening it within seconds.

Meredith kissed him back with everything she had. He felt so good. So solid. So big. So different from herself. So different from all the polished men she'd dated before, who only seemed to care about appearances and social statuses.

When they finally came up for air, Ace's eyes were darker than ever. "Where's your bedroom, honey?"

"Upstairs."

His eyes darkened as he took her hand. But before he made another move, he paused. "This is what you want, right?"

She didn't have a single doubt. "*Oh,* yes."

He smiled. "Thank God."

She grinned, pulling him to the stairs. But just as she took the first step, she noticed a light shining in the kitchen. "Ace, hold on a second. I don't remember leaving that light on." Actually, she rarely turned on the overhead kitchen lights. The fluorescent lights were too strong and if she stood under them for long they gave her a headache.

Dropping his hand, Meredith strode to the kitchen, then gasped. Her back window was broken and there was glass everywhere. It was also obvious that whoever had broken the pane had decided to come in, too. Cabinets were open, food and bills and dishes were on the floor.

Her house had been broken into.

"Babe, what's wr—?" Ace said behind her before letting out a string of curse words. "Meredith, don't go any farther. We need to call the police."

"Should we check upstairs first?"

"I will. But first we're going to give them a call. Okay?"

Trembling, she nodded.

"Do you have the card the cop gave you?"

"Yeah. It's on the counter." She looked at the space where she kept all her mail and calendar, then realized it was scattered all over the floor. Feeling tears fill her eyes, she gulped. "I mean, it used to be."

"We can just call. Do you remember the cop's name?" Ace asked patiently.

"It was Dale Thomas."

"Okay, then." Walking her back to the small living room, he picked up her purse. "Do you want to give him a call, or do you want me to?"

Ace's treatment of her, so kind yet still offering

to let her take the lead, brought herself back together. "I'll call." Getting a grip on herself, she pulled out her cell and skimmed her contacts. Luckily, she'd entered Officer Thomas' name into her phone already.

Two rings later, the receptionist at the police station picked up. "Officer Thomas, please. Is he on duty?"

"He is. Who's calling?"

"This is Meredith Hunt. I talked to him a couple weeks ago about a stolen backpack. Someone broke into my house tonight."

The receptionist's voice turned more intense. "Are you in danger, ma'am?"

"I don't think so. My boyfriend is here."

"I'll transfer you now. Have you already called 911?"

"No."

"I'll call dispatch. Hold on the line."

"All right. Thank you. I'll hold." She looked up at Ace, who was hovering near the stairs. "She's transferring me to Officer Thomas and calling dispatch."

"Okay. I'm going to go check things out upstairs."

"Be careful."

"I will, baby," he said before he strode upstairs.

Watching him go, she let herself imagine for a moment how things might have been different. How they had almost been very different.

Right now she and Ace could have been in her bedroom, on her bed, half undressed. And the heat in his eyes would have looked far different than the anger that seemed to be brewing just below the surface.

"Miss Hunt? Officer Thomas here."

Quickly Meredith filled him in on the situation. By the time she finished, she could hear sirens on the street. "I think the police are here."

"Explain the situation to them. I'm on my way, too."

"Thank you." Just as she hung up the doorbell rang, and Ace was striding down the stairs. "Ace, do you think he went up there?"

"I'm afraid so, honey," he said as he walked to answer the door. "I'm afraid he went through your whole house."

Meredith wanted to put her hands over her face and cry. But experience had told her that crying never helped much. Instead, she walked to Ace's side and introduced herself to the officers and explained that Detective Thomas was on the way.

"I just went upstairs. It looks like whoever was here did a pretty thorough job," Ace said. "Meredith hasn't been up there yet."

"Why don't y'all stay right here and we'll look around," one of the officers said.

Meredith was half sure that Ace would nix that idea and insist on accompanying them through the house. But to her surprise, he simply nodded and wrapped his arms around her from behind. She leaned back against him, taking comfort in his large frame surrounding her.

"Is everything ruined upstairs?"

"I don't think so. It looked like someone was searching for things to rob, not ruin."

A thousand questions ran through her mind. Why her? What did they find? Was it the same man she saw the other night? Could it really have all stemmed from getting her backpack stolen on the bike trail?

It all seemed kind of unbelievable. She wasn't rich, and she didn't have much of value. There were lots and lots of other people in Bridgeport who had bigger houses, more stuff, more expensive stuff.

Why her?

A few minutes later, Detective Thomas entered. After greeting her, he went into the kitchen, then upstairs, too. Seconds later he came down about halfway. "Meredith, I think you ought to come up here, too."

Holding Ace's hand tightly, she walked upstairs, half expecting to see the walls damaged or her bedding ripped. But all she saw were more drawers and closets opened.

"Take your time and look around, Meredith. Let us know if you notice anything gone."

Immediately, she looked for her television and her desktop computer. To her relief, both were there. Older models, they were both heavy and probably weren't worth enough for a thief to lug out of the house.

"Do you have any jewelry or anything that might be missing?"

Jewelry? She didn't wear much, so it hadn't occurred to worry about any of it being stolen. Concerned now, she lifted out a worn cigar box and looked inside. "This is where I keep my jewelry," she told the detective. "I don't have a lot, just some items that my mother . . . " Her voice trailed off as she realized that the string of pearls her mother had given her when she'd graduated high school was gone. "My pearls are missing." With a sense of dismay, she held the box out to Detective Thomas. "I received a strand of really good pearls from my mother. They were her mother's. They were really the only piece of jewelry that was worth anything."

Detective Thomas started writing down notes. "Can you tell me what they looked like?"

"Um, like a strand of pearls, I guess." Shaking her head, she tried to be more specific. "I mean, they were white pearls and had a white gold clasp. They were really pretty." Looking at Ace, she felt her heart sink. "I never wore them, but I guess I should have. Now I feel terrible that they're gone. I don't know what I'm going to tell my mother."

He pressed a hand to her lower back. "That's

why the police are here, Mer. Let them do their jobs."

"Ace is right. Give us a chance to do some investigating. Do you happen to have a picture of them?"

She nodded. "There's a picture in the living room of me on graduation. You can see them around my neck."

"Perfect. Now, look around some more. If he took one thing, he probably took something else."

After she told them about the TV and her computer being accounted for, she looked in her closets. She turned to the police officers in confusion. "Nothing else is missing. At least nothing that I can think of that somebody would want to steal."

Detective Thomas frowned but nodded. "Let's go look around your kitchen and the rest of the house."

For the next thirty minutes, she led Detective Thomas and Ace around her house while the officers took pictures and dusted for fingerprints. But, other than the fact that it was obvious that someone had been in all of her things, she couldn't find anything besides the necklace gone.

Finally, the officers left and the detective sat down in the living room with her and Ace. After sending her graduation photo back to the station with the other officers, Detective Thomas eyed her carefully. "You hanging in there?"

"I don't know. I feel really confused and kind of violated, too."

Detective Thomas nodded. "I don't blame you. I would be feeling the same way."

Though that statement was probably supposed to make her feel better, it didn't. "What am I supposed to do now?"

"It doesn't look like whoever broke in had a key. That's a good thing."

"Is she even safe here?" Ace asked while rubbing her back.

"We'll have a cruiser patrol the area tonight, so I think you'll be safe enough." The detective stared at them both. "But, Meredith, if this happened to my daughter, I'd tell her to lock up the house good and go stay with a friend for the night. What happened to you is nerve-racking. I doubt you'll get much rest if you stay here. We got some good prints. Maybe one of them can get us a match. Let us do our jobs."

Ace nodded. "I think that sounds like a good idea. I'll make sure she's safe."

Meredith glanced at him. Her insides melted a little as she saw both the protectiveness and tenderness in his eyes. Just as if the detective wasn't standing next to them, he leaned closer and kissed her lips.

"You aren't alone, baby," he whispered.

"I'm so glad you were here."

"Me, too."

Looking satisfied that she was in good hands, the detective strode toward the door. "Meredith, I'll give you a call tomorrow evening, if not before."

"Thank you," she said as she walked the stocky man to the door. "Thanks for everything."

"We haven't done anything yet, but we will. Try to stay positive."

"I'll try." She smiled wanly as she waved him goodbye. Then, just as she was about to turn around, she saw Katie and Mike walking over. Just wanting to be alone, she gave a little moan.

"What is it?" Ace asked, coming up behind her. After giving the middle of her back a reassuring rub, he stepped forward and shook their hands. "Ace Vance. Y'all are Katie and Mike?"

"We are," Mike said. "We wanted to make sure everything was all right."

"It's fi—" Meredith stopped herself in time. She wasn't going to fib and pretend everything was okay when it wasn't. "Actually, it's been a bad night," she murmured. "Someone broke in here through the back window."

Katie rushed to her side. "Are you hurt? Is everything okay?"

Meredith shrugged. "I don't know."

"Come on in," Ace waved them in with a hand. "It's cold out here."

Walking through the living room into the kitchen, Meredith told them about what happened, and what the detective suggested.

"Where are you going to spend the night?" Katie asked.

"I don't know. I was just going to speak to Ace about it."

"Why don't you come stay with us?" Mike asked. "It's right next door. If something else happened, you would be close."

"And don't even start worrying that you'd be putting us out. The guest bedroom is already made up."

Meredith glanced at Ace. She'd been about to accept Ace's offer but though she knew she would have been safe with him, it hadn't felt right. It was one thing to be wrapped up in the heat of the moment, it was another to actually pack a bag to stay at his house. She might just be skittish, but it felt a little like too much, too soon.

As if he read her mind, Ace nodded. "I think that sounds like a good plan, Meredith."

She faced Katie again. "Are you sure you don't mind?"

"We're more than sure," Katie said. "Remember what I said a few weeks ago, Meredith? This is what people do for each other. It's not a burden to have the means to help other people. It's a blessing."

She nodded before allowing herself to stew on it any longer. "Thank you. I'd love to stay over tonight."

Wrapping an arm around her shoulders, Ace looked at Mike. "I'll bring her over in about fifteen minutes."

"Good enough. Come on Katie, let's give Meredith some space."

Ace wrapped his arms around her as Mike and Katie let themselves out. "I'm proud of you," he murmured.

"For what? Taking them up on their offer?"

"Yep. I know that wasn't easy. And, though I would have liked to have put you in my bed . . . I would have taken the couch. So I guess my back is thanking you, too."

"Only you could make me chuckle at a time like this."

"How about you kiss me instead?" he murmured as he claimed her lips.

29

From Les Larke's
Terms for Poker Success:

TOC: The Tournament of Champions. These are usually experienced players who know more than most. Take my advice and listen to what they have to say. You might learn something worth remembering.

"I hate leaving you like this," Ace murmured as he pulled her into his arms and nuzzled her jaw. "I need you close."

In spite of her fear and how shaken up she was, she couldn't help but respond to his kisses and the low, gravelly tone to his voice. She knew now that she could trust him. If she told him that she wanted to sleep on his couch—or sleep in his bed while he slept on the couch—he would do that in a heartbeat.

But it still felt too soon. "I'm going to miss you, too, but I really do think taking Katie and Mike up on their offer was the right thing to do." She exhaled a shaky breath. "I don't want to hurt their feelings by refusing. Plus, I'll be right next door. I think I need that."

"I understand. Go get your things together and I'll walk you over."

Glad that she wasn't going to have to be alone in her house for even a few minutes, she quickly changed into comfy sweats, and threw a pair of pajamas and some toiletries into a small tote bag.

After she came back downstairs, Ace helped her lock up and then walked her next door. "Call me if you need anything," he said gruffly.

She knew him well enough by now to know that his order came from concern and not a need to control her. She smiled. "I will."

"You better." Before she could say anything to that, he gave her a kiss that she felt all the way to her toes.

Meredith was sure she was still flushed when she walked inside Mike and Katie's home. After refusing sugar cookies and tea, she quickly got changed and crawled into the comfortable bed outfitted with flannel sheets.

Though she'd brought along her Kindle, she didn't even try to read. All she could think about was the state of her house and the fact that someone had been inside it without her knowledge.

Just as the first tears pricked her eyes, her phone dinged, signaling a text.

She picked it up, sure it was from Ace. But to her surprise, it was from Vanni.

**Mer! I heard about your house.
I'll be over at ten in the morning.
The other girls too. We'll help
you clean up.**

Just as she was about to reply, her phone dinged again.

It was from Carrie, one of the preschool moms.

**Meredith! I'm so sorry! I got
your address from some of
the other girls. We'll all come
over to help you clean tomorrow.
We're bringing donuts from
Holtzman's, too! Don't do a
thing without us.**

More texts came in from other clients. She even heard from Emily and Kurt. She'd barely had time to text her thanks when Ace called.

"Hi," she said, knowing that she probably sounded exactly like she felt—near tears.

"Hey. Are you all right? I know you are in good hands, but it's killing me that I'm not with you."

"You know what? I'm surprisingly okay. You wouldn't believe the number of people who've reached out to say that they will be over tomorrow to help out."

"I might." She could practically hear the smile

302

in his voice. "You're a pretty special person, baby."

Snuggling down deeper into the covers, she said, "Did I even thank you for dinner?"

"You did. Did I thank you for coming over?"

She smiled wider. "I think so."

He chuckled. "I guess I'll have to tell you again when Finn and me stop by in the morning."

"Do you think Finn will want to come over, too?"

"I know he will. He was still up when I got home. He was as fired up as I was when he heard what happened. He wants to help."

Just a few weeks ago, she would have told Ace that she was fine and to tell Finn not to come over. But now, she got it. "Please tell him that I owe him a hug. If he hadn't come back to your house when he did, I would have walked into my house late tonight all by myself."

"That's crossed my mind, too. I would've hated that."

"Me, too."

"You going to be able to sleep?"

She thought of Katie and Mike just down the hall. All of her concerned friends' texts and messages. Now Ace's phone call. "You know what? I think I'm going to be just fine."

"Good night then, baby."

"Night," she said around a yawn. And, true to her word, she slept all through the night.

By the time she got to her house a little after nine the next morning, Meredith was so glad she'd gotten the rest she had. Her house felt different when she walked in by Katie's side. Almost as if it were a stranger's home.

"I'm not sure where to start," she said to Katie.

"Let's start in the kitchen and get some coffee going," Katie said as she set a whole box of black plastic trash bags on one of the kitchen counters. "Everyone is going to need some caffeine for the job at hand."

Liking the idea of concentrating on just one task at a time, Meredith cleared the counter around the coffee maker and got to work. By the time the coffee finished brewing, Carrie had arrived with a giant box of donuts, a vase of pink roses, and three other preschool moms.

After introducing herself to Katie, she took charge of passing out donuts and coffee while Katie gave the other women instructions to toss anything broken in the trash and find a place to put away everything that wasn't broken.

Vanni and Gwen appeared in the midst of it, each holding a bag of groceries. After hugging Meredith, they took over her kitchen. Within the hour, the floor was swept and they were making a pot of spaghetti.

Just as Meredith was attempting to tell them that no one needed to make her dinner, Ace, Finn,

Kurt, Sam, and Emily walked in. Then came Campbell and Troy with a new pane of glass. The men surprised her when the three of them got to work replacing the broken windowpane.

An hour later, five boys from the football team came over to cart all of her trash away so she wouldn't have to worry about eventually carrying it all out to her curb.

By two that afternoon, she had a new kitchen window, spaghetti was simmering on her stove, her house was cleaner and more organized than it had been in weeks, and she was sitting in the living room with Ace, Kurt, and Emily.

"I still can hardly believe what happened," she said.

"I'm sure you're still shaken up," Emily said sympathetically. "I would be."

"No, I don't mean the break in, I mean everything else." She waved a hand. "I can't believe so many people came over to lend a hand."

Ace smiled. "I can. You're a great person, Meredith. Try not to overthink it, okay?"

"I'll try not to."

Kurt grinned. "It really was a great turnout. And, as weird as it sounds, I think everyone had a great time. Hell, I've been to Super Bowl parties that weren't half as fun."

"I really liked all of your clients," Emily said. "Gosh, some of those women almost made me ready to start taking Pilates."

"Anytime you're ready, just let me know."

Just as Kurt was about to say something about that, Meredith's phone rang. "It's Detective Thomas," she announced before pressing the button to answer. "Yes, Detective?"

"Meredith, I want you to know that we just picked up Russell Smith. Does that name ring a bell?"

She shook her head. "I'm afraid not." Reaching out to take Ace's hand, she said, "Is he the one who broke in last night?"

"Yep. The prints we found at your house were a perfect match. It turns out that he's done the same thing all over Cincinnati. He snagged two women's purses in Sharon Woods last month." He paused, then continued, his voice sounding pleased. "After talking to the Cincinnati Police, we were able to locate his apartment and found the guy sleeping on his couch. And one pearl necklace stuffed in the pocket of his jeans."

"You're kidding!" She had already given up hope of ever seeing her necklace again. "Really?"

"Really. We charged him with multiple counts of burglary and assault," he replied, sounding extremely satisfied. "You're not going to have to worry about him showing up at your doorstep anytime soon."

She couldn't stop smiling. "Thank you so much!"

Detective Thomas spoke for a few minutes,

sharing how she might have to meet with some officers again to give a more complete statement.

When she hung up, she relayed it all to Ace, Kurt, and Emily.

Emily beamed. "That's the best news. Now you won't have to be afraid to be all alone here."

As Ace's arm wrapped around her, she nodded and smiled. But not just because the man who'd scared her so badly had been caught. Instead it was because the whole situation had made her realize that it wasn't just her house that made her feel safe and secure.

It was the large group of family and friends. They were the reason she felt so at ease. In the middle of one of the scariest moments of her life, she'd discovered that she was so very blessed.

30

From Les Larke's
Terms for Poker Success:

*Lay Down Your Hand: When a player folds.
This isn't always a bad thing. A good player
always needs to know when to go forward,
and when to cut his losses and concentrate
on something else.*

A week later, Ace's world was rocked to its core. He'd thought nothing could set him off anymore—not after everything he'd gone through with Finn's mom.

But getting the call from Finn's coach had proven him wrong.

"I didn't see any other option," McCoy said, regret in his voice. "The poor kid was in a bad way."

The coach had just told Ace that Finn had collapsed during a workout. When McCoy had tried to revive him, he'd realized that the kid had been burning up with a fever and was struggling to breathe.

When it had looked as if Finn was about to lose consciousness, they'd called 911 and an ambulance had rushed him to the hospital.

It was a struggle, but Ace cleared his throat. "No. No, of course you couldn't have done anything else," he replied, each word feeling like sandpaper in his mouth. "So, y'all are at the hospital now?"

"Yes. Bethesda North. I'm sorry to tell you like this, but we did try to call your cell multiple times. I thought I'd try you one last time before calling the garage's main number."

He'd been under a car. "I'm a mechanic. I, uh, well, I guess I can't always get to the phone."

"Hey, I understand. I'm just glad we got ahold of your buddy."

That would be Kurt. Kurt was listed as Finn's emergency contact. Luckily, he'd answered his cell right away. Ace cleared his throat. "Me, too. I'll be right there."

"Great." Coach McCoy sounded relieved. "Do you know where Bethesda Hospital is?"

He couldn't think. "I'll find it."

"I'll text you the address and a couple directions. I know you could use your GPS and all that, but, hell, sometimes I just want to know where something's at."

"If you could do that, it would be real nice. Thanks." He looked at his watch, which reminded him that yeah, he really had been working under a car for the last three hours. "I'll be there as soon as I can."

"I'll tell Finn," he said as he clicked off.

Setting down the phone, Ace strode into the employee break room. Emerson looked up from his microwave meal. His friendly smile broke off as he noticed Ace's expression. "You okay?"

"I'm fine, but I gotta clean up and go. My kid was just taken to the hospital." Shit. Even saying the words out loud shook him up.

"What? I'm so sorry. Is he going to be okay?" Before Ace could formulate an answer, he shot out another question. "What do you need?"

"Nothing, I don't think. I mean, I'll let you know after I get there." Struggling to find his words, he looked down at his hands—which were still stained with oil and grime. "I need to get cleaned up."

Getting to his feet, Emerson nodded. " ' Course you do. Don't worry about anything here. JD and I've got this."

"The Mercedes—"

"Don't worry about it," Emerson said again. "Go take care of your boy."

With those words ringing in his ears, Ace hurried into one of the two bathrooms and scrubbed his hands raw with soap, then headed to his locker and pulled out a clean shirt, pulling off his uniform shirt in one movement before putting his Henley on over his white T-shirt.

By the time he was striding out the door to his truck, JD had handed him both a bottle of water and cup of coffee. "Here. It's freezing ass outside." When Ace hesitated, his coworker nudged his arm. "It's not sludge. The new kid just made it for you."

"Thanks."

After putting his key in the ignition, he let the truck warm up a few seconds and allowed himself a few sips of the coffee, too. He really was blessed to be working at Bridgeport Automotive.

Cliff, who was recovering well after his procedure, now only came in for an hour or two a day, if that. Otherwise, he'd given Ace his complete trust. That trust had meant the world to Ace. He was coming to appreciate the other men there just as much. By and large, they were all good guys and seemed to care as much about the vehicles they worked on as their paychecks.

Taking the time to make a pot of coffee for Ace was typical of them. The jolt of caffeine, laced with a liberal amount of sugar, did more to calm his nerves than a shot of whiskey would've. Two minutes later, he'd read the directions that the coach had texted him and was driving down the highway.

As JD had said, it was freezing outside. The temperature hovered around fifteen degrees, and a light snow was falling. He forced himself to pay attention to the roads, realizing in the back of his mind that was the best thing he could do at the moment anyway. Worrying about Finn or stressing about why he hadn't realized his kid was so sick could come later.

After quickly parking, he ran into the entrance and gave the attendant his name and Finn's name.

Just as he was waiting impatiently for her to tell him where his kid was, Coach McCoy stepped out of the twin doors.

"Hey, Ace. The doc is with your boy now. They asked me to step out."

Ace held out his hand. "How's he doing?"

Looking pensive, Coach McCoy shook his hand. "He's got a heck of a fever and a bad cough. The nurse thought they might send him for X-rays. We'll see."

"I can't believe this. I had no idea he was sick." But even to his ears, he sounded lame. What kind of father didn't know his kid was that sick?

"To be honest, I didn't either. If I had, I sure wouldn't have had him working out today. He would've been sent right home. Your kid must be tough as nails."

Ace didn't know about that. He wasn't sure what to think at the moment.

A nurse appeared, interrupting his thoughts. "Mr. Vance? I'll take you back now."

"Thanks." Turning to the coach, Ace said, "Thanks again for looking after Finn. I owe you."

"No thanks needed. But look, I'm going to stick around for a few." He gestured over to a small crowd of football players sitting in the back of the waiting area. "No one's going to feel good about leaving just yet."

Touched that so many people cared, Ace nodded. "When I know something, I'll let you know," he said as he followed the attendant through the doors.

He literally felt as if all the air had been pushed out of him when the nurse pulled back the flimsy curtain and he saw Finn lying on the cot on his side. He was still in gym shorts but his shirt was off, and he had what looked like a pair of blankets arranged over his torso.

His eyes were half closed, he was obviously having difficulty breathing, and had a tube of oxygen attached to his nose and a monitor attached to his wrist.

The noise of the curtain moving startled Finn and he focused again.

"Hey, buddy," Ace said softly as he entered the room. He nodded distractedly when the nurse told him that the doctor would return in a moment. "How are you?"

When he realized that Finn was attempting to sit up, Ace rushed to his side and pressed a hand to his shoulder. "No, no. You stay put."

Finn relaxed again as he turned to meet his gaze. "Sorry about this."

"There's nothing to be sorry about, though I think I'm the one who owes you an apology."

Eyeing his boy's flushed cheeks, watery eyes, and pale lips, he frowned. "I didn't realize you were sick. I guess I should've."

"It wasn't too bad until practice today."

"Looks like we might need to do some talking about what you consider too bad, son. I'm thinking you've been real sick for a while."

Finn looked away. "I thought I could handle it."

That floored him. And made him want to cry and yell at the same time. The kid was fifteen. He shouldn't have to think he had to *handle* being sick by himself. What kind of life had he had with Liz?

What kind of relationship did Ace have with him if Finn didn't realize that he could've been more open with him?

As Finn looked like he was attempting to give him another excuse, a doctor who looked to be about Ace's age came in. "Hi. I'm Doctor Perry."

Ace got to his feet. "Ace Vance. I'm sorry I wasn't here earlier."

"I heard you were at work." Smiling at Finn, he said, "Your boy said he knew you'd be here as soon as you could."

"How is he? What's going on with him?"

Dr. Perry held up a folder. "They're bringing in the X-ray monitor so you can both see this, but it looks like we've got ourselves a case of pneumonia."

"What?" After darting a glance at Finn, Ace said,

"That's really serious. I promise, I didn't even realize he was sick. I mean, not beyond a cold."

"Don't blame yourself too much. Finn and I were talking, and it seems he didn't realize his fever has been raging for a few days. I think he had bronchitis and thought it went away."

"I've been working a ton, but I would've taken him to urgent care if I had known he was so bad off."

"I'm sure you would have. Ah, here we go," he said to the orderly who strode in with a monitor on a rolling cart. "Thanks, Evan." After turning on the machine, he slid Finn's X-rays up.

Ace was soon staring at two X-rays of Finn's lungs. Dr. Perry pointed to a cloudy mass. "Here's the infection."

"I don't know much, but even I can tell that looks pretty bad."

"It's definitely not good. That, along with the fever and the preliminary results from his blood work, tells me that we need to keep an eye on him for at least twenty-four hours. I want to admit him."

"All right."

"Can you work with this? Do you have insurance?"

"Absolutely." He pulled his insurance card out of his wallet before he realized that no one in the room expected him to show proof right that minute.

Dr. Perry looked relieved. Turning to the nurse, he started rattling off numbers and codes before walking to Finn's side and placing two fingers on his wrist.

"Do I really have to stay here?" Finn rasped.

"Yep."

"What about school and practice?"

"Nothing matters as much as your health right now," Ace said. "Don't worry about school or practice."

"Your dad is right," Dr. Perry said. "It's Wednesday. Definitely no school until Monday at the earliest."

"But—"

"We'll figure it out, Finn," Ace interrupted. "Right now we need to get you feeling better."

Dr. Perry looked relieved that Ace was being so firm. "Pneumonia isn't anything to mess with, Finn." Looking at Ace, he asked, "Who's your primary care physician?"

"We don't have one. We just moved here from West Virginia a couple of weeks ago."

"Okay. I'll give you some names. In the meantime, Finn, I'll stop by your room in a few hours to see how you're doing."

The doctor handed Ace a business card just as a dark-haired nurse walked in. "Tristen here will give you all my contact information, but take my card in case you need me right away."

"Thanks, Doc."

Dr. Perry smiled. "Hey, that's what I'm here for."

After he left, Finn said, "Dad."

"Hold on, son. The nurse is here."

She smiled at Ace. "Dad, I'm going to ask that you leave us for a bit. We need to get Finn transported up to a room and get him admitted."

"I could walk with him, though. Right?"

She winked at Finn. "He's going to need to put on a gown and get settled. Plus you've got to fill out some forms for us and give the front all your insurance and contact information."

It wasn't what he wanted, but it made sense. "Finn, I'm going to do what she suggested and also fill in Coach McCoy."

Finn nodded, but his eyes were already at half-mast. It was obvious that he was exhausted from fighting the infection and was in the exact place that he needed to be. Ace settled for resting his palm on his son's head for a moment.

"I'll look after him, Mr. Vance. I promise," Tristen said.

After giving her a nod of acknowledgment, Ace walked back out to the waiting room, feeling like he'd been hit by a freight train.

About five pairs of eyes fastened on him as he strode toward the coach. The concern in the boys' eyes was touching, and added another layer of guilt to Ace's shoulders. Had he been so involved with work and Meredith that he hadn't even made the effort to get to know any of Finn's teammates?

Coach looked as agitated as Ace felt. "How is he?"

"He has pneumonia and is going to have to spend at least one night in the hospital." Though the announcement made him feel like crap, Ace forced himself to continue. "Thank you again for looking out for him. I owe you."

"Like I said earlier, you don't owe me a thing. He's a good kid. I'm just glad I was there."

"Me, too." Turning to the other boys, he raised a hand. "I'm Ace Vance. Finn's dad. Thanks for being here."

All the boys got to their feet and walked forward as Coach McCoy introduced them.

"This here is Keaton, Bryan, Hamilton, and Baron."

After exchanging a few words with them, Ace turned to the coach again. "I've got some paperwork to fill out and some phone calls to make. The doc said Finn won't be back at school until Monday at the earliest."

"I'll let the front office know." After shaking Ace's hand again, McCoy shuttled the boys out the door.

Feeling that at least he'd made some progress, he walked over to the nurses' station and was directed to another area, where all the paperwork was waiting for him.

That took a good fifteen minutes. His call to work took another ten, then, after being told to wait in the waiting area until Finn was ready for him, Ace knew he had two more calls to make.

For the first time, he wasn't sure which was going to be harder to make. Figuring both were going to be challenging, he decided to call Liz first. She was Finn's mother, after all.

"Ace?" she said upon answering, sounding happier than he could remember her sounding. "Hey."

"Hey, Liz. You gotta second? I need to talk to you."

"Now?"

"Yep. It's important." He gazed up at the ceiling, right where the wall met the ceiling. Spotted a water stain in the back corner of the room.

After he heard her speak to someone, she was back on. "What happened?"

"I'm in the hospital. Finn's sick."

She gasped. "What's wrong? Is he going to be okay?"

As succinctly as possible, he filled her in on what happened. "I'll text you later after I see him in his room."

"You think he's going to be okay?" she asked again, her voice sounding as stressed as he felt. "I mean, people die from pneumonia, right?"

"The doc didn't sound like Finn was in danger like that. Just exhausted and really sick."

"How come he was at practice if he was so sick?" Her voice hardened. "Did you make him go no matter what?"

"Of course not." It was on the tip of his tongue to say something just as cruel back, but he stopped himself in time. Because he realized then that she was simply doing what he used to do. He'd been a pro at finding fault with almost everything she did regarding Finn. And because he'd always felt so out of control where he was concerned, he'd been real good at asking her questions he'd known she didn't have the answers to.

And here she was, doing the same thing.

"Look. I talked to Finn and the doctor. Both said it hit him pretty suddenly. I just wanted you to know."

"Should I come out there?"

"No reason to."

"A boy needs his momma."

"Boys do. But he's grown up now. That said, if you want to come out, I know he'll be glad to see you."

She paused. "I'll have to check my work schedule," she said. "It might be hard for me to get away."

"I understand." And he did. This was typical Liz. She said all the right things but her actions never matched. "I'll keep you informed on how he's doing."

"Tell him I love him."

"I will," he said as he realized that she would most likely not even call the boy.

"Look, I've gotta go and get back to work." She hung up without another word.

He set his cell phone down and wondered for about the one hundredth time why he'd ever been so infatuated with her in the first place. She was everything he wasn't attracted to.

Everything the opposite of Meredith.

Knowing that phone call came next, he checked the time, and hoped she wasn't in the middle of teaching a class. He needed to talk to her for more reasons than one.

31

From Meredith Hunt's
Guidebook to SHINE Pilates:

Tip #4: Make Space in Your Life for Pilates. For that matter, make space in your life for the things that are really important. Like your family, friends, and faith. Okay, maybe chocolate from time to time, too.

Meredith had just sat down with a large mug of peppermint tea, a basket full of bills and checks, and her online ledger when Ace called. She couldn't pick up fast enough. Though she was good at it, she hated the business side of her studio.

Then there was the fact that she now seemed to spend all her spare time mooning over him like a teenaged girl.

"Hey you," she said. "This is a nice surprise. You're usually working this time of day." She smiled, half waiting for him to tell her that he'd been doing the same thing as her—thinking about their night together.

Well, in a total manly Ace kind of way, of course.

"Meredith, I'm really glad you picked up. I'm at the hospital with Finn."

She leapt to her feet. "What happened?"

"He collapsed during weight training today. His coach had to take him to the hospital himself when I didn't pick up my phone. I was under a freakin' car."

She could hear the pain in his voice. "Ace, I'm so sorry. Where are you? I'll be right there."

After a pause, he said, "There's no need for you to ruin your day. I, well, hell. I don't know why I called you."

It was moments like this when she knew they were meant to be together. There were a lot of things she couldn't do for him. She didn't know how to raise a boy, didn't know how to adjust to living in a new city or state. She sure as heck had no idea about how to repair her old clock radio, never mind a car.

But she did know what it was like to need someone to stand by her side. She also knew how difficult it was to ask for that.

Already moving into her closet, she tsked gently. "I'm only attempting to pay bills, which is a pretty sorry sight. But even if I was in the middle of teaching a class or . . . well, anything, I would stop if you needed me. What hospital?"

"Bethesda off of Montgomery Road. Do you know where that's at?"

"I do. I'm going to throw on some decent jeans

and a sweater that doesn't have holes in it. I'll be there soon."

He sighed. "Thanks."

"Anytime, honey," she said, experimenting with an endearment on her lips. "Now, what do you need?" Thinking quickly, she said, "Does Finn need anything from home? Do you?"

"Kurt and Sam are going to take care of that."

"All right then. Look for me in thirty."

"Mer—"

"No arguments," she teased gently. "I'll be there soon. Bye." Feeling like she was in charge of their relationship for once, she disconnected.

Pulling the first decent pair of jeans and sweater out, she decided to get out of her house fast, and in time to go by the coffee shop and get Ace a mocha latte and a couple of muffins. Her man had a sweet tooth, and if there was ever a time to indulge in it, it was a time like this.

Twenty-five minutes later, she walked into the hospital with three muffins stashed in her bag; a pair of peanut butter chocolate cookies for Finn, on the off-chance he could eat them; a pair of car magazines, a new sports magazine, and a fresh deck of cards in a gift bag; and venti-size mocha in her left hand. After giving her name to several people, she was in the elevator to the fifth floor and walking down the hall to Finn's room.

She heard men's voices before she saw the room number.

Peeking in, she saw that Kurt and his son had beat her there. They were leaning on the metal side rails of Finn's bed. Ace was sitting in a chair, already looking exhausted, and Finn?

Well, poor Finn had an IV in his hand, a monitor attached to his chest, and was wearing both a blue hospital gown and a tired expression.

She knocked on the door lightly. "May I come in, or is this a boys-only zone?"

As she'd expected, all four heads turned her way. Kurt and Sam looked surprised, Finn looked relieved. Ace got to his feet and approached her, wearing a look that could only be described as tender.

"You made it."

"I did." Hoping to tease a smile from him, she attempted to look a little cocky. "Five minutes early, too."

He leaned down and kissed her forehead. "I'm impressed. Thanks." A little more loudly, he said, "And you brought me coffee. It's my lucky day."

"It's a mocha latte. Your secret favorite."

Kurt laughed. "I thought you outgrew that drink when you hit twenty-five."

"I tried," Ace said. "And it ain't like I have them all the time."

But still, he plucked it out of her hand and took a sip.

The expression of bliss that appeared on his face told her everything she needed to know about whether or not she should have stopped to get him his treat.

After smiling at him again, she walked to Finn's bedside and patted his arm. "Hi," she said simply.

"Hey, Meredith."

It was the first time she could remember him saying her first name without prompting. And for some reason, that made her choke up. "I'm sorry you're feeling so bad."

"Me, too."

After Ace gestured for her to take the seat he'd vacated, she sat down and scooted closer. "Is it okay that I'm here?"

"Dad said you rushed over."

"I did." She held up the bag she'd just placed on the floor. "I brought you a couple of things, too."

He looked surprised. "You did?"

Kurt coughed, interrupting their conversation. "Sam and I are going to head on out, Finn. We'll stop by your house tomorrow when you get home."

"Thanks."

After glancing at Meredith and his son, Ace said, "I'll walk y'all down the hall. I'll be right back, buddy."

When she and Finn were alone, Meredith lifted the bag. "Do you still want to see what I brought, or are you too tired? It's okay if you are."

"I want to see." He shifted, attempting to sit up without twisting his gown.

"You use this, honey," she said gently, showing him the electric remote that controlled the bed.

After he sat up, she leaned closer and pulled his sheet and blanket up around his middle again. "Better?"

"Yeah."

Her heart hitched, seeing the same look of vulnerability in his eyes that Ace sometimes didn't hide quick enough. She wondered again just what hell Liz had put these men through. Had she played so many games with their hearts that they didn't know how to be vulnerable? Didn't know how to accept tenderness easily?

Pushing that thought away, she handed him the blue gift bag. "Here's what I brought. Take in mind that one, I never have given a teenaged boy a gift in my life, and two, I was in a super hurry. I just grabbed the first things I saw."

One of his dimples popped in his cheek. "I'll give you a pass and not expect too much." He pulled out the magazines, deck of cards, and cookies. "Thanks."

"You're welcome. I figured you might get kind of bored in here tonight. And it's doubtful you're going to find much selection on the television in here."

"What are the cards for?" Ace asked behind her.

She jumped in surprise . . . and then felt chill bumps form where the warmth of his breath met her skin. How was that even possible?

She turned to smile briefly at him before looking at Finn again. "I thought you might want to play solitaire, Finn. Or we could all play gin or something."

Ace rested a hand on her shoulder. "Do you want to play gin, son?"

He shook his head. "Maybe later. I'm kind of tired right now."

Meredith leaned forward. "Have I tired you out? Do you want me to leave?"

"No, you can stay," Finn said. He looked like he was going to add something, but his eyes drifted closed.

A wave of maternal comfort that she hadn't even known she possessed filtered through her. She sat and watched his muscles ease, then, before Ace could do it, she picked up the magazines and bag from his covers before they slid off the bed.

"He's probably gonna sleep for a while. Let's go sit down the hall," Ace whispered.

She followed him out, noticing that his confident stride didn't seem quite as self-assured as usual. The hall was nearly empty. She could hear several nurses talking at their station. A pair of orderlies were at the far end of the hall, waiting on an elevator.

It felt strangely intimate as he led her to an alcove where there was one of those fake electric fireplaces and a pair of green, cloth love seats situated in front of a window.

Ace sank down on one of them with a sigh. "What a day, Meredith."

She scooted next to him and wrapped a hand around his knee. "Tell me what happened."

Still staring out in front of him, the muscles in his neck worked. "Finn was working on one of the weight machines when he collapsed. The kids got the coach, who quickly surmised Finn had a high fever. When Finn wasn't immediately responsive, the coach tried to call me."

"That had to be a tough thing to hear."

"No, it wasn't that easy. I didn't answer the phone. I was under a car."

It took her a minute to understand why he seemed so upset about that. Then she realized that he was feeling guilty. "So you were doing your job?"

He ran a hand through his short dark hair. "Yeah, but I should've had my cell near me. The coach had to make the call on his own. They called an ambulance." He shook his head again. "I can't believe it."

Meredith was confused. "But I thought Finn was just transferred to a private room."

"That's right."

"So when did they get ahold of you?"

"Oh. Soon after he got to the hospital."

"So how long did they wait to hear from you? Did you hear the phone the second time it rang?"

"No. The coach got ahold of Kurt, who was listed as my backup. He finally got hold of me after Finn had already arrived here at the hospital." He blew out a gust of air. "I can't believe I didn't answer the phone."

"Ace, I'm no parent, but I think you are heaping guilt on yourself, and it's misplaced. You can't be talking on the phone while you are concentrating on your job. That's not fair to your employer or to yourself. You could get hurt."

He shrugged off her words. "Yeah, but—"

"You don't have the only job where you can't take every call right away. Most people don't have jobs where they can pick up the phone whenever they want." She smiled softly as she squeezed his hand. "I don't even do that when I'm teaching Pilates. The schools realize that, too. That's why you have to give them backup numbers."

His voice lowered, turning scratchy. "Meredith, I didn't even realize he was that sick."

"Maybe it happened suddenly?"

His expression hardened. "The doc said it might have been brewing for a while but flared quickly."

Meredith squeezed his hand again. "Ace, answer me this honestly. Did Finn tell you he felt terrible and was having trouble breathing but you refused to let him rest or go to the doctor? If he had told you he felt like crap would you have checked to see if he had a fever? Maybe taken his temperature?"

"Of course."

"I hate to point out the obvious, but he isn't five, he's fifteen. That's old enough to know when he doesn't feel well. You can't read his mind, and you can't be walking around his life, guessing what he needs. He needs to tell you."

"He usually does."

"So he made the choice not to tell you."

"But why would he do that?" He rubbed a hand through his short dark hair. "Do you think he thought I was going to get mad at him or something?"

"You're the parent, not me. I don't know. But I do know, if it was me, if I didn't tell you something like that, it would be because I didn't want to bother you. Would Finn do something like that?"

Ace nodded. "That makes more sense than anything. He knows I would never get mad at him for being sick. But he also knows that I've been working a ton. Maybe he didn't want to worry me."

"That sounds like Finn. Of course, you could always just ask him. That would be the best thing to do."

He groaned. "Boy, for someone who doesn't

have a lot of parenting experience, you are doing a good job."

She smiled. "Thanks." She moved closer. "He'll get better soon."

"I hope so." He glanced at her, his dark-brown eyes looking softer. "I called Liz."

"How did that go?"

"Not great. At first she pretty much told me that I should've known better and then said she didn't think she could take time off work to come out here."

Though she privately agreed with Ace's assessment, Meredith didn't think that would help the situation if she egged him on. "That was helpful."

Ace allowed her a smile before leaning back against the small couch. "She sounded almost pleased about Finn, too. Like she could now feel justified for all the times I called her out for being so selfish."

"She sounds like a piece of work."

"She is. I can't tell you the number of times I've cursed myself for ever hooking up with her. She's like the poster woman for men wanting an easy lay."

She winced at his crude descriptor. "Oh, Ace."

"Sorry. I hate talking about a woman like this, but damn."

"I know. But we both know you don't mean what you're saying. You love Finn."

"Of course I do."

"Then Liz comes with him." She shrugged. "It is what it is."

He sighed. "You're right. I don't know what's wrong with me."

"I do. You're worried about Finn and wish that he wasn't here in the hospital. That's all."

"Yeah." He was silent for a few minutes. After taking a sip of that mocha latte, he sighed. "I'm glad you're here, Meredith."

"Me, too." She didn't know what else to say so she simply scooted closer to him and laid her head on his chest when he curved an arm around her shoulders and pulled her close.

She rested her head on his chest, listened for his heartbeat. They sat like that for a while, not speaking. Not needing to speak.

That's when she realized that she'd had very few moments like this in her life. Moments where she felt like she was really needed, like she was actually helping Ace.

Meredith realized that it was moments like this that she'd been looking for her whole life.

32

From Les Larke's
Terms for Poker Success:

Key Hand: This is the one hand that ends up being the turning point for the player. Keep your eyes open, players, this key hand can change your life for the better . . . or the worse.

A few hours later, Meredith had gone, and Ace had been sitting by Finn's side watching bad TV. After watching some sitcom where the dad had bought a lemon of a car, Ace had muttered, "See that, kid? You get what you pay for."

Finn snorted. "Once again, Grandpa isn't going to believe that you and me both have been quoting him in the same day."

Ace leaned back. "You too? What did you say?"

"I told my biology teacher that I had time to wait." He rolled his eyes. "She gave me this look like she didn't even get what I meant."

Ace chuckled. "If I had a nickel for every time he told me that, I'd be living like a king."

Finn grinned. "That's another one. Grandpa's going to be grinning from ear to ear."

"Let's hope he never finds out then," Ace teased.

"He probably won't, since we won't be seeing him for a while."

Ace knew what Finn had meant, but the words still stung. Though Ace missed his family, he'd thought getting Finn away from his mother had been the right thing to do. He still thought that. But at this moment, with his boy so sick, he was starting to wonder if maybe he'd focused too much on Liz's negative points and not enough on the benefits of the rest of their family.

"Dad, have you called Grandpa and Grandma yet?"

Ace wanted to lie, but he couldn't. "Not yet."

Disappointment flickered in Finn's eyes. "How come? Do you think he's gonna be upset with me?"

"For what? Getting sick? Of course not." Forcing himself to continue, he said, "I was more worried about what Grandma and Grandpa would say to me."

"What do you think they're gonna say?"

"That I should be taking better care of you."

Finn shifted, pushing the remote to adjust his bed to a sitting position. Then he pointed to Ace's phone, which he'd set on his bedside table. "Let's call them now."

Did Ace really want his boy to watch him get chewed on by his parents? No, he did not. "This isn't the place."

Finn rolled his eyes. "Yeah, it is. Besides, if you don't call them, I'm going to."

"You really would, wouldn't you?"

"Yep."

"I'm only giving you your way because you're sitting in a hospital bed," he lied as he brushed his thumb along the screen and pressed his mother's phone number.

It only rang once before she picked up.

"Ace, this is a nice surprise."

Looking at Finn, Ace tried to think of a good way to start the conversation. He couldn't think of one. "Hey, Mom," he finally said. "I've got something I need to talk to you about."

Her voice immediately changed. "What's wrong?"

"Finn is in the hospital. I'm sitting with him."

"What? Hank!"

Covering up the mouthpiece, Ace turned to Finn. "Get ready, boy. I'm going to put her on speaker."

Looking almost amused, Finn nodded.

"Ace, I put you on speaker. Your father's sitting right here. Now tell us what's going on."

"I will, but promise that you won't get all riled up."

"What happened to Finn, Ace?" Dad asked. "Is he hurt?"

"I'm going to put y'all on speaker, too. The two of us are going to tell you what happened." He clicked. "Okay, Finn can hear you now."

"Hey Grandpa and Grandma," Finn said.

"Finn, honey, either you or your father better start talking now," his father ordered. "Grandma is already looking like she's ready to pack a suitcase."

"I passed out when I was working out after school today. The coach got worried, so he called an ambulance."

"An ambulance?" Ace's dad barked while they heard his mother exclaiming and shuffling in the background. "Finn, what's wrong?"

"I have pneumonia."

"How did that boy go from working out in the high school gym to being hospitalized?" his mom asked.

Ace felt his face flush, but he manned up. "Because I didn't keep a good enough eye on him, Mom. I didn't even realize that he was so sick. He had a hundred and two fever when they admitted him." He braced himself. Ready to hear a repeat of what Liz had told him. How he was selfish and no good.

"Finley, how come your father didn't know you had a fever?" Ace's mother asked.

Just as if she'd been standing right in front of him, Finn straightened his shoulders against his pillows. "Because I didn't tell him, Grandma."

"And why not?"

After glancing at Ace, he cleared his throat. "Because I didn't want to bother him."

"Why would you think informing him that you didn't feel well would bother him?"

Ace gripped the phone. "He's sick. I don't think it's time for an interrogation. I'm fully aware that this is on me, by the way."

"No, it ain't," Finn said. "Grandma, I guess I got used to keeping my problems to myself."

"Because . . ."

"Because Mom used to get mad if I complained," Finn said after a sigh.

"Oh my stars, but she is such a witch," she said.

Finn grinned at Ace. "I don't think we're supposed to say that word, Grandma."

"Oh, you." She sighed. "Finley, honey, we're driving out tonight. We'll be there when you wake up in the morning."

Ace closed his eyes. "Mom, there's no need for y'all to drive here in the dark."

"Yes, there is," Dad said. "Finn, you rest. Hear me?"

Finn looked at Ace and shrugged. "Yessir."

"Good. Now get off speaker so I can talk to your dad."

"Okay. Bye Grandpa."

Ace swiped a button on his phone then held it up to his ear. "Dad, it's just me now."

"I wish you would've called us as soon as it happened, but I guess we can talk about that in person."

"All right. But Dad, there's no need for you to

come out here. You know the roads can be tricky in February, and they sure aren't going to be any better in the dark."

"You're right about that. I ain't going to drive a mile in the dark. That's why we're calling Brennan."

He should have known that they'd get his brother involved. "Dad."

"Don't you say a word. Your mother's already on the phone with him and Barbara. You hear me?"

"Yessir."

"Now I'm getting off the phone because I've got things to do. But when I do, I want you to text me the name of the hospital and a hotel nearby."

"You're not staying in a hotel. You're staying with us."

"Brennan and Barbara are going to want somewhere to sleep. And if Lana has her way, she and Curtis will be joining us as well. All the kids, too."

If Ace hadn't been so worried about Finn he would have put up a fuss about that. Instead, he decided to just give in and follow directions. "Yessir. I'll do that right now."

"Good. See you in the morning." He clicked off then.

"What did he say about staying in a hotel, Dad?" Finn asked.

"They're probably going to stay with us, but

Brennan and Barbara are coming. And so is Lana and Curtis. And your cousins."

"Really?"

"Yep." He couldn't help but smile. His family was as bossy as he was. And right now? He was kind of glad about that.

"I can't believe everyone is coming because I got sick."

"Being in the hospital is a big deal. They're all worried about you."

Finn frowned. "They shouldn't be *that* worried."

Pressing his palm on Finn's head, he said, "I'm glad you had me call. It was the right thing to do. You need to be around some people who love you. It will do you good."

"It might do you good, too."

"Maybe so." His mind spinning, he got up. "I'm going to let you rest because I better go get some things done. I'll be back in a couple of hours."

"I'll be fine."

Leaning over, he pressed his lips to his kid's brow. "Try and rest."

"'Kay, Dad."

As he walked to the door, he turned to look back at him. "And Finn?"

His boy opened one eye. "Yeah?"

"I love you."

"I know, Dad." Closing his eyes again, he murmured, "Love you back."

As he walked back out into the hall, Ace

released a sigh. He would have never wanted his kid to be so sick that he'd end up in the hospital . . . but he couldn't deny some good things were coming out of the situation.

Smiling faintly to himself, he thought of another one of his father's favorite sayings. That every gray cloud had a silver lining.

Maybe there was some truth to that, after all.

33

From Meredith Hunt's
Guidebook to SHINE Pilates:

"The mind, when housed within a healthful body, possesses a glorious sense of power."
— JOSEPH PILATES

"Hey, buddy."

Finn blinked as his eyes focused and he remembered where he was. Still in the hospital room. Still feeling like crap. He'd had a really rough night. So rough, he'd been worried he wasn't going to be able to breathe. He'd had to call on the nurse, who'd hurriedly attached the oxygen back to his face and then called for the doctor on call.

The doctor had looked real serious when he'd listened to his lungs and heart. After a couple of minutes, he told the nurses to keep him on oxygen and give Finn a steroid shot to help open the air passages in his lungs.

He'd felt so bad, he could've cared less when the nurse told him to roll over so she could give him that monster shot in his butt. He'd been willing to do whatever it took in order to breathe.

After she'd given him the shot, she'd sat next to him until it kicked in. Luckily, that happened almost immediately. But even though he could now breathe without feeling like the air was coming through a sieve, he'd refused her offer of calling his dad. Dad worked too hard to run up to the hospital just to watch him breathe.

So he'd waited and let the nurse call his father that morning. When Dad got on the phone, asking questions and sounding all stressed out, Finn had told him that he was better and not to worry. But he'd also felt like he'd been run over by a truck.

Most of his morning had been foggy. He vaguely remembered his father sitting by him and talking to him about football games before he fell asleep again.

Now he was achy and sore and staring at Meredith.

"Where's my dad?"

She frowned. "I'm sorry, honey. He had to leave for a while. You're stuck with me." She scrunched up her nose. "He said to tell you that he'd be back as soon as he could, but there was something going on with an Alfa Romeo."

Glad his mind was clearer, he nodded. "Oh, yeah. Dad told me about that car."

"What's special about it?"

"You mean other than it's old and really expensive?"

She looked skeptical. "There's more?"

"Dad said that the car's owner is really rich and had promised him a mint if he got it running by the weekend. Plus, he knows lots of other rich car guys. So if Dad does a good job on it, he's going to get a bunch more business."

She smiled softly. "I hope it happens, then. Though I am sorry he's not here for you. I know he felt bad about that."

Finn shrugged it off. "Did he call you here to babysit me?"

"Since you're fifteen years old, I would say no."

"But—"

"But, to answer your question, yes, he called me and asked if I could come up." Looking like a parody of a tough person, she raised her hand. "And before you start saying things like you're fine and I can go on home, let me just tell you that I wanted to come sit with you."

"Thanks."

Her eyes turned serious. "You had a heck of a night, huh?"

"You heard about it?"

"Your dad called me this morning. He was really worried. I brought him a latte and a couple of egg sandwiches."

Even though he felt like crap he couldn't help but tease her. "Did you bring me one?"

She looked crushed. "No, honey. I'm sorry. When you feel better I'll bring you one."

"You're way too easy to tease, Meredith."

"I know. I was born gullible, I guess. I've been trying to be tougher." She raised an eyebrow. "Do you think it's working?"

He snickered. "No."

"Shoot. How am I going to boss you and your dad around if I'm so noodley?"

"Maybe we don't mind you noodley," he said.

She shook her head. "You are too easy to please, Finn Vance."

He knew he should joke around and let it slide, but something told him that what was happening between them was important enough to take a chance. "Hey, Meredith?"

"Hmm?"

"Dad said you don't have a dad. Like, at all."

Her blue eyes blinked, before turning serious. "He's right. I don't."

"Because he died?"

"He is dead. But he also took off when I was just a little girl. I guess he didn't want to be a parent anymore."

"How old were you?"

"Five, I think."

Finn didn't know much, but even he knew she remembered exactly how old she'd been. "Five is really young."

Looking kind of melancholy, she nodded. "Yes, it is."

"Do you wish he would have stuck around?"

She scrunched up her mouth like she was considering it. "I used to, though now I don't really know. My mother said he had a lot of problems and addictions. Even beyond those things, she seemed to think he wasn't worth much. She said they fought a lot. And since he was the type of guy who left and never looked back, never sent child support, never even sent a birthday card? I think I was better off without him."

He appreciated how she wasn't trying to front with him. She was just putting it out there. It made him feel like they were almost equals. Made him feel like he could be honest, too. "Did you do okay with your mom?"

She shrugged again, a very un-Meredith-like response. "Well enough, I guess. My mom? Well, she wasn't all that into motherhood, if you want to know the truth."

"Like my mom."

Meredith gazed at him for a moment, pulled her bottom lip in between her teeth. "Finn, I'm older than you, so I've had more time to think about my parents than you. And in all of my years of wisdom, I think I figured something out."

"What's that?"

She paused again, then started talking, as if she was trying to weigh every word. "I learned that nobody in the hospital hands parents a guidebook when they have a baby. All those nurses and doctors do is make sure the baby is healthy and the mom is okay. Then, about twenty-four hours after that, everyone is sent on their way. Some people go home with babies with no idea about what to do with them."

"I never thought about it that way."

"Unfortunately, I have. I've thought about it a lot. And what I've decided is that everyone just hopes to do the best they can. Some people read books and have their parents around and, I don't know, are just good at parenting, I suppose."

"But some people aren't."

"You're right. For most people, having that baby at home? Well, it's just fine. They get the hang of it. After all, they wanted to be parents. And they knew for about nine months what was going to happen, right?"

"Right."

She rushed on. "I'm not saying that everyone has a great childhood. It might not be great, or sometimes, one of the parents is a jerk or something, but usually, I think it goes okay."

"Yeah, maybe."

Looking at him carefully, she said, "What I'm trying to say is that it's not always like that. And for the people like you and me? Well, we have to take things into our own hands. We have to kind of raise ourselves and along the way, we find people who care about us. Somehow or other, we make our own families."

"How?"

"Friends. Neighbors. People at church. At school. You take in people in your life who love you in spite of everything and you love them back."

"Is that what you did?"

"Not enough. I kept waiting for things to get better, or maybe even for my dad to come back. Then I just pretended I was fine being on my own. But that wasn't the right decision. Now I know that if I had put more faith in the people who love me, it would have made things easier."

"I have my dad though. And my grandparents and aunts and uncles. I guess I wasn't really alone."

"You're right, you weren't. Your dad loves you a lot." She smiled at him. "See, that's how you're a whole lot smarter than me. You've already looked around and started counting your blessings."

Just as he was about to speak, the nurse popped in. "Oh, good. You're up." She walked right over and placed the thermometer in his ear and took his pulse and blood pressure. "When did you wake up, Finn?"

"I don't know. Maybe five minutes ago?"

"Do you need to use the facilities?"

By now he knew that was code for did he have to pee. "Yeah."

"I'll help you walk to the bathroom." She

turned to Meredith. "Ma'am, if you could excuse us for a moment?"

"Of course. I'll be right out in the hall."

The nurse smiled. "Give us about ten minutes. The doc wanted some blood work."

"Oh. Of course. I'll see you in a little bit, Finn."

Remembering how squeamish she was around needles, Finn nodded. "I'll ask Susan to get you when she's done."

Just as Meredith walked out, she heard Finn say, "Meredith really hates needles and blood."

"Guess it's good she doesn't work in a hospital," Susan said.

"Yeah."

Meredith was still smiling about Finn's comment when she noticed Ace and Finn's neighbor Mrs. Peterson and her daughter Allison. Ace had introduced her to them the last time she'd stopped by.

"Hi," she said as she walked toward them. "Here to see Finn?"

Allison nodded, looking serious. "We were going to go on in, but the nurse asked us to wait a bit."

"That's a good idea. The nurse went in to check Finn's vitals and draw blood."

"Oh." Allison looked up at her mom with wide eyes. "I guess he's still really sick."

Mrs. Peterson turned to Meredith. "How is he?"

"I'm not sure. Ace called me this morning to say that Finn had a bad night. The doctor decided to keep him another day."

"That poor kid."

"I feel so sorry for him," Meredith said quietly. "You know how these things are. They sneak up on you. But Finn is tough and he's in the right place, so I'm certain he'll get through this just fine." Smiling at Allison, she said, "He's going to be happy to see you, too."

Allison bit her bottom lip. "I hope so, but I don't know."

"Al's been really worried about him. We all have," her mother said as she squeezed her daughter's shoulders. "Even the twins were wanting to come here."

Allison rolled her eyes. "I told them no way."

"And I agreed." Smiling at Meredith, Mrs. Peterson added, "We figured the staff here at the hospital could only take so much."

Susan poked her head out. "You can come in now, Meredith."

Just as Meredith was about to usher Allison in, they all heard a commotion down the hall. It was a crowd of six . . . and they all had dark hair and eyes.

She had a feeling Finn was about to get to see all those people they'd just been talking about who loved him . . . all at one time.

34

From Les Larke's
Terms for Poker Success:

Aces Full: A full house with three aces and any pair. Obviously, this is a good thing, though some players have said such a hand can be a little tough to deal with at times.

They came in as a group. Like a herd of deer. Or maybe more like a herd of buffalo, they were so overpowering.

From the moment the slim dark-haired woman dressed in jeans and Uggs and an off-white fisherman's-style sweater called out "Finley!" the whole atmosphere in the room turned on its side. Moments before, when Meredith had been visiting with Allison and her mom, things had been quiet. Orderly.

Now? There was a party going on in room 544. Six people had rushed down the hallway, each bearing gifts, each zeroed in on one person only—Finn.

It was adorable. And, by the smile that had erupted on Finn's face, their arrival was also very welcome.

It was just too bad that the nurse was probably going to shut it down real fast.

If it had been up to her, Meredith would've tried to calm everyone down. But it wasn't.

In fact, as the group crowded around Finn, it felt like she was simply in the way. She wasn't sure what to do. Ace had called her early that morning and asked her to sit with Finn so he could finish a car he was almost done repairing. She'd been happy to keep Finn company so he wouldn't get lonely.

He certainly wasn't lonely now.

But what if he got tired or did too much?

"Meredith?" Finn called out after getting hugged by each member of his family. "Meredith, are you still in here?"

"I'm here," she said. When she felt everyone's attention focus from Finn to her, she raised up a hand. "Just trying to stay out of the way."

Finn rolled his eyes. "You're not in the way. Come say hi to everyone."

Feeling like the Red Sea had just parted, she stepped away from the wall. "Hi, everyone. I'm Meredith Hunt."

"Meredith, this is my grandma and grandpa, Hank and Peggy. That's my uncle Brennan and aunt Barbara, and then that's my aunt Lana and uncle Curtis."

"It's nice to meet you. It's nice of you to come all the way here to see Finn."

Peggy and Hank looked at her like she'd just told them that it was real nice that they'd put on clothes that morning. Ick. Even to her ears she sounded stilted.

After a pause, one of the women studied her curiously. "And who are you? Are you a counselor here or something?"

Finn snickered. "Aunt Lana, she doesn't work here. She's Meredith. She's Dad's girlfriend."

"You're the gal he's been seeing?" Brennan asked.

"Guilty." She smiled, though she feared it looked as strained as she felt inside.

"Wow."

"Where is your father anyway?" Peggy asked Finn. "I texted him that we were almost in Cincinnati."

"He's at the shop. He needed to get a couple of things done," Meredith answered. "He told me he'd be back right after lunch."

"I guess he'll be around here soon then," Lana said. "We'll just have to settle in and wait."

Meredith looked at Finn. "You doing okay?"

"Uh-huh."

"I'll go wait outside, okay?" She knew she should probably leave soon but she'd promised Ace she'd stick around until he came back.

"No need for that," Hank said. "We're looking forward to getting to know you better."

Before Meredith could reply to that verbal

volley, Susan the nurse appeared back at the door. "Sorry to break things up, but you have a girl out here who's been waiting a while to see you, Mr. Popular. Her name's Allison."

"Allison?" Finn blushed. "She's here?"

Meredith pressed a hand to her chest. "Oh, gosh. She's been waiting for over an hour to see you, Finn. She was about to come in when your whole family arrived. I'm sorry, I should have said something."

Susan stared at the assembly. "If I send her in, some of you have to go."

"You know what? Let's all go sit in the hallway and give the boy some privacy," Hank said. "Better yet, Meredith, take us down to get some coffee."

"I can do that. There's a Starbucks here."

Brennan chuckled. "Starbucks at the hospital. Isn't that something?"

And on that note, Meredith found herself escorting Ace's entire family down the hall for a coffee break, hoping the whole time she was going to be ready for the hundred questions about her and Ace that were sure to come.

When Allison came in, Finn forgot all about how he'd been embarrassed for her to see him in a hospital gown. He'd been too busy staring at her. Maybe it was because they were in a different place and situation, but all of a sudden, Allison didn't look awkward at all. Actually, she looked really great.

She might never be the kind of girl who all the guys would call hot, but he realized he liked everything about her. Her long wavy blond hair. The way she didn't wear a bunch of fussy clothes—just jeans, tennis shoes, and long-sleeved T-shirts. She didn't have a bunch of stuff on her face, either. She looked clean and fresh. Pretty.

"I can't believe you came and you've been sitting out waiting to see me for an hour," Finn said.

Allison looked down at her feet like she was embarrassed. "I guess that was too much, huh?" she asked as she pulled back a chunk of hair from her face. "I should have left."

"No. I just feel bad that you went to so much effort."

"Not as much as your family. They came all the way from West Virginia."

"They're all kind of crazy."

Her eyes lit up. "They're loud. Even louder than Phillip and Chloe."

Smiling back at her, he quipped, "Yeah, that says it all."

She sat down in the chair that Meredith had been occupying when he'd woken up. "How are you? My mom talked to the nurses and they said you might not get to go home today either."

"My chest feels like it's got a set of barbells on it." And he felt really weak. And it hurt to breathe, too. "I'll be all right."

Worry filled her eyes. "I hope you get to go home soon."

"Me, too." He studied her again, liking how she wasn't talking his ear off. "How's Maggie and the last pup?"

That brought a real smile. "Maggie's good, and that pup is cute."

"I'm sure gonna miss him."

She bit her lip, then said, "Actually, you're not going to miss him at all."

"Why's that?"

"My mom and I talked to your dad. He's going to let you have him."

"What?" If his chest hadn't hurt so bad, he would have sat up straighter.

She giggled. "Surprise!"

"Wow. I can't believe he'd pay all that. You were selling them for four hundred a pup, weren't you?"

"Yes, but yours is a gift."

She was *giving* the dog to him? As much as he wanted to grin like crazy, he felt bad about that. She'd told him once that she was going to use that money for college. "Al, you can't do that."

"I already did. So you better start thinking of a name for him. As soon as you feel better, you can move him over to your house."

"I . . . I don't even know what to say."

"Just say you want him."

"I do. Thanks. Thanks a lot." That still sounded so lame, though. He swallowed. "I mean, that makes me really happy—*you* made me really happy, Al. Thank you very much."

Her voice softened. "You're welcome." She met his gaze again, and something passed between them that told him that he wasn't the only one feeling their connection.

"Oh! I brought you something." She reached into her giant purse and pulled out a present, wrapped in paper and everything. Smiling slightly, she held it out to him.

He took it. "You didn't have to do this, Allison."

"I wanted to. And it isn't anything big. I . . . well, I just thought it might make you feel better."

Ripping off the paper, he prepared himself. Allison was kind of a goofy girl, so it could be anything.

But when he opened the box and pulled out a stack of magazines, he was pretty surprised. "You got me sports and hunting and fishing magazines?"

"I was going to get you a book, but I thought that might be kind of a bad idea. I mean I know you probably don't sit around reading in your spare time. But maybe you would like to read about sports?"

"I will. Thanks."

"You're welcome." Blushing, she backed off. "I better get going. My mom's out in the hall and you've got all your relatives here. They've probably bought out Starbucks by now."

He chuckled. "Probably. Hey, Allison? Thanks again for the pup and the magazines and for coming here."

"It wasn't anything. Hope you get to come home soon."

"Me, too." Just as she turned, he called out, "Hey, Al?"

She stopped and looked back at him. "Yes?"

"After I get that dog . . . will you help me with him?"

"You want my help?" She sounded both surprised and real pleased.

He nodded. "I don't know much about raising a pup and you know a lot."

"I'll be glad to help you, Finn. Anytime."

"I'll text you soon." He smiled at her and was encouraged when she smiled back before walking out of his room.

Just a few seconds later, Susan came back in. "Whew. You've had a regular revolving door in here, Mr. Finn."

"Yeah. It's been cool."

After she took his vitals, she frowned. "I'm going to have to put my foot down though. Some of these numbers aren't where they need to be. You need some rest."

Feeling dizzy, he didn't even try to argue. "Yeah, I'm kind of tired."

Susan put a hand on her hip. "Can I tell your fan club that you'll see visitors in three hours? That will give you time to take a nap, and if you're up to it, maybe even a shower."

He felt weird talking about showering with her, but he was kind of glad to not be making any decisions. Besides, not having to talk to anyone for a while sounded really good. "That's fine."

Her expression softened. "Take a couple sips of water. I just checked, and you have a full carafe of ice water. Then try and get some rest so we can get you out of here tomorrow."

"Yes, ma'am."

She beamed at him as she closed the door.

He was vaguely aware of being glad that he'd finally met a woman in Bridgeport who didn't get mad at him for calling her ma'am.

35

From Les Larke's
Terms for Poker Success:

Pair: Two cards of the same rank. If you start off a hand with a pair, consider yourself on your way to success.

Ace reached the outside of Finn's room just in time to hear his boy's nurse telling everyone to leave him alone for three hours so the kid could get some rest.

As Ace took in the group assembled in the hallway—Meredith, his whole family, Allison and her momma—he was wondering why the nurse hadn't kicked them all out earlier.

Just as his mom stepped forward, wearing that expression on her face that said she was ready to start asking way too many questions, Ace knew it was time to step in.

"Thanks, Susan," he said as he walked up. "I'll take it from here."

There was no mistaking the look of relief in her eyes. "Thank you, Mr. Vance," she said primly before walking to her station.

Brennan was the first to speak. "Mr. Vance, huh? When was the last time anyone called you that?"

His brother's comment reminded Ace of what he'd told Meredith back the first time they'd met, how no one called him by a name like that. But there was something in his brother's tone that rubbed Ace wrong. Like Brennan couldn't imagine someone looking at him like he was in charge.

"Probably an hour ago, when the man whose car I repaired thanked me."

Brennan's snide expression fell as he stepped forward. "Hey, sorry, bud. You know I was just kidding around."

"Don't worry about it." Turning to everyone else who had been standing by, he cleared his throat. "Mom, Dad, everyone . . . it looks like we need to clear out of here for a while. Nurse's orders."

Allison and her mom stepped forward. "We were just leaving ourselves, Ace," Mrs. Peterson said. "Thanks for letting us stop by. It meant a lot to Allison."

Bending down slightly, he gentled his voice. "Did you even get to see him, Al?"

"I did. I told him about the puppy, too." Looking pleased as punch, she smiled. "He was so surprised."

Boy, he'd been so wrapped up in his worry,

he'd forgotten about that dog. "I'm glad you told him, honey. I bet it made his day."

She blushed again. "Thanks, Mr. Vance."

"If all goes well, Finn will be home tomorrow."

After giving him a pat on the arm, his neighbor and her daughter went on their way.

Taking a deep breath, he looked over at Meredith. As was her norm, she was standing in the background, content to let everyone else do what they needed to do. A wave of tenderness rode through him as he realized that being near her calmed him. And after the strain of the last twenty-four hours, he was eager to touch base with her and soak in more of that calming influence.

But before he could take a step, his parents rushed to his side.

"Our boy looks worn out, Ace," Mom said. "Exhausted."

"I know he does. That's why he needs some rest."

His father walked to his side. "Do you trust these doctors? Maybe he needs to head downtown to Children's Hospital."

"I think he's fine right here. The doctors have been real good about keeping me informed. The antibiotics are working, it's just going to take some time. We need to be patient."

"If you're good, then I am, too," his dad said as he gave him a brief hug. "Hate to say it, but you don't look too good yourself. In fact . . . you look like crap."

Whether he'd meant for that to happen or not, the comment made Ace grin. "Thanks, Dad. Now, look, y'all go on to my house and make yourself at home. I'm sorry, I don't have a lot of food in the fridge, but there's some steak and chicken in the freezer. Maybe—"

"I know what to do in a kitchen, son." Looking at Lana and Curtis, Mom smiled. "I also have a feeling I can get someone to do a grocery run. We'll have something ready when you get home later."

He wasn't sure if he was coming home, but he nodded.

His mother's eyes glinted with unshed tears. "Right." After giving a meaningful look in Meredith's direction, she made a shooing motion to the rest of the family. "Let's go before we get banned from coming back."

"We'll see you, Ace," Barbara said.

"Yeah. See you." He kissed his sister-in-law on the cheek.

"And Ace?"

"Hmm?" he leaned closer.

"We all really like Meredith," she whispered with a smile. "You did good."

He could practically feel his cheeks turn bright red. "I'll see y'all later," he mumbled as he finally headed over to Meredith's side, ignoring his brother's chuckle the whole way.

Luckily, they'd all decided to forgo the elevator and took the stairs. When the EXIT door closed behind them, Ace could practically feel the whole staff on the floor take a sigh of relief.

Meredith's blue eyes were a combination of concern and amusement as she watched him. Before she could ask how he was, he leaned down and kissed her.

After the briefest of hesitations, she placed a hand on the back of his neck and kissed him back. He loved that. He loved how she seemed to forget her natural reticence around him. Loved how she never shied away from his affection but seemed to welcome it, like it was an unexpected gift.

When he raised his head, he rested his forehead against hers. "Tell me the truth, now. How bad were they?"

"Your family? Not bad at all."

"Mer . . . "

"Really." She smiled. "They care and love Finn. It was sweet. I know he was thrilled to see them."

"Were they okay with you?"

"Better than okay. They made me feel like I was part of the family. And, that, you know, is everything."

It was everything.

Somehow, right then and there—in the middle of the hospital floor, Ace knew. The two of them had made it. They'd opened themselves up to new things, new people, new ideas, and a new relationship. And because of that, along the way? He and Meredith and Finn had become their own kind of family. A family of their own.

They still had some things to figure out, but he knew that could be done.

Their relationship wasn't perfect, but it didn't have to be. It was solid and had the foundation to build upon. All they'd had to do was take some chances and look for the positives.

And because they had? Well, he had a feeling they were about to win it all.

36

From Meredith Hunt's
Guidebook to SHINE Pilates:

*"Change happens through movement
and movement heals."*
—JOSEPH PILATES

TUESDAY, THREE WEEKS LATER

"I spied crocuses in my yard," Katie announced the moment Meredith dismissed the class. "We made it, girls. We made it through another winter."

"Hallelujah!" Gwen said as she stood up and stretched. "I was starting to think it was never going to end. When that groundhog signaled that we had another six weeks of winter, I felt like throwing a snowball at him. It was a tough one."

Meredith chuckled as she opened up the new insulated lunch cooler that Ace had bought her for her birthday and pulled out her usual turkey sandwich. "Gwen, not to be a spoilsport, but I'm pretty sure that you said the same thing last winter."

"I probably did." Pulling out her own sandwich, Gwen looked sheepish. "My kids told me I say the same thing every year, too. It's a wonder I haven't moved to Florida."

"I'm glad you don't." She smiled at her group fondly. Today had been a good class. All the members of the Lunch Bunch had shown up, even Pam, who was finally feeling better after her latest round of chemo treatments.

Plus, Gwen wasn't the only person who was feeling optimistic about life. Meredith certainly was! She and Ace now saw each other almost every day, even if it was for a quick cup of coffee in the morning.

"I haven't seen any crocuses, but I do think some of my birds have returned," Katie said. "Mike had to buy new seed."

Meredith was just about to comment on that when she noticed that Vanni not only wasn't eating, she was slipping on a real sweater and shoes over her leggings and tank top. "Vanni, do you have lunch plans?"

"I do. Rick took a half day off. We're going to go down to Paxton's and have lunch together."

"You two are really making progress," Jane teased. "Before you know it, y'all might even graduate to dinner together."

"I know it's been slow, but that's okay. Rick's pretty shy, plus he's so busy training."

They'd all learned after Vanni's first date with

Rick that he wasn't just a mailman. He also worked part time as a youth pastor and competed in Iron Man competitions two or three times a year. Those two things had helped explain a lot about his kindness to Vanni and his incredible body. Rick had it going on.

He also was head over heels in love with Vanni, which they were all overjoyed to see.

Knowing that Vanni would become flustered if they teased her too much about her new man, Meredith said, "I'm glad you're happy, Vanni. That's what counts, don't you think?"

"Yes." She stuffed her hands into the front pockets of her yellow slicker. "But I have to say that as great as Rick is, he isn't the main reason I'm so much happier than I was a year ago. It's because of all of you."

Katie raised her eyebrows. "Us? What did we do?"

"Y'all got me through a really terrible year, gave me something else to think about besides my rat of an ex-husband, and made me stronger, too. It's been more than just a Pilates class that I take twice a week."

"I feel the same way," Jane said quietly. "When I'm here, I can be myself, and I feel like I can talk about anything, too."

"Thank goodness you opened up Shine, Meredith," Vanni said.

When the other ladies murmured similar statements, Meredith felt a knot form in her throat. No, she wasn't going to take all the credit for the Lunch Bunch and the way the class had bonded, but she knew that she'd provided the vehicle for it all to take place.

"I'm glad I opened up the studio, too, but I can't take all the credit for this group. Maybe we were simply meant to be."

Getting to her feet, she pulled a white paper sack out of her desk. "Ladies, I have something for you." Walking around the room, she handed each of them an orange padded coozie. "I asked Kurt Holland the other day if I could have six of them. I just got them last night."

Looking skeptical, Gwen held the one she'd just been handed up in the air. "Meredith, um, though I like a beer every once in a while, I don't play poker at all. Why, exactly, did you think we needed these?"

"Look at what it says," Meredith said.

"Bridgeport Social Club," Katie said dutifully. "Again, isn't that the poker game that Ace goes to once a month?"

"It is. But then, well, I started thinking about the guys' poker nights. Ace always tells me that he never goes over to Kurt's garage just to play poker. He goes to talk to guys like himself and relax. He's made friends there." She shook her head in wonder, "That crazy poker group even sent around a hat and took up a donation when

Finn was in the hospital to help Ace pay the bills. It turns out that they are more than just a group of guys who like to sit around and play cards. They really care about each other and each other's families."

"Like we care about each other," Vanni said with a soft smile. "I get it now. You're saying we're like your guy's poker club."

Meredith nodded. "I know this class isn't really the same thing. I mean, we work out, not place bets. But for me, our Lunch Bunch comes awfully close to Ace's poker group. We talk, we solve each other's problems, and we really care about each other."

Vanni nodded. "I agree completely."

"Look at this," Katie said with a bright smile. She held up her water bottle, which was now neatly encased in the orange coozie. "Turns out this fits my water bottle just fine. I bet it's going to keep my water cold, too. I'm going to use it."

When Pam and Jane did the same thing with theirs, the three of them lifted their bottles. "Cheers!" Jane exclaimed with a grin.

"Cheers!" Pam said. "Here's to the Pilates chapter of the Bridgeport Social Club."

While the other women giggled, Meredith covered her bottle with the orange coozie and held it up high, too. "Cheers! May we all drink our water in good health and stay strong."

Holding up her coozie-covered bottle again,

Katie announced, "Girls, I like this so much, I'm going to get us some matching T-shirts."

"You could sell them up at the front, by your desk, Mer," Gwen said. "Everyone's going to want one."

Their laughter was interrupted by Rick opening the door. "Afternoon, ladies."

"Hey, Rick," Meredith called out.

Obviously looking at their coozies, he raised his eyebrows. "Uh oh. Looks like trouble in here."

Vanni walked to his side. "Oh, Rick. You don't know the half of it."

His eyebrows rose. "Should I get worried?"

She patted his arm. "Oh goodness, no. It's a great story, nothing like when we all called you Mr. April."

He froze. "What?"

Vanni blushed bright red. "Oops. I'll tell you all about it at lunch."

As Rick walked her out the door, she looked back at the five of them and winked.

Practically choking on her last sip of water, Meredith said, "I can't believe she just said that."

"He did look kind of petrified," Pam said.

When the door closed again, they all started laughing harder. "I predict our Mr. April is going to ask to change his route soon," Jane said. "I think there's only so much of us one man can take."

EPILOGUE

From Les Larke's
Terms for Poker Success:

Scoop: To win the entire pot, i.e., the big winner. A word to the wise — the only way you are going to scoop is by going all in. Good luck and good betting, ladies and gentlemen. Play hard, play smart, and above all else? Have a good time.

FOUR MONTHS LATER

"I never pictured you as a fisherman," Meredith told Ace as he held out a hand to help her into the small pontoon on the dock of Lake Lorelei.

He looked surprised. "Really? I grew up in the country in West Virginia. What did you think I did on my weekends when I was growing up?"

She sat down on the padded bench next to a pile of life vests and his tackle box, an army-green monstrosity filled with an assortment of hooks, lures, and various wires, tweezers, scissors, and jars of smelly things she wasn't quite sure she wanted to know about. "I guess I never thought about it too much. Maybe playing football."

He laughed. "I played a lot of ball, but not in the spring, Mer. In the spring, my dad, Lana, Brennan, and I would head out onto a nearby lake and fish for hours."

"Lana, too?"

"Yep. Lana, too." He handed her a life vest. "Better put this on."

She did as he asked, glad for the safety as much as the added warmth it offered. It was barely nine in the morning, but she was dressed like it was already two in the afternoon. She had on a new navy bikini covered by a pair of terry cloth shorts and a tank top.

Ace, who had on a pair of black swim trunks and an old Spartan sweatshirt and dime-store rubber flip-flops, had wrapped her in his arms when he'd picked her up and kissed her like he hadn't taken her out the night before. "Love how you always look so pretty, baby," he'd murmured.

Now they were on his buddy Troy's boat and had plans to float around and fish for most of the day. She'd been excited that Finn had wanted to be there, too. She'd even suggested he bring a friend, but he had shrugged off the offer, saying that his buddies already had plans, and he was going to hang out with Allison that night.

As she watched Ace pull down the ropes next to the dock and start the engine and Finn walk around barefoot, following his dad's direction,

Meredith felt a little lazy. Getting to her feet, she called out, "How can I help?"

"You can sit tight until you get your sea legs, babe," Ace said.

Finn grinned.

She was about to roll her eyes at their macho behavior when they started moving and she almost lost her balance. She sat back down as they slowly edged away from the dock.

There weren't too many boats out on the water, and only a couple of other people out in their yards or next to their docks. The water was smooth and the sun was slowly warming her skin. Little by little, she relaxed, eventually stretching out her feet, liking the feel of the sun warming the tops of her legs.

Ace popped the top of a Sprite and continued to guide the boat through the center of the lake and around a bend. He seemed just as happy to stay quiet and enjoy their surroundings as she was.

After another twenty minutes, he stopped the boat. "This looks like a good place to set up shop."

"It's time to fish?"

Walking back to her side, he nodded. "Yep. Time to fish." Looking over at Finn, Ace said, "You good?"

"Yep."

While Finn opened up his own tackle box and baited his hook, Meredith was happy to let Ace take care of hers. She was thankful that he didn't attempt to give her an impromptu fishing lesson. Instead, he picked up a rod and reel, opened the tackle box and put on a lure and baited the hook with an earthworm. She gave a quick prayer of thanks that it wasn't a live minnow.

After he cast his line, he handed it to her. "Hold it and bob it up and down from time to time." He placed a hand on her wrist. "Like that."

She mimicked the move and smiled at him.

Ace looked pleased as he moved some things around, prepared his fishing pole, then cast off his line, too. Then after an apologetic look her way, pulled out a cigarette and lit it. "Sorry, Mer. This is one habit I can't seem to break yet. I promise I won't have more than two or three today."

"I'm all right." She smiled at him, finding herself smiling at the look of happiness on his face as he smoked his cigarette. There had been a time in her life when she would have never stayed quiet about his habit. She would have reminded him about the dangers of smoking and how she wasn't a fan of secondhand smoking either.

But with time—or maybe it was simply the way that he was so accepting of her own faults—she'd learned to give into some of the things that she used to think she would never put up with.

Instead of dwelling on that smoke, she concentrated on her line, moving her pole around and wishing for a bite. "Nothing yet," she said with a smile at both of the guys.

As she'd hoped, Finn grinned. "Meredith, you've got to learn some patience."

"Seems I do."

Ace's eyes lit up. "Not for me yet either. Guess we just have to settle in and get comfortable."

She kicked off her tennis shoes and picked up her thermos of hot coffee and sipped while Ace carefully extinguished his cigarette and tossed it in the hole at the top of his empty Sprite.

After exchanging a glance with Finn, Ace cleared his throat. "So, I have news," he said.

"You do? What's that?"

"Cliff decided to retire for good. He's letting me buy him out. Bridgeport Automotive is going to be all mine within the year."

"That's wonderful! When did you find out?"

"Yesterday."

"And you didn't want to tell me last night?"

He smiled at her. "I wanted to wait until the right time. Plus, it's a good thing, but, well, me and Finn have something that we wanted to talk to you about while we're out here on the boat."

Meredith glanced at Finn. He looked serious, and maybe a little uneasy, too.

Against her will, she immediately started thinking of the worst. Did they want a break? Slow things down? Tamping those negative thoughts down firmly she put her pole in the metal holder and nodded. "Okay . . . "

Ace moved his rod over the water a bit before turning back to stare at her. "You know, we've all been through a lot these last four months. Finn getting sick, my family visiting, your robbery."

She nodded, the muscles in her jaw and neck becoming even tighter. It had been more than those things, actually. Both of them—maybe all of them—had had a number of changes take place in their lives. They'd each been forced to let go of the old notions they'd held tight to.

She'd had to learn to release all the walls she'd constructed around her heart and learn to reach out to others—and to accept when hands reached out to help her. She'd learned that not every hand that reached for her was eventually going to mean her harm.

Ace had had to get his confidence back, both in himself and in his parenting abilities. She knew that that had been a big step, especially for a man like Ace, who excelled in appearing confident all the time.

And Finn? Well, Finn had learned to not take everything onto his shoulders. He'd had to learn to take things day by day and trust in others.

They'd been three people who on the surface had seemed to have everything—but underneath, there had been so much holding them back from true happiness.

At last she spoke. "I know we've been through a lot, but I wouldn't change a thing."

"I'm glad to hear that, honey. But I'm hoping you'll be willing to change a couple of things."

She darted a glance at Finn. He smiled, but his eyes looked a little worried.

"What do you want to change?" she asked.

"Well, me and Finn . . . we want you to move in with us."

"Move in with you?"

"Dad already said that he'd fix up the living room and make your bedroom more girlie," Finn said. "We're going to finish out the basement for me, too."

"What?"

"I know the house feels like a bachelor pad, but we could make it better for you. And I know you like your place, but my house already has two bathrooms and I think there's going to be more room for everyone."

"And the dog."

Thinking about Henry, Finn's adorable, destructive puppy, she playfully winced. "I don't know. If I moved in, I'd have to watch my shoes and my purses."

Finn laughed. "Allison said she'd help me with that."

Ace looked at his boy fondly. "If Al says she can get Henry to get over his leather fascination, I'd put my money on her. She knows dogs."

"So Henry's kind of a bonus now," Finn said. "Plus he lets you cuddle him, so there's that."

"Still, do you boys think you're ready for another change? I mean, that's a lot of changes. A puppy, owning the shop, finishing out the basement . . . and me." She was only teasing— mostly, anyway. She was also afraid to get her hopes up.

Ace frowned. "You're the main thing, Meredith. Nothing's set in stone. And you don't have to decide on anything right now. But, well . . . "

"Dad's trying to say that things are better with you around," Finn said, his voice cracking. "I like having you around." While she stared at him, he sat up straighter, pulling his shoulders back. "And we're good for you, too. I know we are."

"I know you are, too." She swallowed through the lump in her throat. "I love you, Finn. I love your father, too. You both? Well, you've made me really happy."

Ace reached out and pressed a hand to her bare thigh. "So, will you think about it? About moving in? Because, you see, as much as I like how things are, I think I want something more. I want us to go all in."

She knew now that he was using a poker term. She knew now that Ace using a poker term to describe the rest of their lives wasn't minimizing it in the slightest. It was simply how he thought.

And she realized then that "all in" was a pretty

good way to describe how their lives could be from now on. Nothing halfway. No guards up.

Instead, they were willing to be uncovered, unafraid, messy, and laid bare. Nothing in reserve. Nothing held back, just in case it didn't work out.

But while such a thought used to scare her silly—making her only see the disadvantages—she now realized that it was going to mean the opposite. *All in* meant that she could give 100 percent. Because even if she fell short, she now had two men in her life to catch her.

Just as she was going to be able to catch them. Just as she *had* caught them, too.

"Okay," she said at last.

Ace sucked in a breath. While Finn clanked his pole in its holder and walked over to stand in front of her. "Okay?" he asked. "You're going to do it? Move in with us?"

She nodded, then stood up and pulled that boy close. Gasped when Ace stood up and curved his arms around both of them. Holding them all together.

Right until her fishing pole clanged against its holder. As she and Finn turned to stare, Ace put a knee on the seat and picked up the rod and reel.

"What just happened?" she asked.

"You got yourself a bite, Meredith," Ace said as he handed her the pole.

Her hands were shaking. "What do I do now?"

"Reel it in, Meredith."

She turned to Finn. "Do you want—"

He grinned. "Nope. It's your turn. Let's see what you got."

Looking at her two guys, she started winding the reel, grinning as she did. "It's fighting me, but I've got this," she said.

Ace threw an arm around Finn's shoulders. "Looks like you do. Keep reeling, Mer. Don't lose him."

She reeled it in, all smiles and filled with pride, just as her catch flew out of the water. "Oh!"

Finn laughed full out. "You just caught yourself the smallest fish in the lake, Meredith!"

As the tiny fish flopped around in the air, she squealed. "Ace, what do I do?"

"This, baby." In short order, he unhooked the fish and tossed it back into the lake.

As Finn whispered something to his dad and Ace laughed some more, Meredith slipped her sunglasses back on and leaned back.

The sun was shining, she had these two men in her life, and nothing to do but sit and pretend to fish the rest of the day.

Few moments in her life had ever been so good.

Reader Questions

1. What does "all in" mean to you? When have you had to go "all in" in order to accomplish a goal?

2. Is there a character in the novel who you identified with the most? Why?

3. Why do you think Ace and Meredith were meant to be together, at this time in their lives?

4. Finn's scenes with Allison were some of my favorite ones to write. What do you think will become of their friendship?

5. When Meredith's home is broken into, she learns that she has more support and friends in Bridgeport than she imagined. Has something ever happened in your life when you received unexpected help? Have you ever reached out to help someone, much to his or her surprise?

6. Much of *All In* explores the concept of family, both literally and figuratively. Name two or three people in your life who have given you a strong sense of belonging.

7. Who in the Bridgeport Social Club Series are you looking forward to seeing again in *Hold on Tight*?

Books are produced in the United States using U.S.-based materials

Books are printed using a revolutionary new process called THINK tech™ that lowers energy usage by 70% and increases overall quality

Books are durable and flexible because of Smyth-sewing

Paper is sourced using environmentally responsible foresting methods and the paper is acid-free

Center Point Large Print
600 Brooks Road / PO Box 1
Thorndike, ME 04986-0001 USA

(207) 568-3717

US & Canada:
1 800 929-9108
www.centerpointlargeprint.com